THE *Ties* THAT *Bind*

BOOK SIX OF THE SYDNEY LEGAL SERIES

CHRIS TAYLOR

BOOKS BY CHRIS TAYLOR

THE MUNRO FAMILY SERIES
The Profiler
The Investigator
The Predator
The Betrayal
The Deception
The Negotiator
The Christmas Vigil
The Ransom
The Defendant
The Shooting
The Maker
(Available in Audio)

THE SYDNEY HARBOUR HOSPITAL SERIES
The Perfect Husband
The Body Thief
The Baby Snatchers
The Final Bullet
The Debt Collector
The Lab Test
The Stolen Identity
The Cliff-top Killer
The Likeable Fraudster

THE SYDNEY LEGAL SERIES
An Accidental Murderer
At the Hand of Her Father
A Woman Scorned
Lies and Deception
Ordinary Evil
The Ties That Bind
The Perfect Crime
Malicious Love
Toxic Inheritance

THIS IS WHERE IT ENDS SERIES
Jessie's story

Ryan's story
Holly's story
Sarah's story
Veronica's story

THE CRAIGDON FAMILY SERIES
Callum
Joel
Isabella
Nicholas
Sophia
Flynn
Noah
Logan
Elizabeth

THE BARRINGTON FAMILY SERIES
Broken Lives
Broken Promises
Broken Bonds
Broken Spirits
Broken Vows
Broken Minds
Broken Dreams
Broken Hearts
Broken Homes

Get a FREE book when you sign up for Chris Taylor's
newsletter at: www.christaylorauthor.com.au

Love Audiobooks? Check out Chris Taylor Books on audio
on Audible.com, Amazon.com and the iBooks store.

Join Chris Taylor's Facebook reader group/fan page and be
among the first to receive news of book releases, read and
review books prior to release and other amazing offers. Join
Now at: www.facebook.com/groups/1758023621144744/

Find out more about all of Chris Taylor's books, by visiting her
website at: www.christaylorauthor.com.au/about/books

DEDICATION

This book is dedicated to Pat Thomas, who pushes me to reach for the stars and has made this book so much more than it was.

And as always, to my very own sexy hero: my husband, Linden. I love you to the moon and back.

ACKNOWLEDGMENTS

As usual, no book comes into being without a lot of help and support by my friends and family. A world of thanks must go to my wonderful editor, Pat Thomas. Thank you for everything that you do to make my stories even more amazing than I could ever dare to dream. To former Detective Superintendent Michael Kilfoyle, thank you for lending my story credibility. Any mistakes are wholly my own.

To Damon Freeman, Alisha Moore and all of the staff at damonza.com, thank you for yet another fantastic cover. To my sister, Nicole Guihot and to my friend, Ally Thomson, thank you for your excellent editorial comments, proof reading skills and suggestions. I hope you like the final result.

To Amy Atwell and her dedicated staff at Author E.M.S. who are so much more than book formatters. Amy, once again, thank you for your magic.

To the fantastic writer organizations such as Romance Writers of Australia, Romance Writers of

America and Romance Writers of New Zealand for all the help, support and encouragement they offer new and aspiring writers, including me.

To my readers, thank you for your support and love for my stories. Your encouragement and enjoyment make this journey all worthwhile.

And lastly, to my friends and family, especially my husband and children. Thank you for putting up with late dinners and even later conversations as I've emerged day after day from the sometimes scary but always enthralling world I've created on my computer.

PROLOGUE

Trey Walker's youthful body burned with lust. The feel of Angie's body pressed against his, all soft and perky and luscious, sent blood pounding to his cock. The music from the jukebox had changed to a soppy love song and he took advantage of the slow rhythm to pull her even closer.

He'd had a hard-on all evening, right from the moment he'd picked her up outside her parents' house and noticed her lacy white midriff top and denim mini skirt. She'd given him a smile filled with such promise; his belly had flip-flopped and he'd been hard-pressed not to drive somewhere dark and secluded and take her up on the blatant invitation that sparkled in her warm brown eyes.

Instead, like the gentleman he was, he greeted her with a chaste kiss and asked if she was ready for a night of dancing. They been planning it all week, texting each other madly during school and afterwards, finalizing the details. She'd taken his hand and had squeezed it before giving him a wink.

Fighting the urge to drag her into his arms, he'd put his brand new BMW E64 two-door convertible into gear and pulled away from the curb. The car was an eighteenth birthday gift from his father. Lavish, perhaps, but Trey knew the extravagant gift was meant as an apology for all the other missed birthdays and the general absence of his father in his life. Supreme Court Justice Archibald Frederick John Walker IV was a busy man, a fact his sons knew all too well.

Throwing off the depressing thoughts of his father, Trey had tossed Angie a smile and headed toward their favorite haunt in the city. They'd been dating for more than a month. They spent every waking moment they could together, notwithstanding they were at school six hours a day and only shared a single math class.

Still, ever since he'd found the courage to ask her to go steady, they'd been growing increasingly close and by the way she now pressed her breasts against his chest, dancing cheek to cheek on the makeshift dance floor, he was almost certain the night would culminate in them making love. It would be the first time for both of them. He couldn't wait.

The thought that tonight they might actually go all the way sent another surge of excitement through his body. He moved his hips and brushed against her, leaving her in no doubt as to his aroused state. Her lips parted on a silent gasp and her smile let him know she was well aware of his condition. She moved her body so that they were perfectly aligned, pressed against each other.

It was heaven. It was hell. Trey didn't know how much longer he could stand it. His cock throbbed with a need so great he felt like he might explode. He opened his mouth to suggest they get the hell out of there when he was tapped on his shoulder. With a muffled oath, he turned to see who it was...and grimaced.

"Wade! What the hell are you doing here?"

Seemingly unperturbed by Trey's less than friendly greeting, Wade thumped Trey on the back.

"It's good to see you too, bro. I overheard you and Angie making plans last night. I thought I'd come and join you. You don't mind, do you?"

Wade looked from one to the other, his eyes wide and innocent. Trey bit his lip against the harsh words that filled his mouth. The last thing he needed was his brother turning up and spoiling his night. Wade seemed to be in the habit of doing that lately. Still, Wade was his twin and Trey had been looking out for him all his life. It was what Trey did.

"Of course not," he managed through gritted teeth.

He shot Angie a look of apology and was relieved when she acknowledged it with a brief nod, even as disappointment dulled the excitement that had shone in her eyes only moments earlier.

"How are you, Wade?" Angie murmured.

Wade turned on Trey's girlfriend and gave her an exuberant grin. "I'm doing great, Angie. Thanks for asking. Cool outfit, by the way! I hope you got a discount because they chopped half the hem off your skirt!" He smirked; she looked embarrassed.

Once again, Trey found himself gritting his teeth. Wade seemed to go out of his way to embarrass Trey in front of his girlfriends. This wasn't the first time it had happened. It didn't seem to matter to Wade that his actions irritated his brother.

Trey quietly reprimanded him. "That's not necessary, Wade. You need to apologize to Angie."

Wade looked taken aback. His eyes widened in surprise. "Apologize? Hell, I meant no offense. I was only joking, flattering her, wasn't I Angie?"

To her credit, Angie managed a tight smile. Trey sought to bring the conversation to an end.

"It's nice to see you, bro, but I'm afraid Angie and I were just about to leave."

Wade pouted. "Come on, Trey! I only just arrived! Stay and let's have a drink. You too, Angie. The more the merrier."

Trey compressed his lips into a grim line and shot another look at his date. She appeared equally unimpressed. *Still, what was he to do about it?* This was Wade, his brother. Wade could be socially awkward. For years Trey had been smoothing his path and making allowances. Tonight, it appeared, would be no different.

"Sure," Trey managed.

Wade's face broke into a grin. "Great! I'll meet you at the bar."

While Wade shouldered his way through the crowd toward the bar, Trey turned to Angie.

"I'm sorry, Ange. I didn't know he'd be here."

She offered him a half-shrug, still looking disappointed. "It's fine. I understand. He's your brother. You can hardly ignore him."

"True. And he's not just my brother. He's Wade."

Taking her by the hand, Trey made his way toward the bar, Angie following behind him. He'd have one drink with his brother and that would be it. They'd bid him goodnight and get their plans for the evening back on track. Decision made, he glanced over his shoulder at Angie and smiled.

"One drink, I promise. Then we'll leave. Okay?"

She smiled back and nodded. "Okay."

———————————

It took longer than he wanted, but eventually Trey managed to extricate himself from his brother's clutches and make his farewells.

"Thanks for the drink, Wade," he said. "We'll see you a bit later on."

Wade eyed them knowingly. "Don't do anything I wouldn't do."

He winked at Angie. She blushed. Trey glared at his brother and swallowed a curse then reached for Angie's hand.

"Come on. Let's get out of here."

The cold night air hit him like a blast from a freezer after the moist heat of the crowded bar. He shivered. The objects around him turned fuzzy. Even Angie's face had become blurred. He could see the look of concern that furrowed her brow and wondered at its cause.

"Are you all right, Trey?"

He blinked and shook his head to clear it of the fog that had suddenly come upon him.

"Yes, of course. It's just the sudden change in temperature. It kind of put me off balance." He forced a smile of reassurance and led her to his car. The BMW was parked where he'd left it. Tugging the key fob out of his pocket, he unlocked it with the remote. He jogged around to the passenger side and with a flourish opened the door.

"Milady, your carriage awaits."

Angie giggled and the disappointment and concern lifted from her face. "Did I tell you how much I like your car?" she murmured, running a hand over its shiny exterior.

He grinned and once again anticipation surged along his veins. He strode around the vehicle toward the driver's side and was beset with another rush of dizziness.

What the hell was happening? He'd been fine a few moments earlier. It was so weird.

Determined to get his evening back on track, he squeezed his eyes shut and drew in a deep breath. When he opened them again, the dizziness had eased. He sighed in relief and climbed into the car.

The engine purred to life and he put the car in gear. Pulling out into the light traffic, he reached for Angie's hand. "Did you have a good time tonight?" he asked.

She smiled softly. "Of course. I always have a good time when I'm with you."

Her words warmed him through, but he felt the need to apologize once again for his brother.

"I'm sorry about Wade."

She squeezed his hand. "Hey, it wasn't your fault. Besides, he's not here now,"

The look that accompanied her words said it all and sent a hot burst of desire shooting to his groin. He groaned and tossed her a grin and tightened his hold on her hand. Focusing his attention back on the road, he was startled to discover his vision had once again become blurred. He blinked hard and rubbed his eyes.

"Is anything the matter, Trey?"

He shook his head. "No. Yes. I don't know. I feel weird. Kind of dizzy. And my eyes are blurry."

"Do you think you should pull over?" she asked.

"I don't know. I can still see, kind of. But, it's not clear. Perhaps I should pull over...?"

The car drifted over the center line. The bright lights from an oncoming vehicle blinded him. Angie screamed and he wrenched the wheel. The car moved back in the right lane. More cars sped past him. His head began to throb. Squinting through the darkness, he tried to concentrate on the white line. Once again, he drifted across the center line and was met with the strident sound of a horn.

"Trey! You need to pull over! You're driving all over the road!"

Angie's panicked cry came to him from a distance. His head was full of fog. Her lips were moving, but he could no longer make out the words. Lights burned into his retinas. Pain sheared through his head. The next thing he heard was the sound of screeching metal followed by Angie's terrified screaming.

Then everything turned to black...

CHAPTER 1

Ten years later

Wade Walker took a moment to catch his breath and surveyed the dimly lit bar. The murmur of voices and the occasional burst of laughter filled the room. A good-looking barman with black hair that shone beneath the overhead lights smiled and joked with the patrons, particularly the women. The tinkle of crystal champagne glasses accompanied the melodic sound of conversation.

The Chill Factory was a popular nightclub and as usual on a Saturday night, was crowded with people: the young and rich and beautiful, the people with more money than sense. Most of them didn't lift a finger through the week, except to attend their hairdresser or masseuse, or to work on their golf handicap. Still, they liked to let their hair down on the weekends. Tonight was no different.

He moved on silent feet, working the crowd like a pro. A wave here, a smile there and for that pretty girl on the barstool, a wink. She'd been eyeing him all night, although she'd made a fair attempt to hide it. Seated at the bar beside an equally attractive woman he guessed was her friend, the mystery woman had stolen moment after moment to watch him and his progress around the room. He could tell she was intrigued by him. She must have assumed from his popularity with the crowd, he was *someone*. She just didn't know who. And it was obviously killing her.

Just don't stuff this up, Wade. A few moments of conversation and she'd be his...

Moving inexorably closer to her on the pretext of refreshing his drink, Wade narrowed the distance between them until he was only a few feet from where she was perched. His gaze swept over her long, tanned legs. They were crossed at the knee and one Christian Louboutin-shod foot moved up and down to the heavy beat of the music. The short black leather mini skirt was almost indecent as it rode high up on her thighs. The skirt was coupled with a sheer, black lace corset that was threaded with leather ties all the way up her back.

She looked sexy as hell. It was the reason he'd chosen her out of a crowd full of strangers. It was obvious she was out for a good time, and so was he. *What better way to spend a few hours on a Saturday night?*

He sidled up to the bar and pretended not to notice the women. It was a trick he'd perfected long ago. A beautiful woman expected to be noticed, *needed* to be noticed. She was put out when things didn't happen that way and it usually only served to increase her curiosity about who he was and why he ignored her.

"Hey! Can we buy you a drink?" one of the girls offered.

Wade hid a surge of satisfaction and turned toward them in mock surprise. He widened his eyes innocently. "Are you talking to me?"

The girl in the leather giggled and gave him a quick once-over. He returned the compliment and when his eyes once again met hers, frank interest sparkled like diamonds in her gaze.

"Yes, I'm talking to you," she said in an arrogant tone.

Wade turned side-on and leaned against the bar. The action pulled his white Calvin Klein T-shirt tight across his chest, emphasizing the impressive muscle tone beneath.

"What's your name?" he asked, his gaze never leaving Leather Girl's face.

"I'm Heather. And this is my friend, Naomi."

Wade dipped his head in acknowledgement. "Well, it's nice to meet you Heather and Naomi. I'm...Trey."

Leather Girl giggled again. "Trey. That's a nice name."

Wade smiled inwardly. It wasn't the first time he'd impersonated his brother. "Almost as nice as Heather," he quipped.

She blushed charmingly, but didn't drop her gaze. She was a bold one, that's for sure. Just the way he liked them.

"So, do you want a drink?" she asked again.

He once again focused on her. "Sure," he replied. "Make it a rum and coke."

"A rum and coke it is," she murmured and signaled the barman.

The man hightailed it over. When Heather pulled out a gold American Express card, Wade knew why he'd been in such a hurry.

"My friend would like a rum and coke... And get us another bottle of Veuve Clicquot. We seem to have finished the last one."

"Of course, ma'am," the barman replied, reaching for the girls' dirty champagne glasses. "I'll bring you fresh ones," he tossed over his shoulder.

Wade raised a lazy eyebrow. "Fresh glasses? You must have been treating him right."

Heather shrugged insouciantly, like only the very rich can. "I do my bit to pay his rent."

Wade chuckled. "So, you're on the champagne. Would you like a little something extra to spice up your Saturday night?"

Both girls immediately looked interested. Heather shot him a smile. "Well, Trey, aren't you full of surprises?" She tossed him a sly look from beneath her lashes. "What did you have in mind?"

Wade reached into his pocket and pulled out a small plastic bag. "Just a couple of E's to get things happening. What do you say? Do you want one?"

He directed his question to Heather, but both girls eagerly held out their hands. They swallowed them dry without hesitation.

Not the first time they've done that, I bet...

He kept the thought to himself. He didn't judge others for the choices they made in life. Given their age and their access to ready cash, it was hardly surprising. Despite all the warnings on TV, no one took the risks seriously. Besides, he knew firsthand the guaranteed buzz was worth any risk they might end the night in Emergency. He tossed an ecstasy tablet down his throat in full view of the girls. They giggled.

The drinks arrived and, at Wade's suggestion, they moved away from the bar and found a secluded spot at a booth in the far corner of the room. Naomi reached over to refill her glass and sloshed half of it over the side. She giggled again and Heather joined in and then took the bottle from her. When Heather also sloshed the expensive champagne all over the place, the girls almost bent double with laughter.

They're already wasted… This probably wasn't such a good idea, after all.

The thought formed in his mind, but he struggled to hold onto it. The E was already doing its job, along with his fourth rum and coke. He had a good buzz on, for sure, and he was seated with two beautiful women, both looking for a good time. He might as well make the most of it.

"So, Trey!" Heather slurred. "What do you do for a living?"

He smiled and shrugged. "Who cares?"

Once again, the girls bent over with laughter. "You're so funny!" Heather gasped.

"Don't make me laugh so hard!" Naomi complained. "I'm going to pee my pants!"

This set both girls off again and Naomi slid across the leather seat and stood. "I need to go to the bathroom." She wobbled unsteadily on her feet.

"Do you want me to come with you?" Heather asked.

"No." Naomi hiccupped. "I'll be fine. Stay here and keep Trey company. We don't want him running off."

Heather giggled and slid closer to Wade. Her breast pushed up against his arm and her bare thigh brushed against his Levis. His cock instantly hardened.

"Take all the time you need, Naomi. I'm not going anywhere." The last, he said to Heather and she gave him a saucy smile and moved even closer. Another inch and she'd be in his lap. That suited him just fine.

He stretched his arms out and let one fall across her shoulders. Pulling her in against him, he caught a whiff of her expensive perfume. It was rich and sweet and *oh so erotic*. His cock throbbed with need.

"You're a sexy minx, aren't you?" He growled in her ear.

She giggled and pressed herself even closer. Her hand drifted to his crotch. Concealed under the table, she fondled him through the denim.

"You're not so bad yourself," she replied in a breathy little voice.

He shifted in his seat in order to get more comfortable and to allow her greater access to his cock. When she popped the button on his jeans and undid his zip, he almost cried out in relief. Keeping up the pretense of normality, he picked up his glass and took a drink. All the while, her pretty little hand worked its magic.

"This isn't the first time you've done that," he murmured, taking another sip.

She gazed at him with eyes that were wide with innocence. "Are you complaining?"

"Not at all. I could tell the first moment I saw you that you were the one I wanted."

"And why was that?"

"You just had that air about you—one that screamed you wanted cock."

She smirked. "You're pretty confident, aren't you?"

"With reason."

"What about Naomi?"

He shrugged. "What about her?"

"She's a hot girl. Why did you pick me?"

"Yeah, she's hot, but you're hotter and I can tell you'll know just how to suck my cock."

Shock widened her eyes, but the smile remained on her lips.

Oh, yeah, she's interested all right. A few more drinks, another E and she'd be his.

"I don't feel so good. I'm going home."

Wade blinked and sat upright. At the same time, Heather removed her hand. Naomi stood beside their booth. It took him a moment to realize she was the one who'd spoken.

"Oh, I'm sorry," he managed.

"Are you sure?" Heather asked her friend. "The night's only just beginning."

Naomi grimaced. "Yeah, I'm sure. I have a splitting headache. I can't bear to think what I'll feel like in the morning."

Heather made sympathetic noises, but when her hand stole once again inside his jeans, he knew she was glad her friend wouldn't be bothering them again that night.

"Do you need a ride somewhere?" he offered. He didn't have the least intention of driving her home, but the girls didn't need to know that.

"Oh, that's so sweet of you," Heather crooned. Her hand tightened around his cock.

Oblivious to all that was going on under the table, Naomi shook her head. "No, but thanks for the offer. I don't live too far away. I'll catch a cab."

"Are you sure?" Wade persisted. "Because I don't mind driving you. I haven't had that much to drink."

Naomi smiled, then winced and reached for her head. "I'm sure. I guess I'll catch you later, Heather. Trey, it was nice to meet you. Maybe I'll see you around sometime."

Wade inclined his head in her direction and gave her his sexiest smile. "Maybe you will."

With that, Naomi turned away, headed for the exit. Heather renewed her efforts on his cock. In the dimness, he reached out and fondled her breast, his fingers finding her nipple through the thin lace. He flicked at it with his finger and it pebbled beneath his attention. He smiled with satisfaction. Still, it wasn't enough.

His cock was throbbing so hard, it felt like he might come there and then. He wanted to feel her lips around him, bury himself in her wetness. His hand stole down across her thigh and slowly slid upwards. She moved, opening her legs to allow him greater access. Beneath the table, his hand shifted higher, up the length of silky smooth thigh. Higher still, until he found her center. Pushing aside her panties with his fingers, he slid one across her swollen flesh.

She gasped and tightened her hold on him. Her chest rose and fell with her breaths. With his gaze fixed on hers, he found her opening and thrust his fingers inside. This time, her gasp was audible and he leaned over and sealed it in with his mouth. His lips moved over hers and she opened her mouth and invited him in. His tongue slid in without hesitation and began to imitate the thrust of his fingers. She groaned and released his cock and her arms came up around his shoulders.

Dragging him toward her, she clung to his neck and kissed him like she was drowning and he was an oxygen tank. In a far distant part of his mind, he remained aware of his surroundings. They were in a public bar. They could hardly fuck each other there.

"Hey," he muttered and withdrew his hand.

She made a murmur of protest, but he ignored it and reached for her hands. Extricating them from around his neck, he gently set her aside.

She pouted. "What is it? Don't you want me?"

"Of course I do." He reached for her hand and mashed it against his erection. "Isn't that proof enough?"

He set her hand back in her lap and continued. "I want to fuck you like there's no tomorrow, but I can hardly do that here."

She looked around them and slowly nodded. "You're right." Her gaze came back to his. "How far away do you live?"

He smiled and shook his head. "Too far. But don't worry. I have a better plan."

She brightened. "You do?"

"Yes. Now, drink up and let's get out of here."

Leaning over her, he refilled her glass and watched as she emptied it in three swallows. He filled it again and she laughed.

"What are you trying to do? Kill me?"

He laughed with her. "Of course not, silly. I just hate to see good champagne go to waste."

With a shrug, she finished the second glass. When it was empty, she shot him a triumphant grin. "Waste not, want not."

He grinned. "Exactly."

He reached into his pocket and pulled out the small plastic bag. There were two tablets left in it. "Want another?" he asked, waggling the bag in her face.

She smiled. "Why not?"

He handed her an ecstasy tablet and took the other one for himself. They grinned madly at each other, like two naughty kids. He reached for her hand and together, they stumbled outside.

CHAPTER 2

The night was soft and balmy, but Wade barely noticed the warm spring breeze that gently lifted his hair. Tugging Heather by the hand, he led her down an alley that ran alongside the bar. It was a place he knew well. This wasn't the first time he'd taken advantage of its many dark and concealed places. She stumbled along behind him in her four-inch heels, laughing all the while. For her, this was a magnificent adventure.

He drew her deeper into the alley until he came to his favorite spot. Drawing her close, he pushed her up against the wall and immediately crowded her with his body. He placed his hands flat against the wall on either side of her head and kissed her again. Just the memory of her hand around his cock drove him wild. And then he remembered how she felt, how his fingers had slid in and out of her opening. She wanted him as much as he wanted her and he couldn't wait to have her.

Opening his mouth, he pressed his tongue against her lips, demanding entry. She turned her head to one side and started to struggle against him.

"No! No, stop! I-I can't breathe."

"Hey, babe. It's all right. Just open your mouth. I want to see that pretty mouth wide open. Sucking on my cock. I'm so hard for you, I don't know how much longer I can wait. Come on, babe. Give it to me. You know you want to."

Heather's struggling increased and she managed to get her hands between their bodies. She pushed against him and when that had no effect, she began to pummel his chest.

"Please! Please, stop! I told you I can't breathe! I think I'm going to be sick!"

Wade cursed under his breath. *Great. Just what I need.* He released his hold on her just in time for her to turn her head and vomit all over the street. The acrid stench rose up to meet him, but he was drunk and high and pretty much beyond caring. Her corset had loosened in the struggle, exposing her breasts and once again, he grew hard.

She leaned against the wall, trying to catch her breath. "Do you have a handkerchief?"

He reached into the pocket of his jeans and pulled one out.

"Here." He offered it to her.

She took it gratefully with a murmur of thanks and swiped it across her face. As soon as she was done, she handed it back to him, but he merely shook his head.

"Keep it." And with that, he put his hands on either side of her hips and drew her close.

Lowering his head, he went in for another kiss, but this time, he went for her neck. She turned her head away.

"You've goddda be *khidding!*" she slurred. "How can you think of that now? All I want to do is go home and have a shower and sleep this off."

Wade stared down at her in disbelief and slowly shook his head. "Oh, no you don't. You want this as much as me. A moment ago you were begging me for it! This doesn't stop until I say so."

Fear flashed in her eyes, but he was beyond caring. She had him so worked up, there was no way in hell he was going home until he'd gotten what she'd promised. Shoving her roughly against the wall, he jammed his leg between her thighs. She gave a little yelp, but he ignored it and bent his head and nuzzled her neck. She tensed, but he continued.

"Come on, babe. You know you want it. You were all over me back in there. You couldn't keep your hands off me."

"But-but t-that was before... Before I was sick. Now I just want to go home."

She looked so forlorn, he almost gave in, but he'd already spent far too much time and effort on this one. He'd be damned if he were going home empty-handed.

"Shut up," he muttered, his voice rough.

Holding her against the wall with one hand, with the other, he popped the button on his jeans and unzipped his fly. Pulling out his cock, he reached between her legs and tore down her panties. They still smelled of her arousal.

"You say you don't want this, but your pussy says otherwise," he murmured.

In the next instant, he jammed his cock inside her and almost groaned with relief. She was warm and wet and slippery. She felt amazing.

With nothing more than his occasional grunt to break the silence, he fucked her until he was done. As he released her, she slid slowly to the ground. Her head lolled to one side and he realized she was almost unconscious. He bent low and slapped her across the face in an effort to wake her up.

"How much did you have to drink, you little slut?"

She made a gurgling sound in her throat. Her eyes rolled back in her head and she slumped over.

He surged to his feet, panic flooding through him. "Fuck! Fuck! Fuck!"

What the hell was he going to do now?

The little slut had passed out on him. *What if she'd reacted badly to the E's? What if there was something in them that had set her off? He felt nothing more than the usual buzz, but what if there had been something else in hers?* He couldn't let her die there, in the gutter. His father would never speak to him again. Even worse, he'd cut off his allowance. The very thought filled Wade with panic.

With his mind racing a mile a minute, he did the only thing he could think of: He called his brother.

Trey Walker cast a casual glance through the window of his vintage red Mustang as he made his way slowly through the quiet Sydney streets. It was late, past one in the morning. There was hardly a soul about. He'd just come from the bed of one of his work colleagues, where he'd spent a very pleasant few hours. The single malt whiskey had slid down his throat with ease and Mary-Jane's enthusiasm in the bedroom was something else. Even better, she had no interest in a long-term relationship and that suited him just fine.

He thought of the comfortable super king-size bed in his penthouse apartment overlooking Bondi Beach. He longed to lay his head down on his pillow and get some rest. It had been a long week, with work piled up on his desk and if Mary-Jane hadn't called him and begged him to come over, he probably would have spent a quiet night in.

The sound of his phone ringing snagged his attention and he reached over and answered the call.

"Hey, Wade. You're calling late. What's up?"

"Trey! Thank God you're still awake! I need your help!"

Trey heard the urgency in his brother's voice and sighed inwardly. *What trouble had his brother gotten himself into now?*

"What's the matter, Wade?"

"Trey, you have to help me! You need to come fast!"

"What's happened?"

"I can't tell you over the phone. Just get over here. Quick!"

Wade rattled off an unfamiliar address in an upmarket part of town and Trey pulled over long enough to enter it into his in-car navigation system. Doing a U-turn, he headed toward the city.

He arrived at his destination forty-five minutes later. As he drove past an alley, he saw his brother standing over a girl. Parking the Mustang on the street and hoping like hell no one stole it, he climbed out and headed back. Upon spying him coming toward him, Wade's face flooded with relief.

"Trey! Thank God you're here!"

Trey sighed. "What is it, Wade? What's going on?"

Wade looked frightened. "I don't know! I met this girl in a bar. We had some drinks and got talking. She followed me outside. We started kissing and, you know, making out and then she kind of fainted. I don't know what happened. And now I can't get her to wake up. You gotta help me!"

A surge of alarm went through Trey. "Help *you*, like hell. I need to help the girl!"

While hurrying toward the figure slumped on the ground, Trey tugged out his phone. Dialing Triple zero, he waited for the call to connect.

"Police, fire or ambulance?"

"Ambulance! I need an ambulance!"

"What seems to be the problem?"

"I'm not sure. There's a girl. She... She's unconscious."

"Does she have a pulse?" the operator asked.

Trey knelt down on the side of the gutter and felt for a pulse in the girl's neck. He was relieved when he found one. He spoke into the phone. "Yes. Yes, she has a pulse."

"Okay, that's good. Is she breathing?"

Trey stared down at the woman and was relieved to see her chest rise and fall. He returned his attention to the phone. "Yes, she's still breathing."

"All right, then. Stay with her. An ambulance is on its way."

With the immediate emergency now dealt with, Trey surged to his feet and turned on his brother.

"What the hell happened, Wade?"

Wade shrugged and stared at the ground. "I don't know. She seemed fine when we were inside."

"Well, she's certainly not fine now."

"Is the ambulance coming?" Wade asked.

"Yes. They're on their way."

Wade looked relieved. "Thank God! I didn't know what was happening! One moment we were both having a good time and the next she was on the ground."

Trey sent him a hard look. "Did you give her anything? The paramedics will want to know."

Wade shook his head. "No! Of course I didn't! What do you take me for?"

Unconvinced, Trey held his brother's gaze. Wade didn't flinch.

Trey's shoulders slumped on a sigh. For all of their lives, he'd been rescuing Wade out of one bad situation after another. But they were no longer little kids getting into scrapes around the neighborhood. They were twenty-eight years old! When was Wade going to grow up?

The sound of sirens rent the still air and Trey sighed quietly with relief. At the same time, Wade's face filled with panic.

"I've gotta get out of here!"

Trey shook his head. "No way! What if the paramedics have more questions? I don't even know who the hell she is. You're not going anywhere."

"Trey! You know how much I hate needles! I hate anything to do with hospitals! Ever since I had to visit Mom in there, right up until the day she died… I can't stay, Trey! I just can't!"

Trey's hands clenched into fists as he fought hard to hold on to his temper. It was late and he was tired and he'd been in this position with his brother way too often.

"You're not going anywhere, Wade. This is your mess. This has nothing to do with me!"

Wade slowly backed away from him, shaking his head. "I'm sorry Trey. I'm really sorry. I wish I could…" With that, his brother turned and ran.

Trey cursed aloud and thrust his hands into his hair. After all these years, he should be used to this by now. He'd lost count of the number of times he'd rescued his brother, and lately the incidences were becoming increasingly serious. Wade had fallen in with the wrong crowd and ever since, his life had spiraled out of control. And now he had a girl who'd passed out in the street and God knows what the two of them had taken...

"Please! Please help me!"

The woman's weak, panicked cry broke into his thoughts and he hurried over to her side. Cradling her head in his hands, he tried to reassure her.

"It's all right. The ambulance is on its way."

She blinked and opened her eyes and stared up at him in the dimness. A streetlight, not far away, cast his face in shadows, but still her eyes widened with recognition.

"You! Get away from me!" she shouted, turning her back on him. She huddled against the wall. "Help! Someone, please help!" she cried, choking on her tears.

At a loss, Trey stood and moved slightly away. No doubt she thought he was Wade. It was an easy mistake to make. After all, they were identical twins.

CHAPTER 3

The wail of several sirens got louder and all of a sudden, the night was filled with blue and red and white strobing emergency lights. They bounced off the tall buildings in a rhythmic motion that reminded Trey of light from a disco ball. He squinted against their brightness and waited for the cavalry to arrive. It wasn't long.

An ambulance filled the narrow alleyway, followed almost immediately by two police cars. The ambulance pulled up a few yards from where Trey stood. Two paramedics alighted and jogged toward him.

"She's over there," Trey said and pointed to the girl who remained hunched up on the edge of the cracked pavement.

"What's her name?" one of the paramedics shouted over their shoulder.

"I don't know," Trey responded.

The paramedics reached the girl's side and kneeled down beside her. Trey watched from a short distance away as they assessed her condition.

They took her vital signs and peppered her with questions. He couldn't hear what was being said, but there was no mistaking the glare she sent his way. Almost simultaneously, both paramedics turned to look at him. Their eyes glinted with anger and disgust.

Trey moved a little further away from them, hating the rush of guilt that flooded his veins. This had nothing to do with him. He wasn't responsible for his brother's actions, twin or no twin. He didn't even know what the hell she was upset about.

Two uniformed police officers, and two wearing plainclothes, appeared out of the darkness. Two of them approached the girl. The other two came toward him.

"I'm Detective Sergeant Jett Craigdon and this is Detective Harry Boule. We're from the City of Sydney Police Station. What happened?"

Trey eyed the detectives warily. Craigdon was about Trey's age. Tall and broad shouldered and exuding an obvious air of authority, the detective's automatic expectation of cooperation filled Trey with unease. He instinctively guessed Craigdon was a man to be reckoned with; a man who would pay attention to every word Trey said. The detective wouldn't be put off by vague answers. Boule was much older and more laid-back, but there was nothing to say that wasn't a ruse he used to encourage people to drop their guard.

Panic nipped at Trey's toes. *What could he say that wouldn't incriminate his brother, or himself?* He had no idea what had gone on or how Wade was involved. His brother had sworn he hadn't given the girl anything. He said the girl had been friendly and that nothing untoward had gone on, but how was Trey to know for sure? And now the only person other than the woman who knew the truth about what happened had disappeared.

Trey held the detective's gaze, though it was an effort. "I'm not sure what happened, Detective. I only just happened along. I saw the girl on the ground and stopped to see if she needed help. That's the first time I set eyes on her. I made the emergency call."

The detective's expression didn't change. "What's your name?"

"Trey Walker. Spelled T-R-E-Y."

"Where do you live?"

Trey gave him his address and phone number.

"What were you doing out here this time of night, Trey?" the other detective asked in a conversational tone.

Trey took a breath and forced himself to relax. He had to separate his circumstances and actions from those of Wade's and keep telling himself he'd done nothing wrong. And telling them the same.

"Like I said, I was just driving past. See, that's my car over there." Trey pointed in the direction of his Mustang, still parked on the opposite side of the road at the street end of the alley. Both detectives looked in the direction he indicated.

"Nice car," Detective Boule murmured.

"Thanks."

"So, you were driving past and happened to look down the alley and you saw the girl on the ground. Is that it?" Boule asked.

"Yes. That's it."

"So, you don't know anything about her?" Craigdon asked.

Trey shook his head. "No. I saw her there and I thought she might need help. I pulled over and came closer. Then I called the ambulance."

Detective Craigdon tossed a glance in the direction of the girl who remained surrounded by the paramedics. His gaze returned to Trey. "What made you think she might need medical attention?"

Trey shrugged. "I don't know. I guess I just thought she might. She was just crouched there on the pavement, in the dark. I thought she might be hurt."

"Did you speak with her?" Craigdon asked.

"No. Yes."

Craigdon shot him a wry look. "Which one is it?"

"Yes. I mean, I told her I'd called the ambulance. That was it."

The sight of the paramedics lifting the girl onto a stretcher and wheeling her into the back of the ambulance snagged everyone's attention. Detective Craigdon glanced back at him. "Wait here," he said and moved over to where the other two officers stood near the gurney. Detective Boule remained where he was.

Trey watched from a distance as Craigdon conferred with the other uniformed officers. The paramedics went about their jobs securing the woman in the ambulance before departing with lights and sirens blazing.

A few moments later, Detective Craigdon returned to Trey's side. His eyes bore into Trey's and the unmistakable anger behind them turned Trey's gut inside out.

"It seems you've been telling me a whole lot of bullshit, Trey Walker," the detective stated angrily. "I've just spoken to my colleagues. They've interviewed the girl. The one you said you didn't know; had never set eyes on before. She tells a different story."

Trey tried his best to maintain eye contact, but it was impossible. He had no idea what the detective was talking about and he had a sinking feeling that his brother had been less than forthcoming with the truth.

The detective pulled a set of handcuffs from his belt. They glinted silver in the strobe lights. Trey tensed and his body flooded with panic. "What the—?"

"Trey Walker, you're under arrest."

Trey stared at the detective in shock and with ever-increasing alarm. "What the hell are you talking about? I did nothing wrong! I stopped and tried to help the girl. That's all. I swear!"

"Heather Lockhart has a different version," the detective stated flatly.

"Who's Heather Lockhart?" Trey asked.

The detective leveled him with a deadly look. "Heather Lockhart is the girl you raped."

Trey backed away in panic. "*Raped?* What the hell? No way! You've got it wrong! I tried to help. I swear I did nothing but call for the ambulance."

The detective stepped forward and snapped the handcuffs around Trey's wrists. They closed tightly, pinching his skin. Unmindful of his discomfort, the officer dragged him toward one of the police vehicles.

"You're coming back with us to the station where you'll be asked to participate in a record of interview." Craigdon snarled each word.

Trey looked about him frantically in search of an ally, but there was no one. His panic increased.

"There's been some mistake! I swear, I had nothing to do with this! Whatever she said, it isn't true. I've never even met the girl!"

"Save it for the judge," the detective replied coldly and shoved Trey into the back of the police car. Without another word, Craigdon slammed the back door shut. The sound of it crashed into Trey's head and sent a shiver of foreboding down his spine.

What the hell had his brother done?

It was more than two hours later that Detective Craigdon presented outside the jail cell where Trey had been unceremoniously dumped to cool his heels upon arrival at the City of Sydney Police Station. Sharing the small concrete space that smelled of an awful mixture of vomit and urine and bleach, with six other prisoners in various stages of inebriation and each one vying to be heard, Trey was more than relieved to see the detective.

The rattle of the key in the lock was barely noticeable over the din.

"Hey! Keep the noise down!" the detective shouted. He pulled the steel door open and eyeballed Trey.

"You! Walker! Come with me." He unceremoniously snapped the handcuffs back on and then turned his back and left the way he'd come.

Trey followed him into an interview room. It was sparsely furnished with a gray Formica table and four hard plastic chairs, one of which was occupied by Detective Harry Boule.

"Mr Walker, I trust you're ready to talk to us," Boule said in an even tone.

Trey nodded. "I have nothing to hide, Detective. Ask away."

Craigdon closed the door and took a seat across from Trey and dropped a blank legal pad and a pen on the table.

"Mr Walker, am I correct in assuming you're willing to participate in a record of interview?"

Despite the nerves that swirled in his gut, Trey held the detective's gaze and nodded. "Yes, Detective. That's correct."

Craigdon nodded. "Very well. The normal procedure is that we electronically record these interviews. Do you have any objection to that?"

Trey shook his head. "No."

"Good," Craigdon replied and went about checking the recording equipment. When he was satisfied all was well, the interview began.

"The time is half-past four in the morning on Sunday, September, fifth. I'm Detective Sergeant

Jett Craigdon. With me is Detective Sergeant Harry Boule. This is a record of interview with Trey Walker who has been brought in for questioning with regard to an alleged sexual assault which occurred this morning in Drury Lane, Darlinghurst. For the purposes of the recording, Detective Boule and Trey Walker will identify themselves."

Boule leaned slightly forward. "I'm Detective Sergeant Harry Boule of the City of Sydney Police Station."

Detective Craigdon nodded toward Trey. He cleared his throat of a sudden rush of nerves. He forcibly reminded himself he'd done nothing wrong. Craigdon shot him a pointed look. Trey drew in a breath and spoke. "I'm Trey Walker."

"Before we start, Trey, I'm required to ask you if you want to contact a lawyer," Craigdon said.

Trey had already thought about this very thing during his time cooling his heels in his cell. If he requested a lawyer, the cops would think he was guilty. Why else would he feel the need to have legal representation? It would also mean he'd spend the rest of the night in jail. There was no way any lawyer would crawl out of bed at half-past four in the morning to attend a record of interview.

The last thing he wanted was to delay things and spend any time that wasn't absolutely necessary in this place. No, he was best to get this over with as soon as possible. Answer their questions and get the hell out of there. He shook his head. "No, I'm fine."

Craigdon raised his eyebrows briefly and glanced toward his colleague. Trey's gut immediately filled with dread. He clenched his fists beneath the table and prayed he'd made the right decision.

Craigdon took charge of the interview. Upon request, Trey supplied his full name, address and date of birth.

"What do you do for a living, Trey?" Craigdon asked.

"I'm an advertising executive with Baker & Saddler."

Craigdon acknowledged his response with a nod. "I want to take you to a time earlier this evening, Trey, when you said you came upon the woman, Heather Lockhart, lying in the alleyway outside The Chill Factory nightclub. For the purposes of the record of interview, can you tell us again what happened?"

Trey drew in another deep breath and released it slowly, taking his time to respond. Though he longed to speak the truth, as ongoing protector of his brother, Trey couldn't do that to him. Wade had called on him for help. He'd needed him. Just like Trey had needed Wade a decade earlier.

Crystal clear images of that terrible car accident flashed through his mind. The fear, the pain, the screaming... No matter how much he wanted out of this situation, Trey couldn't rat out his brother. Wade had saved his life.

Finally, he spoke. "I have to take your word that her name is Heather Lockhart. We didn't ever get around to making introductions. The first time I saw her was in the alleyway. I was driving past and happened to look in that direction. I saw her on the ground. I parked my vehicle and got out and came toward her. At the same time, I pulled out my phone and called the ambulance."

"What were you doing there?" Boule asked.

Trey did his best to hold the man's gaze, but failed. He ended up staring somewhere in the direction of the floor. He strove to keep his voice casual. "Like I said, I was just driving by."

"At *two* in the morning?" Craigdon asked, his tone deceptively lazy.

Trey forced himself to remain calm. He shrugged nonchalantly. "It's Saturday night. I was on my way home from visiting a friend."

"Which friend?" Boule asked.

"Her name is Mary-Jane O'Shaughnessy."

Craigdon made a note on the pad in front of him. "Where does she live?" he asked.

"She lives in Maroubra."

Once again, Craigdon made a note. After he'd finished, he looked up at Trey. "You said you lived in Bondi. Is that correct?"

Sensing a trap, Trey proceeded with caution. "Yes. That's correct."

"So you visited this friend at her place in Maroubra?" Craigdon asked.

Trey nodded. "Yes."

"And you were on your way home. That's what you said, wasn't it?" Craigdon continued.

"Yes, well, kind of. I left her place and was driving around."

"So, you weren't headed for home?" Boule asked.

"Yes. No. I-I was driving around."

"So you were driving from Maroubra in the eastern suburbs toward your home in Bondi, which is also in the eastern suburbs and somehow you ended up in Darlinghurst. Is that right?" Craigdon asked.

Trey cursed silently under his breath. A fresh wave of nerves filled his belly. If he were truly driving home from Maroubra, he shouldn't have been anywhere near Darlinghurst. The inner-city suburb was nowhere near where he'd been and in a completely different direction to where he was supposed to be headed. It wasn't logical and he didn't know how to make it appear as if it were. He should have thought about that before he opened his mouth. Now he was stuck with it. He did his best to recover.

"Like I said, detectives. I'd been at my friend's place in Maroubra. I said goodnight and started to head for home. At some point, I took a different turn and headed toward the city. I ended up in Darlinghurst. I happened to drive past The Chill Factory and I noticed the girl on the ground."

Craigdon eyed him with suspicion. "You see, this is what I don't get, Trey. You made the call to emergency services at two-fifteen in the morning. Even driving slowly, it must've been after one when you left Maroubra for you to be in Darlinghurst by that time. It seems odd to me that a man would head in that direction, away from his home, at that time of the morning with no firm destination in mind, and no fixed purpose for being there."

The detective eyeballed him. Trey did his best not to squirm. "It was after one when I left her house and I just wasn't tired. Knew I wouldn't get to sleep easily."

Craigdon's gaze grew more intense. "You're lying to me, Trey. And I want to know why."

Despite Trey's best efforts to remain calm and cool and collected, sweat popped out on his upper lip. Reaching for his handkerchief, he pretended to cough and surreptitiously swiped at the dampness. Despite his efforts, he was almost certain the eagle-eyed detectives had noticed it.

Fuck.

What the hell was he doing? He should have just lawyered up and refused to answer their questions. *Why did he think he could talk his way out of this?* He'd never been the kind of person who was comfortable concealing the truth. His friends were always ribbing him about having to work on his poker face. The cops knew he was hiding something. He could see it in the open distrust on their faces and the way they kept narrowing their eyes. *What the hell was he going to do now?*

Boule cleared his throat. "So, Trey. Let's just get this straight. You spend an evening with Mary-Jane in Maroubra and sometime around one in the morning you head for home. But instead, you change your mind and turn toward the city and end up in Darlinghurst, correct?"

Trey nodded. "Correct."

"So, you had no particular purpose for being in Darlinghurst?" Craigdon asked.

"No. I was merely driving around."

"So, while you were merely driving around in Darlinghurst, you happened to look across and see Heather Lockhart in the alley. That's correct, isn't it?" Boule asked.

"Yes, that's correct."

"Lucky you," Craigdon murmured.

Trey eyed him warily. "Actually, I think *she* was the lucky one," he quipped.

Craigdon eyed him with disgust. He leaned across the table until their faces were inches apart.

"See, Mr Walker, Heather Lockhart tells a different story. She says the two of you were drinking together inside The Chill Factory nightclub. She said she and her friend, Naomi Marchant, met you there. You shared a few drinks, talked for a while and then you gave her some ecstasy tablets. You then suggested she follow you outside and you took her into the alley and raped her."

Fear rushed through Trey's veins and settled as a hard cold lump of dread in his gut. As if from a great distance, he saw the oncoming vehicle again, felt himself wrench the wheel... *The BMW swerved, but not enough. The squeal of metal on metal would stay with him the rest of his life. Angie was screaming... And there was Wade, racing toward him, dragging him out of the car. Saving his life.*

Quite simply, without Wade, Trey wouldn't even be there. And there was no way Trey was going to betray him now. With a mammoth effort, he maintained eye contact with the hard-nosed detective.

"No, that's not what happened. I already told you. The first time I saw the woman was when she was in the alleyway. I didn't go into The Chill Factory. I didn't meet with her or her friend. I didn't share drinks, idle chitchat or ecstasy tablets. I did none of those things. Until almost one in the morning, I was with a woman by the name of Mary-Jane O'Shaughnessy. If you don't believe me, call her."

Craigdon eyed him coolly. "Oh, don't you worry, Mr Walker. We'll certainly be talking to Mary-Jane."

Boule pushed the blank legal pad toward Trey. "What's her number?"

Trey wrote down the number from memory and at Craigdon's request, read it aloud for the purposes of the recording. He wondered silently how much longer he was going to be kept there.

As if reading his mind, Craigdon shot him a hard look. "This isn't the end of this, Mr Walker," Craigdon promised. "Heather Lockhart is undergoing a medical examination as we speak. I requested a rape kit. We'll find out soon enough if you're telling the truth. It's hard to get that close and personal with someone and not leave some trace of yourself behind. Believe me, if it's there, we'll find it."

He eyeballed Trey, his expression relentless. Trey's heart raced a mile a minute and once again, sweat popped out on his upper lip. He was the first to look away. Silently, he cursed Wade for the mess his brother had dropped him into. For all the stupid stuff Wade had gotten mixed up in over the years, this had to be the most serious.

"What's that on your arm?"

The question came from Craigdon. Trey looked down at his left forearm and noticed the fresh scratches visible there. The dread in his gut increased.

Fuck.

He'd forgotten about them. They hadn't meant anything at the time. Now they looked downright suspicious. He drew in a deep breath and told the truth.

"I tried to rescue a stray kitten from a storm water drain yesterday afternoon. She wasn't too happy with my efforts. She scratched me." He shrugged. "That's it."

Both detectives regarded him with dubious expressions. It was obvious neither of them believed him. He tried again.

"I don't know what else you want me to say. It's the truth."

"Can anyone verify that?" Boule asked.

Trey shook his head. "No. At least, I don't think so... Maybe Mary-Jane noticed them while we were together. Please check with her. It happened outside my apartment block. I didn't notice anyone around at the time."

"Do you mind if we photograph the scratches?" Though Craigdon's words were posed in the form of a question, Trey knew he wasn't meant to refuse.

He kept his gaze steady on the detective's. "Sure. I have nothing to hide."

Boule pushed away from the table. "I'll go get the camera," he said and closed the door behind him, leaving Trey and Craigdon alone.

Craigdon remained silent. Trey did his best to do the same. Still, it wasn't easy. He fought against the urge to fill the silence—and lost.

"I know how bad this looks, Detective," he said. "For some reason, this woman has accused me of rape. I don't have a clue why. I swear, I just happened upon her in the alley. I now wish to God I'd never stopped. All I was trying to do was help her. Look where it's gotten me."

Trey shook his head in exasperation, frustrated that his Good Samaritan act had caused nothing but trouble. The detective remained silent and Trey wished he'd done the same. It was obvious both detectives had already made up their mind about his guilt. There was nothing he could say that would exonerate him at this point, other than waiting for the test results and handing over his brother.

The latter was something he simply wasn't prepared to do.

Wade had sworn he'd done nothing wrong and eventually—if he told the truth—the evidence would prove that to be correct. Maybe they'd give him a polygraph. That would surely point to his innocence... But they might also ask questions that pointed to Wade...No, that test wouldn't be an option.

Trey swallowed a sigh. His head pounded. His eyes were sore and gritty. All he wanted to do was go home and sleep and try and forget this nightmare had ever happened.

The door to the interview room opened and Boule came back in, carrying a camera. He asked Trey to take off his white T-shirt and Trey willingly complied. He stood against the wall of the interview room while Boule photographed the scratches on his arms. Angry and red, they looked suspicious as hell. Still, there was nothing he could do about them. Besides, they'd already started to heal over. Surely a medical expert could see that they were more than a couple hours old…

"We'd also like to take a DNA sample from you, if you don't mind," Craigdon said.

Trey silently debated his options. Submitting to a DNA sample without a court order was optional, but if he refused, he'd only ignite the detectives' suspicions further and after all, he had nothing to hide. He'd done nothing wrong and neither had his brother. With a nonchalant shrug, he agreed.

With quiet efficiency, Craigdon produced a sterile swab and asked Trey to swipe it around the roof of his mouth. Trey did as he was asked and handed the swab back to the detective.

"Can I go now?" he asked.

Craigdon glared at him. "Not so fast."

Boule cleared his throat. "Trey Walker, you're going to be charged with the sexual assault of Heather Lockhart. You'll be brought before the court in the morning where you can apply for bail. In the meantime, you'll spend the rest of the night in the lockup. You'll…"

The detective continued to speak, but the rest of the man's words were drowned out by the rush of noise in Trey's head. He gaped at the detectives in shock, unable to believe what was happening.

He was being charged with rape! How could it have come to this? It was her word over his! Why didn't they believe him? Surely the tests would exonerate him?

In a daze, he felt himself being led away. He was fingerprinted, photographed and finally taken back to his cell, still handcuffed. The same motley crew of drunken idiots filled the small space. They howled and heckled Trey as Craigdon released the handcuffs and then unlocked the door to the cell. With a shove to his back, Trey stumbled inside. Craigdon secured the door behind him.

Still shocked and confused, Trey made his way to a far corner and sat down on the floor. He tried not to think about how quickly his life had spiraled out of control. He tried not to think at all.

Chapter 4

Trey opened the plain yellow envelope handed to him by a uniformed officer and dumped the contents onto the counter. He slipped his watch over his wrist and pushed his wallet and car keys into his pocket. He threaded the black leather belt through the loops of his jeans and pulled it tight. He slipped on his Italian leather loafers and picked up his phone. There were four missed calls from his secretary and two from Mary-Jane. He sighed. He could just about guess the content of the messages.

He'd been taken to the bail court earlier that morning. Appearing before the judge as an accused was a strange and totally uncomfortable experience and one he didn't want to repeat. Still, the judge had released him on bail and for that he was grateful.

"If you just sign here at the bottom of this page, Mr Walker, you're free to go."

Trey picked up the pen and added his signature to the line the officer indicated. The constable handed him a copy of the paperwork and Trey stuffed it into his back pocket. With the briefest of nods in the direction of the uniformed officer, he turned and left.

He took the stairs two at a time, in a hurry to get away from the place. When he reached the pavement, he once again tugged out his phone. He dialed into his voicemail and braced himself for what was to come. The first message was from Mary-Jane.

"Hi there, Trey. It was soooo great to see you again. I've missed you. We must do it again sometime."

Her voice was low and full of innuendo and if this had been a normal day in a normal moment in Trey's life, he might have smiled slowly and called her right back to take up her offer. But his life had been turned upside down and he doubted anything would ever be normal again. The next message from Mary-Jane was much terser.

"Trey, I just had a call from a detective asking me about whether you were with me last night. I told them you were. I hope that's all right. What's going on? Are you in some kind of trouble? Please, call me."

Trey sighed. He was sorry that Mary-Jane had been dragged into this, but he was glad she'd verified his alibi. At least, until one o'clock.

The rest of the messages were from his secretary, Constance Worthington. The first call expressed mere curiosity as to why he was running late. Each subsequent message got increasingly annoyed. The last one was filled with concern.

"Where are you Trey? I'm worried about you. The executives from Colgate are waiting for you in the boardroom. You have that presentation today, remember? Call me."

Trey bit his lip. With a bit of luck, his early-morning appearance in the bail court would go unnoticed. His father might be a former Supreme Court justice, but Trey had always kept a low profile and after all, only the lowest of legal aid lawyers turned up to the bail hearings at that hour and they were unlikely to be in contact with his work colleagues. Still, he owed his secretary an explanation. With a sigh, he dialed her number.

"Baker & Saddler, Trey Walker's office."

"Connie, it's me."

"Trey! The bosses from Colgate have been waiting for more than an hour. They're royally pissed. Where are you?"

Trey sighed. "I'm sorry, Connie. You have to give them my apologies. I'm... I'm sick. I must've had something bad to eat last night. The seafood must've been off. I'm sorry... I've been on the toilet all night with a bucket in my hand. I'm not sure which end will come out first."

"*Ewww!* Too much information...Trey. I can do without that image!" Connie complained.

Trey smothered a grin. The thought of a severe gastric bug would be enough to garner the sympathy of most people, including, he hoped, the executives from Colgate.

"Are you sure there isn't anyone else I can send in there instead?" she asked. "What about Jeremy Jones?"

Trey groaned. "Connie! Jeremy Jones is an idiot! Besides, he knows only the barest of details about my presentation."

"Better than no one, Trey! Do you really want me to go in there and send those people away? They might not come back."

"I don't care. You're not sending in Jeremy."

She sighed heavily on the other end of the phone and Trey was filled with guilt. It wasn't Connie's fault that his brother was a fuck-up and that Trey was stupid enough to come to his defense yet again. That's what happened when you owed your brother your life. You never stopped feeling obligated to him for it.

"Hell, Connie. I'm sorry. I'm being an ass. It's not your fault. Send Jeremy in if you have to. It will be on me if he messes up."

"Good," she replied.

"I'm sorry to ask you this, Con, but can you reschedule all of my appointments? I'm just not going to be able to make it into the office today."

"Of course. You poor thing! Do you need anything?"

"No, but thanks. I appreciate your concern."

The blast of a car horn right beside him made him jump. He moved further away from the street and put a finger in his ear to block out some of the noise from the morning traffic.

"Where are you?"

Connie's question forced his attention back to his phone. She'd obviously heard the traffic noise over the phone. He was supposed to be on death's door. She assumed he'd called from home, not from a couple blocks from their building. He thought fast.

"Sorry, I have the TV up too high."

The lie fell off his lips all too quickly, but it left a bitter taste in his mouth. He wasn't used to being deceitful and never liked it when he was forced into a situation where he had no choice. Still, the dishonesty had the desired effect.

Connie's answering sigh was full of sympathy. "You poor thing. Make sure you keep your fluids up. Plenty of water and some clear soup, if you can keep it down. You don't want to dehydrate. Are you sure you're going to be okay?"

"Yes, I'm sure. But thanks. I appreciate your concern."

"Anytime. Let me know if you need anything."

"Sure. And thanks again. Have a good day."

He ended the call and dropped the phone back in his pocket. He caught a cab to Darlinghurst and was surprised and relieved to discover his vintage Mustang was still parked at the curb across from the alleyway outside The Chill Factory nightclub where God knows what went on the night before.

He still couldn't believe he'd been charged with rape. It was unthinkable! He refused to believe his twin was capable of it either. Wade had done some stupid stuff over the years and lately he seemed to be traveling even more off course than usual—but rape? No way!

There must be some mistake. It was the only reasonable explanation. Either that, or Heather Lockhart had known his brother previously and was exacting revenge for some earlier slight. *Who the hell knew?* Trey just wished to God he'd been kept out of it.

Tugging his key fob out of his pocket, he unlocked the Mustang and slid behind the wheel. Before he pulled out into the traffic, he dialed his brother's number through the car kit. The call rang out in the silence. Trey counted nine rings before it diverted to voicemail. Trey punched the steering wheel in frustration.

"Shit! Pick up the phone, dammit!"

Unmindful of his irritation, Wade's voicemail beeped, indicating Trey should leave a message.

"Stop whatever it is you're doing and call me," he snapped. With that, he ended the message, tossed a look over his shoulder and roared away.

He stood under the shower in his condo for so long the water went cold. No matter how many times he lathered himself up, it seemed he still couldn't get the smell of the jail cell out of his skin. It was like it had seeped into his pores and up the shafts of his hair while he'd fitfully tried to sleep. He shuddered at the memory and prayed he'd never find himself in that situation again.

Finally, he turned off the water and toweled himself dry. Stepping out onto his balcony dressed only in a pair of black satin boxers, he let the glorious view of the Pacific Ocean, sparkling like diamonds in the sun, soothe his soul. The blue sky stretched from the horizon all the way to heaven. People sunbaked or jogged or walked their dogs along the beach. Freighters dotted the horizon, on their way to Port Botany, or even further south, to Wollongong. It was a view he never tired of and he was forever grateful for the generous salary he earned at Baker & Saddler that allowed him to live in such a fine place.

It wasn't as if he hadn't worked hard for those generous dollars, but not all advertising firms rewarded their staff like Baker & Saddler. It was one of the reasons advertising gurus from all over the country vied for a position there. Trey counted himself among one of the lucky ones. Now it seemed like some of that luck had run out.

He'd have to tell his bosses about the sexual assault charge. Now that it was on the public record, it was only a matter of time before someone realized he was *that* Trey Walker and then would leak the story to the media. All hell would break loose. Not only on the work front, but at home, too. His father would have a fit.

With a sigh, Trey opened the double, sliding glass door and went back inside and fetched his phone. Once again, he dialed his brother. This time, Wade answered.

"About time. What the hell have you been doing?" Trey asked by way of greeting.

"Well, good morning to you, too, big bro. What are you in such a snit about?"

Trey shook his head in disbelief. Wade was unbelievable.

"What the hell happened last night, Wade? And don't give me some bullshit that nothing did. I've spent the night in the lockup. The police have charged me with sexual assault."

"What the fuck...? You have to be kidding!" Wade exploded.

"I wish I was. That girl you were with outside the bar pointed the finger at me. She told the police I raped her."

"She's lying! I swear! I never set eyes on her until last night and she and her friend were all over me. Then her friend went home sick and she and I started to get it on. She couldn't keep her hands off me. I suggested we take it outside, where we could have a little more privacy."

"That's why you were out in the alley?" Trey guessed.

"Yeah."

"What happened next?"

"I don't know. It kind of gets a bit hazy after that, but there's no way in hell I raped her."

He sounded so convinced, Trey couldn't help but believe him. Besides, his brother had never exhibited signs of violent behavior before. Trey wouldn't believe he had it in him to force himself on a woman.

"How much did you have to drink?" he asked.

"Not much. A couple of rum and Cokes. That's it."

"Then why is everything hazy? What aren't you telling me? The police said the girl told them you'd given her speed."

"Yeah, I probably did. Like I said, it's all a bit hazy. I definitely had some E's on me and I can't find them now, so it's quite possible we shared a buzz."

Trey's anger came from deep inside him. He guessed he'd been holding it back since the night before when the police took him in for questioning over an alleged offense that had nothing to do with him.

"You told me last night you gave her nothing!" he shouted. "You lied to me, Wade!"

"Yeah, sorry. I panicked. I didn't know what to do. She was perfectly fine and into me and then all of a sudden she was on the ground. I didn't know what was happening. I should have told you the truth."

"What you should have done was sort this mess out on your own. This was all your doing, not mine. Why the hell did you involve *me*? Now look what's happened! I've been charged with a serious offense. If this gets out, my career, my reputation—everything will be ruined. And it will be all your fault."

"Surely the police don't really believe you raped her. You weren't even there."

"The girl identified me at the scene. After you ran off like a coward, I stayed behind to help her out. How stupid could I have been?"

"You weren't to know the silly bitch was going to cry rape. Besides," Wade added, his voice filling with hope, "you have the golden tongue, the gift of the gab. You can talk your way out of anything. Dad's always said that."

Trey snorted in disgust, hardly believing what he was hearing. Wade had gotten him into this mess, but Wade believed it was up to Trey to get himself out. Typical.

"You just don't get it, do you, Wade? This is serious shit! This kind of thing could ruin everything I've worked for."

"I'm sorry, Trey. I really am. I wish I'd never called you. It isn't fair that you've been dragged into this."

The contrition in Wade's voice sounded genuine and Trey felt himself relenting, like he always did. He sighed heavily. He was the older twin by three minutes. It felt like he'd been looking out for Wade all of his life. Twenty-eight years and counting. And then there was the added obligation because Wade had saved his life...

"What are you going to do, bro?" Wade asked, his voice cautious.

Trey compressed his lips into a tight line and slowly replied. "Find myself a good lawyer, I guess."

———————

Kiesha Munro twisted an errant strand of hair around her finger and tried to concentrate on the words in front of her. Even the view of leafy Hyde Park and the glimpses she had of the botanical gardens from her corner office couldn't hold her attention. She'd just received word that her application for a position as a District Court judge had been successful, effective the beginning of next year. In a few short months, she'd be the first aboriginal woman to take the bench in the District Court of New South Wales. The very idea of that made her head spin.

She came from a long line of high achieving relatives, including her uncle, Duncan Munro, who'd been the first aboriginal male to be appointed as a judge to the District Court. He'd been on the bench since the mid-90s. It had taken more than two decades for the court to recognize that aboriginal women had just as much to offer.

She looked around her and released a small sigh. She enjoyed working at Sydney Legal and had risen to the highest ranks. In fact, had her aspirations not been toward the bench, she was sure she would have been offered a partnership. After all, she'd been with the firm since she'd graduated law school seven years earlier and had brought in millions of dollars in fees over that time.

But it was the courtroom that called to her and being in charge of her own domain would be a dream come true. She'd had doubts that it would ever happen. Though there were a small number of aboriginal women who'd been appointed magistrates over the years, none had made it as far as the bench in the District Court. She couldn't believe she'd be the first.

Her father, Percy Munro, would have been so proud. It was sad that he was no longer around to celebrate her achievement. He'd died three years earlier of a heart attack at only fifty-one. It had been a difficult time for everyone.

She'd settle for Uncle Duncan's congratulations. Those would have to be enough. After all, Uncle Duncan knew exactly what she'd had to do to achieve such lofty heights in the legal profession.

She couldn't wait to take up her post.

The phone at her elbow pealed and she reached over and answered it. "Kiesha Munro."

"Kiesha," Suzanne Peterson said. "I have Trey Walker on the line."

"Okay, do I know Trey Walker?"

"I'm not sure. He's not a client. He's asked to speak with you."

"All right. Put him through."

"Ms Munro. Thank you for taking my call."

"What can I do for you, Mr Walker?" she asked politely.

"Please, call me Trey. I know we don't know each other, but... I need your help."

She frowned. "What's this about, Trey?"

There was another pause on the other end of the line. She was about to ask if he was still there, when he spoke again.

"You're not going to believe this. In fact, I'm still having difficulty believing it myself. Last night... I was charged with the sexual assault of a woman I've never met."

She blinked in surprise and cast around for something to say. "I... I... I don't know what to say."

"Yeah, tell me about it." His voice was low and filled with disbelief.

"How does something like that happen?"

"I don't know," he replied. "Late last night, I stopped in the street to give a woman some assistance. The next thing she's accusing me of rape. The police have charged me with sexual assault. I was released on bail this morning."

Kiesha's eyes widened more with every word he uttered. It was like something out of a movie. And then she had an uneasy feeling and wondered what he wasn't telling her. They weren't living in a police state. In her vast experience, and from dealing with law enforcement, she knew criminal charges were only laid with just cause. Not only that, if she were to believe what he said, it would mean the police facts had been surveyed by the judge who'd freed him on bail. If there was anything odd about the charge, it would have been raised in court, the case dropped... Something didn't add up.

"I want you to represent me."

Trey's somberly voiced statement interrupted her thoughts. She blinked and cast around for something to say. She latched onto the first thing that came to mind.

"I'm sorry, I'm leaving in a few months to take up a new position. I'm not taking on any new cases."

"Oh. When are you leaving?"

"At the end of the year."

"This is only September. With a bit of luck, you'll have this thing tossed out of court before then."

Kiesha cleared her throat. "Trey, I don't think you understand. It doesn't work that way. I can't—"

"Please, just let me come and talk to you. To explain. You're the best criminal defense lawyer in town. And right now, you're exactly what I need."

CHAPTER 5

Kiesha bit her lip and stared blindly out the window, the receiver still in hand. The sun was big and bright, framing the perfect blue of the sky around it. She wished she could give him a flat-out no. After all, what she'd told him was true. Now that her appointment to the bench had been confirmed, she wasn't taking on any new cases. She hadn't had a chance to inform her partners, but she was sure they'd understand and would wish her well. After all, it was always handy to have an ex-employee on the bench.

The silence between them lengthened while she vacillated back and forth.

"Please, Ms Munro. I'm begging you..."

It was the quiet desperation in his voice that finally weakened her resolve. Though she didn't know him, she imagined it would be difficult for anyone to beg a favor from a stranger.

It was obvious how much he was in need of her help. She wasn't swayed or flattered by his reference to her being the best criminal defense lawyer in town. That was merely a statement of fact and she was proud of the hard work she'd put in to earn it. There was no need to deny the truth or to try and justify it. Still...

As if sensing her indecision, Trey spoke quietly again. "Please... Please, Ms Munro. Ten minutes of your time is all I ask. Just hear me out..."

She felt herself relenting and with a sigh of resignation, she agreed. "All right. Meet me here in an hour." She hung up the phone.

———————

In order to make Kiesha's tight deadline, Trey drove into the city. The Mustang was quicker than taking public transport, but finding a parking spot within a mile of the Sydney Legal building proved difficult. The first two parking lots he tried were full. His luck was with him in the third. He found an available spot on the top floor of the building and quickly made his way outside. With two minutes to spare, he arrived at Sydney Legal, puffing slightly. He took the elevator up to Kiesha Munro's floor and waited for her secretary to advise her he was waiting.

He'd already made the phone call to his boss. Being the son of a former Supreme Court justice meant that there was a very real likelihood someone in the court registry might make the connection. All it would take was a phone call to one of the media outlets and his fall from grace would be all over the news. He'd wanted to do the right thing and come clean to his boss before that eventuality.

Charles Baker II was suitably taken aback when Trey told him about what had happened. Trey had been quick to reassure the man that it had all been a mistake and he was sure things would be cleared up as soon as possible. After a brief silence, his boss had suggested he take a leave of absence until the matter was sorted out.

Trey had wanted to protest, but in the end had kept his mouth shut. After all, what Baker said was true. Baker & Saddler couldn't afford any hint of scandal. They had a reputation to protect. A reputation they were proud of. A reputation that had stood for more than twenty years. They sure as hell didn't need to hit the front pages of the newspapers for the wrong reasons.

Trey understood all of this and reluctantly agreed to Baker's suggestion. He'd take a leave of absence without pay, or he could choose to take his holidays. Either way, he was no longer to represent Baker & Saddler in any way, shape or form until the mess had blown over. His clients would be discretely shared out among his colleagues until such time as he could take them over again.

A tall slim woman with smooth, golden brown skin and hair the same color pulled back into a loose bun, strode down the short corridor toward him. Her almond-shaped, blue eyes sparkled with intelligence. The sensuous lines of her full lips were emphasized with golden brown lipstick.

When she reached him, she held out her hand. "I'm Kiesha Munro. You must be Mr Walker."

The pictures he'd found of her on the Internet during his search for a lawyer hadn't done her justice. With nerves flooding his stomach at her beauty, in a daze, he nodded and shook her proffered hand. "P-please, call me Trey," he reminded her with a stammer, still taken aback by her stunning looks. Remembering his manners just in time, he added, "Thanks for seeing me."

She merely inclined her head slightly and turned away from him, heading back the way she'd come. He followed behind her, unable to keep his gaze off her. She wore a cream-colored designer suit, the jacket tailored to fit her body. The tight narrow skirt ended at her knees. The cut of the expensive fabric fit her perfectly and clung to her in all the right places.

He immediately felt an acceleration in his pulse and cursed silently under his breath. Now wasn't the time to appreciate the finer points of Kiesha Munro's decidedly attractive figure. After all, he was here because of her sharp mind, nothing else.

Oblivious to his thoughts, she opened the door to a corner office and invited him to precede her. He accepted her unspoken invitation and was immediately captured by the breathtaking view that unfolded outside her windows.

She had an amazing office. He was sure she'd earned it. She hadn't become known as the best criminal defense lawyer in town without reason—and she'd been rewarded accordingly.

She offered him coffee, which he declined.

With a shrug, she took the seat behind her desk. Trey sat opposite her and tried not to fidget. Drawing her chair up closer, she leaned her elbows on the pale Tasmanian oak and steepled her fingers beneath her chin. She regarded him steadily.

"Like I said over the phone, Trey, I'm not sure I can help you. It's not that I don't want to. Your case sounds...interesting and I am certainly sympathetic to your plight. But, I'm leaving Sydney Legal in a few months. I'm reducing my workload and I'm not taking on any new cases. I need to tie up loose ends in the cases I'm currently involved with before the year comes to an end. I simply don't have the time to take on anything new. I hope you understand."

Trey had a sinking feeling in his stomach. *She wasn't going to take him on after all!* Panic flooded his veins. He sat forward in his seat.

"Please," he entreated her, "you agreed to hear me out. I've looked into your professional bio. You've done some amazing work. You pride yourself on taking on difficult cases, of setting right the wrongs. We have that in common. I also can't abide injustice. It's a wonder *I* didn't become a lawyer." He paused.

He knew exactly why he'd stayed well clear of the legal industry and it had everything to do with his father.

He cleared his throat and forced himself to focus on the task at hand. "Unfortunately, this is one hell of a wrong that needs to be righted and I need your help to do it."

To his relief, she gave an imperceptible nod. Leaning back against her seat, she crossed her arms in front of her and eyed him steadily.

"Okay, Trey. You've done your research. And while my head isn't turned by flattery, I'll give you the ten minutes you asked for. Tell me what happened."

He drew in a deep breath and eased it out between taut lips. The muscles in his neck were tight with tension, but he fought against it, knowing that this was the only shot he'd get. If he didn't manage to convince her, he'd be stuck trying to find some other lawyer, someone who wasn't as good. He'd studied the bios of hundreds of lawyers earlier that day. She was the best. She had to represent him. If there was one thing he was sure of, it was that he needed the best.

As briefly as possible, he outlined for her what had happened, leaving Wade out of the story. Old habits died hard. Even now, he felt the need to look out for his brother. The fact was, Wade had assured him he'd done nothing wrong and Trey was confident the physical evidence would support that. It could take time to get forensic evidence analyzed. He just had to bide his time and see this thing through to the end. In the meantime, he wanted to have Kiesha Munro on his side, breathing down the detectives' necks.

She regarded him with a sardonic expression. "So, you're telling me you just happened along late last night and spied a woman in an alleyway you thought needed your help. You stopped to speak to her and then called an ambulance.

When the police arrived, she accused you of rape. Did I miss anything?"

With difficulty, Trey held her gaze. "She also told the police I was with her in a nearby nightclub and that...I gave her speed. That's it."

"Right," she said dryly. "I take it you're denying that as well?"

"Of course I am. I don't do drugs and I swear, the first time I saw her was in the alleyway."

Her frown deepened and she shook her head in consternation. "It doesn't make sense. What aren't you telling me?"

Trey lowered his gaze to the desk and hunted around for something to say that wouldn't incriminate his brother. "Nothing. It doesn't make sense to me, either," he said. "That's what happened."

"Who was the arresting officer?"

"Four police officers attended the scene. Two of them were plainclothes detectives. I only spoke to Craigdon and Boule from the City of Sydney Police Station. They were the ones who conducted the formal interview and eventually laid the charges."

The furrows on Kiesha's brow became more pronounced. Once again, she shook her head. "I've known Jett Craigdon for years. He's a good cop. So is Harry Boule. They're not rookies and they sure as hell don't go around laying charges without evidence to back it up."

Her gaze had narrowed on his and it was all he could do not to squirm. "You're right," he admitted. "I looked into Craigdon and Boule this morning. Both of them have impeccable records. Under different circumstances, I'd feel the same way you do. But for some reason, last night they decided to single me out. They've charged me purely on the say-so of the girl. They don't have any other evidence. They made a mistake and I need you to prove it."

"Are you known to the police? Do you have a criminal record?"

Trey wondered if he looked as shocked as he felt. "No! Of course not! The worst I had was a parking ticket and that was at least five years ago."

She continued to regard him skeptically. "Then why would the police target you? It doesn't make sense. I'll ask you again. What aren't you telling me?"

"Nothing!"

Unable to hold her gaze a moment longer, he stared at a spot on the floor and fought hard against the guilt that threatened to overwhelm him. He wished he could tell her the truth, but his father had made it clear what he expected Trey to do. Besides, turning Wade into the police would be like pointing the finger at a recalcitrant child. The best thing to do was keep his brother out of it for as long as he could. Hopefully Kiesha Munro could produce a miracle and make this mess go away without Wade.

He risked a glance in her direction and was once again taken aback by her understated, elegant beauty. She remained silent for a long time. He held his breath and tried not to think what he'd do if she turned him down. His career, his reputation, his very life was on the line. He needed her.

After what seemed like a decade, she blew out her breath on a heavy sigh. "Okay, let me read the brief of evidence. After that, I'll decide whether or not to offer you representation. If what you say is true, the detectives involved have some explaining to do. On the other hand, if the evidence shows that you're a filthy liar, I'm going to be royally pissed and you're going to be left hoping like hell you never come before me in my courtroom. Do you understand?"

Trey compressed his lips and held her gaze, hoping to God his brother hadn't lied to him about anything else. "Yes, ma'am. I understand."

———

Trey squinted against the bright sunshine and hunted around in his pocket for his sunglasses. Slipping on his Maui Jims, he headed in the direction of the parking lot. His step was much lighter than it had been half an hour earlier, when he'd arrived, unsure of the reception he would receive. Now, Kiesha Munro had agreed to take on his case—or at least to read the brief. He was confident that once she'd seen the evidence, or lack thereof, she'd fight tooth and nail to clear his name.

His phone vibrated in his pocket, reminding him he still had it set to silent. Pulling it out, he glanced at the screen and grimaced. It was his father.

Archibald Frederick John Walker IV was a retired Supreme Court judge whose sons were well past the age of consent, but that didn't stop him from having an opinion on everything they did and wanting to intervene at the drop of a hat.

His father also knew that Wade was a fuck-up, but Archibald Frederick John Walker IV expected Trey to bail his brother out, regardless of the mess he was in. Trey had taken on the responsibility without a word of complaint, and until now, his brother's wayward actions hadn't affected him in any serious way. He wondered if his father had heard about Wade's latest escapade and was already working out ways to prevent his younger son from bringing shame upon the Walker family name.

With a sigh, Trey hit the button to answer the call. "Hi, Dad."

"Wade called me," his father replied without preamble. "What the fuck is going on, Trey?"

He waited a beat before answering. "It's a long story, Dad."

"Well, you'd better start talking. I could hardly understand a word Wade said. He kept going on about some girl he'd met in a bar. Somehow things went off course. He said the police were called. Do you know anything about it?"

Trey grimaced. So, Wade hadn't gotten around to telling his father *everything*. Typical.

"Yeah, I know something about it." As succinctly as possible, Trey filled his father in on what happened. "The cops think it was me. They've charged me with sexual assault."

"*What the fuck!* How the hell did you let something like that happen? What were you thinking! What the hell do you think's going to happen when the cops realize you have an identical twin brother? I thought you were the one with all the brains. The one who could talk your way out of anything. What happened to that slick tongue of yours last night?

"Wade's going to be dragged into this and all hell will break loose. He'll end up saying something stupid. He can't defend himself like you can. It's just not in him. He'll end up admitting to everything. For fuck's sake, Trey! Is this the best you could do?"

Trey clenched his jaw against his father's outrage and fought off his own anger. He wished his father would take his side, just once. *Why was it always Trey's fault when Wade got in trouble?* For twenty-eight years, it had been no different. Add to that the burden of knowing Wade had saved his life…

Through gritted teeth, he forced himself to reply. "Wade's the reason both of us are involved in this, Dad."

"I thought you said he didn't rape her?"

"Yeah. That's what he said."

"What? Don't you believe him?"

"Of course I do, Dad. Wade wouldn't do something like that, even if he was wasted."

"Wasted?"

Trey sighed. "Yeah, Dad. He took speed. So did the girl. He supplied her."

It was his father's turn to sigh. "Great. Just fucking great. Still, this means her memory is as foggy as his about what happened. I take it both of them were drinking, too?"

"Yeah. I believe so."

"Let's hope there isn't any physical evidence indicating rape," his father said.

"Yeah. That's exactly what I'm hoping, too."

"Listen, Trey. No matter what, you're going to have to keep Wade out of this."

It wasn't a request. Trey swallowed another sigh. "Yes, Dad. I'll keep Wade out of this, no matter what. Just like I always do," he added under his breath, too low for his father to hear.

"It's the only way forward, Trey," his father continued as if Trey hadn't spoken. "Wade's not smart like you. The worst thing that could happen is for the police to get wind of Wade's existence. He'll end up convicting himself by his stupidity. I'm retired for Christ's sake. I don't need the stress at my age."

"Yes, Dad. I understand."

"Good. Well, let me know what happens. I'm sure it will all blow over soon and we can forget about it."

"Yeah. That's it, Dad. Let's all forget about it." His tone dripped with sarcasm. In disgust, he ended the call.

CHAPTER 6

Four weeks later

In stunned silence, Kiesha turned over the final page of the last statement contained in the brief of evidence prepared by the police in the case against Trey Walker. She was filled with a sense of disbelief that quickly morphed into white-hot anger.

He'd lied to her.

Trey Walker had sat in her office, eyeball to eyeball and *lied* to her. She couldn't believe how badly she'd misjudged him! She was just as angry at herself for being taken in by his sinful good looks and hard-luck story. She should have known better. He wasn't the first man to try and hoodwink her with charm and persuasion.

She'd read through the statements given by both detectives and the alleged victim, Heather Lockhart. There were also statements from Sam Frost and Naomi Marchant. Frost had been the barman on duty the night Trey said he didn't attend The Chill Factory nightclub in downtown Darlinghurst. Marchant was the alleged victim's best friend. Both Frost and Marchant had independently identified Trey Walker as the man who'd been in the club with Heather on the night in question. Marchant went so far as to say the man had introduced himself as Trey.

Then there was the doctor's report. A comprehensive medical examination had been performed. Seminal fluid had been found in Lockhart's vagina. It was obvious a condom hadn't been used. The report went on to say that no abrasions had been found on Lockhart's body, nor any foreign material located under her fingernails. Though it was obvious the two people had engaged in sex, it was one word against the other that it was consensual.

The final statement in the brief was a report from a DNA lab. According to the report, there was a 99.9% probability that the DNA located in the seminal fluid found in Lockhart belonged to Trey Walker...

Once again, her anger found its head. The son of a bitch had lied to her.

"Shit. Shit. Shit."

The lying, scheming bastard. He'd sat there, looking all desperate and distressed, begging for her to believe him. He'd told her it hadn't been him; that he hadn't been at the club that night. He told her his only involvement was to pull over and help someone he thought was in need. The Good Samaritan who'd been betrayed for his efforts.

If anyone had been betrayed, it was her. The evidence spoke volumes. It told her where the real deceit lay and it wasn't with Heather Lockhart.

With another angry curse, she reached over and picked up the phone. She punched in Trey's number. He answered on the second ring.

"Hello?"

"You piece of shit!" she shouted without preamble. "You lied to me. You looked me in the eye and said you never touched her. You said you weren't even there. You said the first time you saw her was in the alleyway. Well, the evidence doesn't lie. I have a report in my hand that tells me there is a 99.9% probability that the semen found inside Heather Lockhart is yours. And don't *dare* tell me you don't know what I'm talking about."

If Trey was surprised by her harsh accusations, it didn't show in his voice. Instead, he sighed heavily in her ear.

"I'm sorry, Kiesha. This is going to make you even madder, but I don't have a clue what you're talking about. I... I can only guess it has something to do with my brother."

She frowned. "Why the hell would it have anything to do with your brother?"

"His name is Wade. I should have told you earlier. I'm sorry. I've battled with the right and wrong of it for a month. If you'll let me, I'd like to explain."

A surge of impatience went through her. She'd had enough of his games. Enough of *him*. "Explain what?"

Once again, she heard him sigh. "I'm sorry, I was hoping to keep him out of it."

Her patience came to an end. "What the hell are you talking about, Trey? Spit it out or this conversation is over. Period."

"All right, all right. I'll tell you everything, but I'd prefer not to do it over the phone. Could you meet me at Jacobs Café? It's not far from your building."

Kiesha couldn't believe how calm he sounded after all the things she'd just thrown at him. He still insisted he was innocent. Was he *insane*?

"If this goes to trial, Trey, and you're found guilty—"

"But it's not going to get to trial, Kiesha and I sure as hell am not going to be found guilty. The evidence you have before you is bullshit and once I'm finished talking to you, you'll know what I mean. I'll see you at Jacobs in twenty minutes."

Trey arrived at the appointed meeting place early. He was already in the vicinity, meeting with his father. Archibald Frederick John Walker IV lived in a penthouse apartment within walking distance of Circular Quay. Floor-to-ceiling plate glass windows captured the spectacular one-hundred-and-eighty degree view of the harbor.

Ever since the incident back in September, his father had demanded regular updates on the case. Until now, Trey had nothing to report. The police had been given the usual month to provide the brief of evidence to his lawyer. From Kiesha's recent phone call, it was obvious she'd received it and read it—and the news wasn't good. His brother had lied. Again. First about the speed and now about the fact he and the girl had engaged in sex.

Trey's gut filled with dread at what the brief might contain. Test results didn't lie and the police now had DNA evidence that linked him to the crime. No wonder Kiesha was so furious, so insistent that he'd lied.

A wave of anger and disbelief washed over him. He closed his eyes against it. *Oh, Wade, what the hell have you done?*

He found a table away from the other diners in the far corner of the room. Thankfully, the lunch rush was over and there was only a handful of patrons there. The tinkle of the bells that hung above the door of Jacobs Café snagged his attention and he watched as Kiesha made her way across the polished concrete floor toward him. A rush of nerves filled his gut.

She wore another expensive-looking power suit, this one in pinstriped gray. Her hair swung in a loose ponytail, giving her a youthful air. He didn't know how old she was, but he guessed she was about the same age as him, maybe a little older. Sometimes it was hard to tell.

She pulled out a chair and sat across from him. The expression in her eyes indicated the depth of her anger.

"Right, you'd better start telling me the truth, or I swear I'm out of here. And if you tell me you don't know what the hell I'm talking about, this ends quicker than you can blink."

Trey looked at her somberly and forced himself not to react to her nearness. "I'm sorry. I should have told you about my identical twin brother."

It took a second or two for his words to register in her brain. When they did, he heard her sharp intake of breath and saw surprise widen her eyes.

"You have an identical twin brother?" The words were flat and came out with anger still coating her tone.

He held her gaze steadily and answered with just one word. "Yes."

"And you didn't think to tell me this *before*?" she shouted. "What the hell were you thinking? Identical twins carry identical DNA. It's his, isn't it? It's his DNA?"

Trey nodded. "Yes." He sighed. "Wade called me the night it happened. I was on my way home and arrived in the alleyway to see the girl, already there, just as I told you."

"Yes, but what you didn't tell me was that you have an identical twin brother with identical DNA who was with the girl that night and who might very well have *raped* her."

Trey compressed his lips and let her anger wash over him. He understood the way she felt. He'd blindsided her and she was none too happy about that. If their positions were reversed, he wouldn't have been happy, either.

Quietly, he told her what happened. By the time he was finished, her anger had faded and was replaced by bewilderment.

"Why didn't you tell this to the police?"

He shrugged. "He's my brother. What do you expect me to do?"

"Well, he certainly hasn't had any compunction dragging *you* into all of this. One of the witnesses said the man she met that night introduced himself as Trey."

Trey reeled back in shock. *What kind of game was his brother playing?* This had gone far beyond a joke.

"Does he even know you've been charged?" Kiesha continued, oblivious to his thoughts.

"Yes. He knows. He insists he didn't rape the girl. They met, shared some drinks, got high and that was it. He's as much in the dark as to why she cried rape as I am."

"Except they obviously had sex. Did he tell you that?"

Trey compressed his lips together in an effort to hold back another rush of anger at the thought of what Wade had held back. "No, he didn't."

She stared at him, her blue eyes searching his. "He's lied once for sure. How do you know your brother's telling you the truth about the rest of it?"

Once again, Trey held her gaze. "We're twins. Identical twins. It's hard for people like you to understand. If he were lying to me, I'd know."

She made a sound of impatience. "But he *did* lie and you *didn't* know. So, why not just tell the police, let them question him? If he's telling the truth, he has nothing to hide."

"No. Wade's not like me. We might be identical in our physical appearance, but that's where the similarity ends. He's not...strong. And he's been in trouble lately. In fact, he's been in scrapes most of his life. Nothing serious, but he wouldn't be able to cope with a police interrogation. He'd end up saying something stupid and getting himself locked up for years." He paused and then added, "There's also the fact that when I was eighteen, he saved my life."

"What happened?" she asked in a calmer tone.

Trey sighed. "I had a car accident. I was pretty badly injured. The front of the car took the brunt of the impact. I was trapped behind the wheel, unconscious. The car caught fire. Wade was the first one on the scene. At no little risk to his personal safety, he dragged me and my girlfriend from the burning car and then gave his own blood to keep me alive. He's screwed up nearly every day of his life, but that one time, when it mattered, he was my hero. I won't forget it."

Kiesha's expression softened. "Okay, I get it. What he did was no little thing and you're grateful. But it doesn't mean you need to take the fall for him this time. We're talking about a serious criminal offense. If you're found guilty, you're going to jail." She shook her head slowly. "You need to think about yourself and how this will impact your life. You have to put yourself first. By withholding Wade's existence from the police, you're making this much more difficult than it needs to be. Especially for you."

He nodded. "That might be so, but I'm not going to turn over or abandon my brother. Not now, not ever. If he'd put himself first when he came upon my accident, if he hadn't done what he had, I wouldn't be here. It's as simple as that."

Kiesha stared at Trey across the table. While loyalty was an admirable quality for anyone to possess, he was making a terrible mistake. She was relieved to discover he wasn't the lying cad she'd thought him to be, but still, he should have told her everything right from the very start. She was his lawyer, after all... Well, kind of.

She'd agreed to read the brief. He should have trusted her enough to tell her everything. To tell her the truth, the whole truth. She'd busted his balls about being deceitful, when all along it was loyalty and gratitude to his brother, however misguided, that had kept him silent. As much as she wanted to, she couldn't censure him for that.

A waitress appeared and took their order for coffees. Kiesha couldn't help but notice how the young woman's gaze lingered on Trey far longer than necessary. Kiesha cleared her throat and the woman blushed and hurried away.

Without conscious thought, Kiesha's gaze traveled over him. His curly brown hair was messy and had either been ruffled by the light breeze that had drifted in from the harbor, or else he'd run his hands through it more than once. Her gaze moved lower, across his broad shoulders and trailed down his strong chest.

He wore a plain blue T-shirt with "Nike" scrolled across the front and a pair of faded Levis. His clothing fit him well and emphasized the strength and athleticism of his body. He looked more like an athlete preparing for the Olympic Games than he did an advertising executive who spent most of his time behind a desk.

She could understand the waitress' interest. He was good looking, with an air of authority and understated confidence that appeared natural. He was sexy without trying to be. His lack of show made him even more attractive. There was plenty to like about Trey Walker.

She blushed and heat crept across her cheeks at the waywardness of her thoughts. More than likely her strong reaction to him was because the last time she'd been with a man was back before the dinosaur age.

He moved to run his hand through his hair and she swallowed a smile. A tease of his spicy aftershave, or perhaps it was his cologne, wafted toward her. Either way, it filled her senses and made her think of naughty things she was better off to leave alone. She refused to have such thoughts about her client, and that was that.

Besides, she was about to embark on a whole new career—the moment she'd been waiting for her whole life. In a few short months, she was to become the first female aboriginal judge to preside over the District Court. Just the thought of it filled her with pride. She'd worked darn hard to get there and she wasn't going to let anything or anyone jeopardize it, no matter how good looking. She couldn't afford a distraction in the form of the way-too-sexy Trey Walker, or the problems he faced.

Still, she couldn't help but feel for him and the serious dilemma he now found himself in. The police had done the right thing by charging him. Little did they know he had an identical twin brother who carried identical DNA. It wasn't their fault that Trey hadn't shared the information with them. Although surely with a little more in-depth police work, they could have found that out.

She was certain an online search would have given them the very information he'd shared with her and she kicked herself for not doing the same thing the very first time they met. It would have saved her a whole lot of angst thinking he was a lying son of a bitch.

The waitress returned with their order and with only the briefest of glances in Trey's direction, set their coffees before them and turned and left. Kiesha added one sugar to her latté. She noticed Trey drank his black.

"Tell me about the rest of your family," she said.

Trey took a sip from his coffee and then set the mug slowly back down. He shrugged.

"What do you want to know?"

"Do you have any other siblings?"

"No. Just Wade and me."

"What about your parents? Are they still alive?"

"My father is. He's a former Supreme Court judge. You might have heard of him. Archibald Frederick John Walker IV."

She shook her head. "No, I'm sorry; I don't know him."

"No matter. He didn't do criminal work. He was exclusively probate. He retired a few years back. As for my mother, she died from meningococcal disease when I was seven." He paused and then added, "I always thought she died of a broken heart."

Kiesha started in surprise and sat back in her seat. "Why would you think that?"

"Let's just say, my father didn't believe in his vow to remain faithful to his wife. There was a long string of women in and out of my father's life, even when my mother was still alive. I was only young, but I was old enough to know what was going on. I asked my mother about it once. She told me my father was a complicated man."

"She accepted his infidelities?"

"No, I don't think she ever accepted them. She just didn't think she had the wherewithal to fight them. Or perhaps she knew there was no point?"

"That's so sad," Kiesha murmured, thinking about her own parents. They'd been married nearly thirty years when her father died and after being together all that time, they'd still held hands when they walked together. She wanted that kind of marriage one day.

"Anyway, that's my family," Trey said with forced cheerfulness. "Now, tell me about yours."

She smiled. "Do you really want to know?"

He grinned. "Of course."

"Well, my parents are Percy and Eileen Munro. Dad passed away three years ago, but Mom's still alive and well. She lives on the family farm outside Bourke in western New South Wales."

"Wow, is that where you grew up?"

"Yes."

"So, you're a country girl."

She laughed. "Through and through. I go back and visit as often as I can."

"What brought you to Sydney?"

"College. I went to law school at Sydney University."

"I went to Sydney University, too. I did a business and marketing degree."

They shared a smile. "What year did you graduate?" he asked.

"2011."

His smile widened. "You were a couple years ahead of me."

Her lips tugged upwards. "That explains why we didn't know each other then."

He chuckled. "So, do you have any brothers and sisters?"

"I sure do. The Munros are good breeders. I have three brothers and two sisters. I'm the second oldest. Then there are my cousins—thirty-five on my dad's side and twenty-nine on my mom's."

"Wow! That's a lot of cousins! I can count mine on one hand."

Once again, they shared a smile and the spark of heat that had ignited between them earlier suddenly came to life. Kiesha tried to look away from the mesmerizing green of his gaze, but for the life of her, she couldn't. Trey seemed to be struggling in the same way.

Her heart beat faster and her palms went damp. Tingling centered in her core. She shifted in her seat in an effort to move to a more comfortable position, but the movement only made things worse. The friction of the seat against her bottom drew attention to the aching in her clit. It was embarrassing how quickly and completely her body had responded to him. She really needed to start dating again. Casting around for something to say that would take her mind off the moist heat between her legs, she latched onto the first thing she thought of.

"I assume your father's reasonably well known in the legal fraternity. I mean, his name wasn't familiar to me, but there must be a number of people who know him—and you. When word gets out about what happened, and the fact the former judge's son has been charged, it will only be a matter of time before someone mentions you have an identical twin. What will you do then?"

His expression became shuttered. "I don't know. Neither Wade nor I have ever had a high profile in the media. Not like Dad. I'm hoping we both might just fly under the radar until we can get this thing thrown out."

"But if your brother did rape the girl, he's committed a serious crime. What message are you giving him if you help him get away with it? Have you thought about that? And even if you don't say a word, all that has to happen is for some over-eager journalist do a little digging on the Internet and he's going to discover your brother's existence. Then everything you'd hoped to keep from the courts will likely come out. What will you do then?"

Trey stared at her, his expression filled with determination. "I don't know, but you and I are going to work harder than we ever have before to make sure this thing goes away before that happens. I have to take care of my brother. I have no other choice."

She stared right back at him, refusing to back down. "Of course you have choices. You could go to the police right now and tell them. They can start looking at Wade. If he's told you the truth about what happened, he has nothing to worry about and you'll be off the hook."

Anger flashed in Trey's green eyes. She braced herself for his outburst.

"You're not listening, Counselor. Wade stays out of this. In fact, if you're going to continue to represent me, that's a non-negotiable term of your engagement. You can represent me only if you take my brother off the table."

Annoyance at his arrogance flooded through her. "Of all the conceited things to say! I haven't even agreed to *be* your lawyer! I promised to read the brief of evidence. That was it. You're being mighty presumptuous to suppose I'm going to see this thing through to the end."

"I'm sorry. You're right. I had no right to say that. I'm the one who needs your help. I'm in no position to be making demands. Please, forgive me."

His voice was low and contrite. He held her gaze, his green eyes wide and appealing. She stared at him. She wanted to turn him down. There were so many reasons why she should. It was the sensible thing to do.

Just open your mouth and say no, Kiesha. It's easy.

She opened her mouth. "Okay, I'll do it. I'll represent you."

"Thank you."

Trey's slow and sexy answering grin sent her nipples hardening reflexively. She wondered whether she'd end up regretting her decision and was almost certain she would.

And then his smile faded. "Does this mean you're fine with my condition?"

A reluctant smile tugged at her lips. She shook her head. "Hey, I'm the one doing *you* a favor, remember? You don't get to set conditions."

His gaze remained steady on hers. "I understand, but this is really important to me. If you're as good as they say you are, you should be able to win this without Wade. I'm innocent, after all. Do we have a deal?"

His green eyes filled with emotion. She found it impossible to look away. She drew in a shaky breath and slowly released it.

"Okay, I'll keep your brother out of this."

He held out his hand. "Let's shake on it."

She stared down at his hand for a long moment. A million reasons why she should refuse battled inside her head. And then she found herself wrapping her hand in his. "Deal."

Warm tingles spread up her arm, trailing heat in their wake. From the slight widening of his eyes, she could tell he'd felt it, too. Once again, she wondered if she'd come to regret being taken in by this man with a pair of sexy green eyes and a smile she felt all the way down to her toes.

Chapter 7

Trey hopped on a bus on Elizabeth Street and headed for home, his mind still filled with all that had transpired between him and Kiesha.

What the hell was his brother thinking when he pretended to be Trey? Especially when the little idiot was getting up to such mischief—taking illicit drugs, having sex with strangers and the like. He wondered how many other times that had happened.

The fact that Wade had lied to him about having sex with Heather Lockhart also made him furious. He'd specifically asked his brother if he'd touched the girl. Wade had flat out denied it. And yet, the DNA tests proved his brother had lied. Again.

What else was he lying about? The fact that Trey no longer knew or could rely on his brother's forthrightness or his own twin intuition was troubling. It was time Wade gave him some honest answers and Trey wouldn't be put off with trite replies.

A surge of determination went through him. He pulled out his phone and dialed his brother's number. The call rang out and finally diverted to voicemail. He cursed under his breath and ended the call without leaving a message.

Wade had to stop hiding behind their father. He had to come out and take responsibility for his actions. If he wasn't going to answer his phone, Trey would go around and visit him and do everything he could to make his brother see sense. This ridiculousness had gone on long enough. Trey wouldn't turn his brother in to the police, but if Wade manned up and decided to go to them voluntarily, Trey would encourage him all the way and give him the help and support he needed. That plan might not sit well with their father, but right at that point in time, Trey couldn't care less. Kiesha was right. This was his life they were fooling around with. He'd had enough.

He tugged on the bell rope above his head to signal to the driver that he'd get off at the next stop. The bus pulled to halt a short time later and Trey jumped off. He flagged down a taxi and gave the man Wade's address. In less than fifteen minutes, the cab pulled up outside Wade's grungy, inner city apartment block.

He spied Wade's beat-up Honda parked on the street a few doors down and hoped that the presence of his brother's car meant Wade was home. Still, given the mood Trey was in, he was prepared to sit on the doorstep and wait for his brother all night if need be. This had to be sorted out, once and for all.

Jogging up the cracked and dirty steps that led into the three-story walk-up, Trey buzzed for his brother. To his relief, Wade's voice came over the intercom.

"Yeah?"

"It's me. Trey. Open up, Wade."

The buzzer sounded above the door, and Trey let himself in. Wade's apartment was on the third floor. Trey took the stairs two at a time. He'd barely broken a sweat when he arrived outside Wade's front door and rapped on the panel.

The door opened. Wade muttered a brief hello and then turned his back on Trey. Trey followed his brother down the short hallway that opened into a combined kitchen and living room. The space was small, and Wade had made it seem even smaller by jamming every conceivable object he owned in it: two overstuffed couches that had seen better days; a coffee table covered in dirty plates, cups and cutlery—like someone had enjoyed several TV dinners and then left the used crockery behind after each one; a worn countertop strewn with half-eaten food and opened boxes of cereal. A carton of juice also sat there open to the elements. Pizza boxes, beer cans, and more discarded food overflowed the trash can. The smell was awful.

Trey made a sound of disgust. "For fuck's sake, Wade! Do you have to live like such a pig? When's the last time you had a clean-up, man?"

Wade thrust out his jaw at a stubborn angle Trey knew all too well. "You don't have to live here, bro. What's your problem?"

Wade's surly tone irritated Trey no end. He tried hard to contain a sudden spurt of anger. He'd had just about enough of his brother's childish attitude. Wade might have once saved his life, but this had to stop. Right here. Right now.

"Look at me, Wade."

Trey's voice brooked no refusal. Slowly, his brother turned to face him. Trey took in the dilated pupils, the wasted look on his brother's face and cursed again in disgust.

"For fuck's sake, Wade. What the hell are you doing with your life? You're high as a kite! What the hell did you take this time?"

Wade stared at him with wide eyes in a poor attempt to look innocent. Trey would have none of it.

"Don't even bother to try and deny it! I can smell the shit on you. Is that all you took? Or are you mixing it up with something else now?"

Ignoring him, Wade stumbled over to the couch and sat down among the piles of dirty clothing and other discarded waste. As if oblivious to the filth, he leaned his head back on the back rest, closed his eyes and sighed.

"Don't carry on, Trey. I have the worst headache in the world. Please, leave me alone. This isn't a good time."

Trey stared down at his brother and once again snorted in disgust. The anger that had been simmering in his gut ever since his meeting with Kiesha once again stirred to life. The fact that his brother was wasted on drugs didn't excuse anything. Wade needed to take responsibility for his actions and now was as good a time as any to bring that up.

"I just had a meeting with my lawyer," he said. "You had sex with that girl from the club."

Wade stirred on the couch. His eyes opened slightly. He squinted at Trey. "No, I—"

"Don't bother to deny it, Wade. Your lies won't work on me this time. The lawyer had a DNA report she'd gotten from the police. You fucked that girl outside the club and there's DNA evidence to prove it. The only thing is, the police think it's mine."

Wade's only reaction was to shrug and to once again, close his eyes, as if by doing so he could block out all the problems Trey had brought to his door. A fresh wave of anger surged through Trey. He rushed over to the couch and grabbed Wade by his shirtfront and shook him.

"Trey! What the fuck? Let go of me!" Wade protested weakly.

Trey shook his brother hard once more and then released him. Wade fell back against the couch. Trey's anger continued to surge through him, looking for a release.

"For fuck's sake, Wade! Have the decency to show some remorse!" he shouted. "This is my life we're talking about! You don't seem to give a damn! You don't seem to care whether my career goes down the toilet or that my reputation is torn to shreds. The cops think it was *me* who raped that woman. They're gearing up for a fight and they won't let up until I'm behind bars! Does that make you happy?"

"I didn't rape anyone," Wade protested. "That slut was all over me. We were having a good time. Okay, I might have fucked her. I can't remember. But if you said it happened, who am I to argue? But it definitely wasn't rape. If you don't believe me, go to hell."

Trey's breath came faster with the force of his anger. He turned away and did his best to calm down. It wasn't often he lost his temper with anyone, let alone his twin, and the unfamiliar feeling put him off balance. When he felt more in control, he turned back to Wade again.

"You told me you didn't touch her," he said in a low, controlled voice.

His brother threw up his arms in defeat. "What do you want me to say, man? I was wasted! I didn't have a clue what I'd done, but I sure as hell know I didn't rape her! Do you honestly think I could be capable of that?"

Wade stared at him and Trey stared back. He wanted to issue a swift denial. Of course his brother wasn't capable of such violence against a woman. It wasn't possible. Just like Trey could never bring himself to do something like that.

But something inside him made him hesitate and the words of reassurance just wouldn't come. He hated himself for it. Wade noticed his hesitation and came off the couch, his eyes blazing.

"You're kidding me? You're fucking *kidding* me! My own brother thinks I could be a rapist! Well, thank you very much! Here I thought you were the one person I could count on, no matter what. And you've betrayed me in the worst way possible. Talk about gratitude. You wouldn't even be here if it hadn't been for me. How quickly you forget, bro."

Trey had every right to say those same words to his brother, and yet he was stricken with guilt to hear them. Once again, he was bombarded with images of the burning wreck, the smell of fuel, the taste of fear... His shoulders slumped.

"Wade, please... You told me you hadn't touched her and then I find out you had sex. You told me you hadn't given her anything. And surprise, surprise, guess what showed up in her blood? It was only later, when I pressed you that you conceded you'd probably given her speed. You also failed to mention you introduced yourself to both women as Trey." He shook his head in disbelief, struggling once again to hold on to his temper.

"What the fuck, Wade? Why would you tell people you were me? You're in a nightclub looking for good time, with illicit drugs in your pocket that you're freely sharing around and all the time everyone there thought you were me! Rape or no rape, at what point do you think that's okay?"

Wade had the decency to look embarrassed. His gaze dropped and he half-turned away.

"I'm sorry," he mumbled. "It's just that you're so God damn perfect. I wanted to feel what it was like to be you, just once. I swear it hasn't happened before. I don't know why I did it that night. I shouldn't have. It was wrong of me."

"You're damn right it was wrong!" Trey blazed. "It's fraud, that's what it is! We used to pull those kind of stunts when we were kids, but those were nothing to this! In those days nobody got hurt. It was for fun! This is so much different, so much more serious. Do you understand?"

Wade nodded, his expression filling with remorse. "Of course I understand, Trey," he mumbled. "It was done in fun. There's no other reason why the hell I did it. I guess… I guess I was jealous of your perfect life. You're a smart and successful advertising executive. You never have trouble getting girls. Everyone who meets you loves you. I just wanted to be that person for one night. I'm sorry, okay?"

The anger went out of Trey then and he let out a heavy sigh. He moved back toward the couch and perched on the very edge of it, mindful of the filth that lay thick on the fabric.

"We're identical twins, Wade. Don't you get that? You can be whatever kind of man you want to be. You've been given just as many gifts as I have. No one helped me get through college or handed me a job. I worked my butt off. Something you know nothing about. Get off your ass and do something with your life. Go back to college, finish your degree. Or get a trade. Anything. Stop sitting around feeling sorry for yourself and expecting me and Dad to bail you out. I've had enough. I'm telling you, Wade. I've had enough."

Something in the sad resignation in Trey's tone must have impacted inside Wade's brain. He stared at Trey in panic, desperate tears flooding his eyes.

"Trey! You can't mean that? I saved your life!"

Trey shook his head slowly with disgust and disappointment. "I'm sorry, Wade. You're my brother and I love you, but I just can't be around you anymore. Yes, you saved my life and I'll be forever grateful, but that's not enough anymore. A pattern is becoming clear. You've lied to me over and over about this and other things, and you don't seem to care. You sit around all day in squalor and it doesn't occur to you to get out and get a job. If it weren't for Dad paying your rent and utilities, you wouldn't even have this roof over your head. It's time you grew up. You're twenty-eight, for fuck's sake. I'll be thankful all my life for what you did, but I've repaid you over and over again. How long is it going to be before you stand on your own and start acting your age?"

With a final shake of his head, Trey stood and picked his way through the debris that littered the floor. He walked down the hall. Wade came running after him and grabbed his forearm.

"Please, Trey! Don't leave me like this! I need you! I'm sorry, okay? I shouldn't have lied to you or those other people. I know that now. Please, don't leave. Not like this."

Trey regarded him solemnly. "You need to do the right thing and come forward, Wade. Tell the police you were there. You saved my life once and I've never forgotten it, but this is different. This is *serious*, Wade. If I'm convicted, they'll send me to jail."

"But what about *me*?" Wade cried. "If I turn myself in, *I'll* be the one sent to jail! I've seen those TV shows! They'll beat me up and rape me! I know they will! I can't do it, Trey! I can't!"

His brother backed away from him, shaking his head from side to side. Trey stared at him and disappointment like he'd never known welled up inside. His brother was a coward. Wade was determined to hang him out to dry. It was time Trey accepted that and acted accordingly. At least, that's what his head told him. He only hoped he could convince his heart.

With a heavy tread, Trey turned away in silence. He opened the door, stepped through the opening and quietly closed it behind him. Once outside Wade's apartment building, his gut continued to churn with disappointment and disgust. He had a terrible feeling there might be more to the rape charge than he wanted to believe. It was obvious he couldn't rely on Wade's memory of that night. His brother claimed he could hardly remember what went on.

Great. Just great.

He should have listened to Kiesha. She'd urged him to go to the police. It would make it so much easier for him if he could tell them about Wade… This whole nightmare would go away.

But where would that leave his brother? And more importantly, where would that leave him? He'd have to live with the guilt of being responsible for sending his brother to jail—the brother who'd risked his own to life to save him and Angie from a burning car.

If Wade went to jail, it was likely his father would never speak to him again. That wouldn't exactly be a terrible thing—the two of them had never been close—but apart from Wade, Archibald

Frederick John Walker IV was the only family Trey had. *Did he really want to lose the only two people he had left in the world? Was his freedom worth that price?*

Trey wished he could simply throw Wade to the curb and let him fight his own battles. After all, Wade had caused this mess all on his own. He was an adult. High on drugs or not, he should be forced to take responsibility for his actions.

If only it were that easy…

Trey blew out his breath on a heavy sigh. Flagging down a passing cab, he climbed into the back, no closer to making a decision.

———————————

Kiesha poured herself a second glass of Merlot. Taking a sip, she savored the warm, rich taste. From her position on her balcony, she stared out across the dark waters of the harbor from her position on her balcony and listened as the waves gently lapped the shore. She contemplated all that had happened in the past few hours and in particular, Trey's court case—the one she'd had no intention of seeing through to the end. *Ha! So much for that!*

When she'd first agreed to read the brief of evidence, she admitted it was mainly because of the facts of the case and the utmost belief Trey had in his innocence. She'd always hated any sign of injustice and she'd been more than intrigued by his story.

He'd sworn he'd never met the girl until the moment he'd spied her in the alley and yet, he'd been charged with her sexual assault. *How could the police have gotten it so wrong?* The detectives involved were trained professionals with many years of experience in policing behind them and they were officers who took pride in the quality of their work. They weren't a couple of rookies who leaped in and laid serious charges without the evidence to back them up.

Still, according to Trey, that's exactly what happened and she'd wanted to get to the bottom of it. Now that she'd read the brief, and Trey had told her about his twin, she understood exactly how things had turned out the way they did.

At the scene the alleged victim, Heather Lockhart, had accused Trey of raping her. She was the first one to identify him as her attacker. Further inquiries made by the police had revealed that Heather's friend, Naomi Marchant, and the barman, Sam Frost, had also identified Trey as the man she'd been with on the night in question. And then there was the DNA evidence, and that certainly didn't lie. The only thing was, the police weren't aware Trey had an identical twin brother. Once they had that knowledge, all their preconceptions about this case would have to change.

But Trey had made her promise not to reveal Wade's identity, or even to suggest to the police that he might exist. While she admired Trey's loyalty to his brother, she couldn't help but wonder what that loyalty would cost him.

Right now, the detectives were absolutely certain they had the right man. In their eyes, this was no longer a case of mistaken identity, but an issue of consent. The DNA evidence put Trey squarely at the scene and proved the couple had engaged in sex. That was a completely different argument from the mistaken identity defense Trey had first proposed to her.

Just how far was Trey prepared to let this go? Would he cover for his brother to the point he went to jail for him? Surely not. She understood all about family loyalty—she came from a family of six: three brothers and two sisters. All of them were close. She'd do anything for them... *But jail time?* Probably not.

What was it about Trey's brother that inspired such blind loyalty in Trey? Such a desire to protect him, even at his own expense? All of a sudden, she wanted to know.

Setting her wine glass down on the table beside her deck chair, she padded across the balcony on bare feet, through the sliding door, and into her living room where she retrieved her laptop from the couch. She headed back out onto the balcony, switched it on and waited for it to boot up.

Clicking on a search engine, she plugged in Wade Walker's name and received several hits. Most of them were from Facebook. She clicked on one of the links and a moment later, caught her breath.

Wade's likeness to Trey was uncanny. In fact, had she not known better, she would have thought it was Trey: the same curly dark brown hair; the intriguing bright green eyes; the perfect tanned skin; the slow and sexy smile. She shivered with awareness.

She scrolled through what little information was available to her, given that she wasn't Wade's Facebook friend. One thing she couldn't help but notice was that he had only nine Facebook friends, two of whom were family.

Not that it was a crime or said anything in particular about him, just that he either spent very little time on the social media platform or that he truly didn't go out of his way to build friendships—either online or in the real world. From what Trey had said about his brother being socially awkward, she tended to believe it was the latter. In that respect at least, the twins couldn't be more different.

Trey struck her as someone very self-assured and confident. He knew his place in the world and was comfortable with that. She guessed it was one of the reasons being the subject of a rape investigation had rattled him so much. He wasn't familiar with being on the wrong side of the law or being accused of a heinous crime he didn't commit.

On impulse, she typed Trey's name into the Facebook search bar. A few seconds later and she found him. There he was, smiling that sexy smile. The profile picture looked like it had been taken recently. He wore a smart suit and tie and his curly brown hair was ruffled. She used to think it was from the wind—or perhaps stress caused the messy look—but she was beginning to realize this was just the way his hair was. There was something about the wildness of it, the unrestrained freedom in his curls that tugged at something deep inside of her, something that had been long denied.

She pulled a face. She really needed to start dating again. That was the reason she reacted so strongly to Trey's nearness. It had been too long time since she'd been with a man. She was merely frustrated, tense with pent-up desires. Her body needed release. That's all this was. A mere physical reaction to a very attractive man from a woman who could barely remember the last time she'd had an orgasm.

Still, the feelings he stirred inside her were unwelcome and only served to distract her from the task at hand. If she were going to give her very best to Trey's case, she needed to be on top of her game and completely objective. That meant forgetting all about how attractive her client was and focusing on the facts.

Skimming Trey's profile information, she wasn't surprised to see he had more than a thousand Facebook friends, many of them women. A flash of jealousy took her by surprise. She grimaced, annoyed at herself. *What did she care if Trey had more than his fair share of female Facebook friends? They might not all be ex-lovers.* And even if they were, it was none of her business.

She needed to remember that.

Compressing her lips, and determined to get Trey Walker off her mind, she typed the name "Heather Lockhart" into the Facebook search bar and waited for the results. Several entries were listed. She didn't know what Heather looked like, but from the witness statement the woman had given to the police, Kiesha knew Lockhart was in her early twenties and lived in the exclusive suburb of Double Bay. No doubt she had a bank account to match.

Clicking on one entry after another, Kiesha finally struck pay dirt. A beautiful glamorous young woman with blond hair and expertly applied makeup filled the page. The woman had listed her age as twenty-three and her address matched the one given in the statement. It was her.

Curious about the woman who'd cried rape, Kiesha scrolled through the information available to her. There were plenty of photos of Heather taken with other glamorous women in exclusive nightspots, both around the city and overseas. From the iconic buildings and structures in the backgrounds of the pictures, it was obvious some of them had been taken in Paris and London and two of them showed Heather and another young woman on a boat with the Statue of Liberty in the background. For a girl so young, she'd traveled extensively and as Heather's occupation was listed as socialite, Kiesha could only assume it was on someone else's dime.

Since when had being a socialite become an occupation? It had started with Paris Hilton. Now with the advent of TV shows such as the *Real Housewives of Beverly Hills* that had expanded to include shows set in Melbourne and Sydney, it seemed it was a perfectly acceptable way for some people to spend their time.

A show like that would probably be right up Heather Lockhart's alley. The girl likely had more money than sense. Still, no one deserved to be raped—if that's what really happened. According to the doctor's report, there was no evidence of sexual assault—no abrasions or other physical injuries. It could have been consensual.

Was Heather Lockhart the kind of woman who accused men of rape when she knew darn well it hadn't happened? Was she the type of woman capable of such deceit? It always blew Kiesha's mind when she came across such a person and during her time as a criminal defense lawyer, she'd met a few.

In her experience, such callous and dishonest actions were normally driven by a need for revenge or for attention. An ex-boyfriend who'd moved on to another woman—a payback for cheating; a spiteful and insecure woman who didn't want the relationship to end or who wanted the limelight...

The list of excuses was endless, but the fact was, there was a certain kind of woman who found it acceptable to accuse a man of rape, knowing full well he was innocent. The accuser didn't necessarily want the man to go to jail, but she sure as hell wanted to turn his life upside down, to ruin his reputation and possibly his career. And when the women were finally exposed for the liars they were, hardly any of them expressed remorse.

Was Heather Lockhart that kind of woman? Could she cry rape merely for the fun of it? Or was she telling the truth? Had Trey's brother raped Heather and later just denied it?

Kiesha took another sip from her wine glass and set it back down beside her. Pulling the laptop closer, she plugged Heather's name into a search engine. Apart from the Facebook profile, the other hits that filled Kiesha's screen were from the social pages of popular magazines—Heather at movie premieres, opening nights, art exhibitions... As Kiesha clicked on each link, she saw time and again the smiling glamorous Heather in expensive designer clothes with an equally attractive man on her arm, a different one at each event.

So many men, so little time...

With a sigh, she dug a little deeper and discovered a handful of newspaper articles about Heather's family. According to the articles, she was the daughter of a prominent heart surgeon and came from old money. John Lockhart was the head of cardiothoracic surgery at the Sydney Harbour Hospital. His wife was the daughter of a well-known TV executive who owned several stations. There were pictures of Heather's father with the state premier, a famous cricketer, the jockey who'd most recently won the Melbourne Cup. The man had friends in high places and would fight hard for his daughter's name. Old money. Old pride. It was a dangerous combination.

A surge of nervousness flooded through her and she hastily gulped at her wine. This fight was going to get ugly before it was over. She hoped Trey was prepared for that. And more importantly, that she was.

Once the media got wind of it, this case would be high profile. The people involved would be front page news, maybe for the duration of the trial. Every word, every action of hers would be scrutinized, analyzed, commented on during talkback shows.

Is that what she wanted for the last case she would ever try? She had a District Court appointment to think of. It was the most important accomplishment in her life. *Was she prepared to jeopardize everything she'd worked for by taking on this case?*

But if she dropped the case, an innocent man would be prosecuted for a serious crime he didn't commit. *How could she walk away from that?*

It concerned her deeply that she had no answers.

CHAPTER 8

Unmindful of the perspiration that poured off him in sheets, Trey increased the speed and incline of the treadmill. His arms pumped in a rhythm to match the pounding of his feet and yet still, it wasn't enough. The anger inside him needed an escape and what better way to achieve that than by punishing himself in the gym? Staying fit was important to him and he regularly worked out, but today his angst was all about Wade.

Being banned from the office also meant Trey had far too much time on his hands to think and the issues concerning his brother dominated his every thought. And thoughts of the impending court case inevitably brought thoughts of Kiesha Munro.

He knew better than to get involved with a woman who was integral to securing his freedom, no matter how beautiful and desirable. There were plenty of beautiful and desirable woman in the world. *Why did he have to center his attentions on this one?*

It was just that there was something about her that drew him and he wished he knew what it was. Something indefinable, almost spiritual that touched him deeply. And irritated him to no end.

Women had always come easy to him, but he'd found it harder to keep them. Even as a teenager, though girls had flocked to him, they inevitably broke things off before too long without a word of explanation.

He'd searched his brain for a reason, but couldn't come up with even one. *Why was it that the girls he dated seemed to enjoy his company for only a short time?*

Things didn't change when he got to college. There were plenty of girls eager to go out with him, but only a few weeks in and they bailed. A short, terse text was the usual method of communication, letting him know they were over. Every now and then he'd find the courage to ask the girl why, what had he done wrong, but the usual response was even terser than the first and he was left none the wiser.

It had meant that in adulthood, he'd become a lot choosier about the women he asked out and dated far less often than he wanted to. Having lost his mother at such a young age, he loved the company of women, but he didn't like the feeling of being dumped without rhyme or reason and he'd learned to stand back and protect his heart.

Now dating had become something of a game. He went out with women who were looking for nothing more than a casual fling, like Mary-Jane. It was easier that way. There were no expectations of a future—on either side. It would have suited him just fine if he weren't so lonely. There were only so many times he could tell himself it was best this way—easy come, easy go, with no complications in between.

The truth was, he longed to find a woman he could settle down with. He yearned to have someone to come home to; confide in; share his burdens. He wanted fun and laughter and love— all the things that had been missing from his life for a long time. If it weren't for his twin, he'd be lost. And now even Wade had let him down.

Their conversation the week before had shocked him. For all his twin intuition, he'd had no idea Wade felt jealous of all Trey had achieved. As far as Trey was concerned, Wade had been given all the same opportunities. He'd just not capitalized on them the same way.

But Trey hadn't been lying when he told his brother he'd only gotten there with a lot of hard work. It seemed, as close as they were, Wade's ability to get out and do what needed to be done to make things happen hadn't kicked in like it had in Trey. He could only guess it was because their father had often made things easier for Wade.

Wade had been born the much smaller twin and had struggled in his first few months of life. For a while there, his parents hadn't known if he'd survive. Wade had been kept in the ICU for many weeks after his birth. He'd been tiny and severely underweight so their mother had spent hours and hours at the hospital by his side, hoping and praying for him to pull him through.

When Wade had eventually been well enough to come home, his parents had been overjoyed. Trey had been only a baby himself, of course, and had no memory of the time, but it had been much talked about in the early days when his mother had still been alive. Trey was left in no doubt that it was a miracle his brother had survived.

This increased concern for Wade's welfare had continued throughout his life and even after their mother died, their father, for all his ruthlessness on the bench, made extra allowances for the weaker of his sons.

As far as Trey was concerned, the soft attitude toward Wade and making excuses for him hadn't done Wade any favors. In fact, Trey believed it had only contributed to Wade's slack attitude. Wade always seemed to have his own excuse: The work was too hard; life was too difficult; things just didn't come easy enough...

Which was total bullshit. There was nothing physically or mentally wrong with Wade now and there hadn't been for most of his life. Okay, so the early days after his birth had been touch and go, but that threat had long since passed.

And yet, it was almost as if Wade relied on that excuse of weakness as a reason for all his failings and their father continued to think his son too fragile for this world, as if at any moment Wade might leave it. Though Trey recognized where the attitude came from, it still frustrated him no end.

It was obvious to all concerned that Wade was now a healthy adult, with all the abilities and opportunities that any other young adult had.

He'd proved his capabilities when he'd unselfishly rescued Trey and Angie from their burning car.

Added to that, Kiesha certainly didn't regard his brother as having any kind of handicap. Of course, she didn't know him like Trey did, but still, she continued to urge him to turn Wade in to the police. And even though Trey knew it was the right thing to do, to force Wade to take responsibility, he just couldn't bring himself to do it. Hence, the anger that kept surging through his veins and had him punishing himself in the gym.

With his chest pounding from exertion, Trey slowed down the treadmill and when it came to a stop he stepped off. Striding over to the bike, he programmed it for a fast and hard six-mile trek. His legs pumped hard, round and round and sweat once again poured off his face. And still, he pictured Wade before him: helpless, vulnerable, selfish, sulky, spoiled… In an effort to rid himself of the images, he focused on something else.

Kiesha.

His smart and beautiful lawyer who only complicated things. He wondered if she were single. He hadn't noticed any rings on her fingers. In fact, she wore very little jewelry at all. So far, all he'd seen was a simple gold cross on a fine gold chain around her neck. The jewelry had picked up on the golden tones in her skin.

Trey recalled what he'd discovered about her while he'd been researching lawyers on the Internet. She was from an aboriginal family and it had been announced she was soon to be the first female aboriginal District Court judge. That was quite a feat, but on further investigation, it became obvious she came from a long line of impressive high achievers.

All five of her siblings were professionals and had graduated college at the top of their class. All of them were highly regarded in their chosen careers. Two of them were doctors, two of them were lawyers and one of them had followed their father and worked to develop their family farm.

Such accomplishments were no easy task for people who sadly still faced prejudice and difficulties in society because of the color of their skin. It obviously hadn't held them back, Kiesha included. Their drive to succeed said a lot about their character and their upbringing. They seemed like the kind of people he'd like to meet.

Kiesha was just another example of that can-do attitude. Intelligent, determined and beautiful. *What was there not to like?* All the other women he dated paled to insignificance. It was as though he'd spent all his time dating girls and now he'd found a woman—poised, mature, gorgeous. He was filled with a rush of nerves every time he thought about her. It was so unlike him.

He was the one normally in control, the one who called the shots. He chose women who were looking for a good time, not a long time. He wished he knew what category Kiesha fell into. She had him so stirred up, so confused and uncertain. Never had he felt like that around a woman. Not with Anastasia and Mary-Jane. And that was unsettling.

It was also stupid even thinking of her as a potential romantic interest. She was his lawyer. He needed her to stay focused, clearheaded, determined. He needed her to bring all of her considerable skills to get him out of this fix without involving his brother. He hoped his confidence in her wasn't misplaced and that she'd help him come out on top.

Was he being naïve? Or just plain stupid?

Maybe, both. But he had to give it his best shot. She had to prove to him she couldn't win this fight without his brother. Then and only then he might concede to her advice. It would be done only as a last resort.

———

Kiesha chewed on the end of her pen and at the same time, frowned at the police statements spread on the desk before her. Once again, she'd been going over the evidence in the case against Trey Walker and once again, she was concerned about the DNA report.

Without evidence being introduced that Trey had an identical twin brother, it would be impossible to persuade the jury that another man had been involved. The jury would simply believe he lied and that it was Trey who'd been with Heather Lockhart that night. He was gambling his whole future, his life, almost certainly his freedom, on Kiesha's ability to pull a rabbit out of a hat. She was good at her job, the best, in fact, but she wasn't a magician.

There was nothing else for it. She needed to persuade Trey to either prepare his defense on the basis that he had been there, but the sex was consensual, or turn in his brother. There were no other options.

A knock on the door interrupted her morose thoughts. She bid the person to enter and looked up in time to see her friend and fellow lawyer, Anastasia Swift, enter the room. They were close in age and had started about the same time at Sydney Legal. The woman's long blond hair and make-up were impeccable, as usual, and her custom tailored navy-blue suit fit her body to perfection.

Kiesha couldn't help but wonder how many hours Anastasia spent at the gym. Way more than she did, she'd bet. Still, she welcomed the interruption. Her lips tugged upwards in a smile.

"Hi Ana. It's good to see you. It's been ages. What brings you up here?"

Ana walked toward her in her four-inch heels and with a heavy sigh threw herself down in the chair opposite Kiesha's desk.

"Oh, you know how it is. I've been in court all day listening to one boring witness after another. I'm in the middle of a drug trial and we're still working our way through the scientific evidence. You know how long and tedious that can be. I swear I even saw Judge Watkins nod off a couple of times. I don't know how we expect the jury to stay awake." She rolled her eyes and grinned.

Kiesha smiled back. "Oh yeah, I know exactly what you mean. Although it's been at least a year since I did a drug trial."

Anastasia leaned her elbows on Kiesha's desk and sighed again. "Lucky you. It's beyond tedious. What are you working on?"

Kiesha grimaced. "I'm meant to be tying up loose ends, finalizing my current cases." She flicked a glance in Anastasia's direction. "You heard about my appointment?"

Anastasia nodded. "Yes. I was there when the partners made the announcement last month. Congratulations. It's about time they put an aboriginal woman on the bench. Any woman for that matter. There are nowhere near enough of us in positions of influence and power."

Kiesha nodded. "Yes, you're right. And thanks. It's quite an honor. I look forward to taking on the role and hopefully making a difference."

"You'll be great. I can't think of a more deserving candidate."

Kiesha regarded the woman warmly and with more than a little surprise. Though the two of them were friends and colleagues, they'd never been particularly close.

"Thanks, Ana. That means a lot. You're every bit as deserving as me and hopefully one day soon you'll be offered the same opportunity."

Anastasia looked unconvinced. "I'm not going to hold my breath," she muttered.

Silence fell between them and then Anastasia broke it. "So, what are you working on if it's not tying up loose ends and finalizing open cases?"

Kiesha pulled a face. "I agreed to take on Trey Walker's sexual assault case. Do you know him?"

"Um...maybe. Does he work for Baker & Saddler?"

"Yes."

Anastasia grimaced. "Then, yes. I know him. Along with a long list of other women. He's a serial dater."

Kiesha blushed and quickly averted her gaze, hoping Ana wouldn't notice. She should have known better.

Anastasia's eyes widened in sudden comprehension. "Oh, my goodness, Kiesha Munro! Don't tell me you've also succumbed to his charms?"

Kiesha's embarrassment deepened. She cast around for something to say. "I've done no such thing. I've merely agreed to represent him. He's a client, nothing more. Okay, I admit, he's good looking and way too charming, but that's it. I swear."

Anastasia looked at her knowingly. "Kiesha Munro, I don't know if you're lying to me or if you're lying to yourself, but either way, I don't believe you. I can tell by your reaction when you talk about him. You like him way too much."

"No, you're wrong," Kiesha protested weakly.

Ana looked back at her. The expression on her face told Kiesha her colleague remained unconvinced. And then, Ana's expression sobered.

"Listen, Kiesha. As your friend, I feel the need to warn you. Trey Walker isn't the smooth and charming man you think he is. He's a desperado, trying to latch onto any woman who'll give him the time of day. He doesn't come across like that initially. I think we're all taken in by his good looks, but believe me, I know what I'm talking about. Why would you risk your career on someone like him?"

Kiesha frowned. "What do you mean?"

Anastasia shook her head, her expression grim. "You're about to embark on the most important step of your career. You don't want some nobody hanging off your coattails, driving you nuts with his needs."

"His father's a former Supreme Court judge. He's not exactly a nobody. And anyway, that kind of thing doesn't matter to me. There are plenty of people in my life who remember full well when *I* was a nobody. I'm *still* a nobody."

Anastasias shrugged nonchalantly. "Suit yourself. But I'm telling you I have firsthand information. Trey Walker is bad news."

"When you say firsthand information, what do you mean?"

"Trey and I dated for a while."

Kiesha started in surprise, though Anastasia fit the profile of the kind of women who appeared on Trey's Facebook page.

"You speak in the past tense," she murmured.

"Yes. It didn't last. The first couple months were great. We got along well. But then he started to get too needy. He even thought he was in love." She scoffed. "Fancy that. All I wanted was a casual relationship and he wanted me to walk down the aisle. What a joke."

Anastasia paused to draw in another breath. "As your friend, I think you should know. You're putting a once-in-a-lifetime appointment to the District Court on the line for a sad and desperate loser."

Kiesha blinked in surprise. Anastasia's description of Trey was far removed from her own character assessment of the man. She didn't see him as desperate at all. In fact, quite the contrary. He always came across as sophisticated, suave and confident. If anything, Ana's description more aptly befitted what she knew of Wade.

Was Kiesha blinded by her burgeoning feelings for her charming and sexy client? Or was there more to Trey and Anastasia's breakup? Something that made Anastasia so vindictive...? Not knowing where the truth lay irritated the hell out of her and soured her mood.

"Have you looked through the evidence against him in the sexual assault case? What does it say?" Anastasia continued.

Kiesha drew in a breath and eased it out slowly. With reluctance, she met her friend's somber gaze. "The DNA evidence points to Trey," she conceded.

The other woman shook her head in disgust. "See, what did I tell you? That desperado has taken to forcing women! I can't believe you'd want to defend a sick bastard like that."

Kiesha opened her mouth. The words revealing the existence of Wade were on the tip of her tongue, but something held her back. She closed her mouth. Trey had revealed Wade to her in confidence. As her client, he was entitled to the same rights of legal professional privilege and confidentiality as any other person she represented. She couldn't be sure if Anastasia knew about Trey's twin.

"How long did you two date?" she asked casually.

Anastasia shrugged. "About three months."

Kiesha blinked in surprise. Three months and yet Trey appeared not to have revealed the existence of his identical twin brother to his girlfriend during that time. Still, it was none of her business what Trey shared or didn't share with the women he dated.

All of a sudden, Anastasia leaned forward, her expression full of concern. "You need to excuse yourself from this case, Kiesha," she said in an urgent tone. "It's for the best. This is not going to end well, for either of you. Trey will be convicted of rape and you'll be forever known as the lawyer who defended him. You don't want to take that kind of baggage with you to the bench."

Kiesha regarded her steadily, her heart beating fast. She was suddenly suspicious of her friend's motives.

"What do you care?" she asked.

"I just don't want you to get hurt," Anastasia replied impatiently. "He's a sexy charmer, there's no denying that, but it's all an act. He'll turn your life into a living hell with his neediness and representing him will ruin your career. You've worked so hard to get here. I'd hate to see that happen."

Kiesha merely compressed her lips and nodded. "Okay, well, thanks for the warning."

Anastasia shrugged and gave her a tight smile. "No worries. What are friends for?" With that, she pushed away from the desk and left the room, pulling the door closed behind her.

Kiesha stared into space, her head spinning. Though she'd defended Trey to her friend, Anastasia's words rang loud and clear. It seemed like Trey Walker was dangerous in more ways than one. She'd best keep her distance from him and get this case over with as soon as possible. Then she could escape with her heart intact and life could return to normal.

Somehow the thought didn't seem as exciting as it should have.

CHAPTER 9

Sore and tired from yet another punishing session in the gym, Trey drove to his brother's place. They hadn't spoken since they'd argued over a week ago and Trey could only assume Wade's twin intuition told him that his brother was far from happy with the way things had gone.

Wade's street was filled with parked cars and Trey had to drive more than a block away before he found somewhere he could park. He climbed out of the Mustang and locked it and walked back to Wade's apartment complex.

The sun was warm on his face. There wasn't a cloud in the sky. It was another beautiful spring day. It was a shame he wasn't in the frame of mind to enjoy it. He was still far too worked up about the rape charges hanging over his head and the fact his brother continued to refuse to do the right thing and come forward.

A brand new cherry-red Porsche caught his eye. It was parked beside the curb outside Wade's apartment block. It looked incongruous among the rundown buildings, broken sidewalk slabs and overgrown grass. He wondered who owned it.

To his relief, Wade answered the buzzer and let him in without an argument. Trey hadn't called ahead of time. Wade hadn't been answering his calls, anyway. He'd come there to try and reconcile with his brother and to find some way to resolve this mess and he didn't want to start things out with Wade on the defensive.

"Thanks for letting me in, Wade. It's good to see you," he said as Wade opened the front door to him. "What's with the car downstairs?" he added. "It's a beauty."

Wade offered him a half-grin. "It's good to see you, too, bro. I've missed you."

He dragged Trey in for a hug and Trey sighed and hugged him back. He hated being at odds with his twin. Even though Wade had driven him nuts for most of his life, getting into one scrape after another and expecting Trey to bail him out, he was still his brother and nothing was going to change that.

Wade turned and headed back down the hallway and Trey followed him in. The apartment was as dirty and smelly as it had been on his previous visit, only this time, the smell of marijuana hung thick in the air.

Trey's shoulders slumped. He stared at his brother's back, willing him to turn around.

"Don't tell me you've been taking that shit again, Wade." His voice sounded as disheartened as he felt.

Wade spun on his heel, a belligerent expression on his face. "Don't give me a hard time about it, Trey. My life's gone to shit right now. Everyone's on my back. You, Dad. I need something to distract me, to take my mind off it. I thought you'd understand. Thank God Dad finally does."

Trey frowned at him. "What's that supposed to mean?"

"The sports car outside. Dad bought it for me. We argued last week about...you know. He knew I was feeling down. He had my old Honda towed and replaced it with the Porsche. He thought it would cheer me up."

Trey shook his head in disbelief. "You have to be fucking kidding? What the hell? Who does that? How the hell are you ever going to be forced to take responsibility for your actions if Dad keeps doing stuff like that?"

Wade's expression turned pouty and he swiftly turned away. "I knew you wouldn't understand," he muttered.

"*Understand?* You have to be fucking *kidding?* How the hell would you expect me to understand that it's right to be rewarded for behavior that could see me go to jail? It's just possible you raped an innocent woman, at least the police seem to think you did, and Dad goes and rewards you with a two-hundred-and-fifty thousand dollar car! It's totally unbelievable!" Trey shook his head in disgust.

What the hell was he doing here? Why had he even bothered? It was obvious Wade was never going to man up and act his age. It had been that way all their lives. And his father willingly went along with it! Why would Trey expect this time would be any different? After all, they were only talking jail and the end of Trey's career and life as he knew it. No biggie.

With a sigh of disappointment, he tried again. "Wade, listen to me, mate. This is serious. The evidence against you—against me... It's serious. The police know you were there. They have your DNA."

Wade's grin was unrepentant. "No, bro. You have it wrong. They know *you* were there. They have *your* DNA."

Anger surged through him and it was all he could do to control it. "You seem to have forgotten, Wade, the only reason I was there that night was because *you* called me asking for help. I was on my way home, ready for bed, minding my own business. But you called and said you needed me and I came right away. I came to help you, just like you once helped me. That's why I was there. The *only* reason I was there. And that's why the police have what they think is *my* DNA."

Wade had the decency to look embarrassed. "Okay, okay, bro. You don't need to remind me. I know what happened."

"Then why the hell aren't you *saying* something? Why are you hiding behind this ridiculousness? Why are you letting me take the rap for this and pretending you weren't even there?"

Wade merely offered a helpless shrug. "You know what I'm like, bro. I'm not like you. I'm not strong and smart with the gift of gab. I'd only end up saying the wrong thing. Then where would I be?"

Trey stared at him, hardly able to believe the words that were coming out of his brother's mouth.

"Where the hell do you think that leaves *me*?" he snarled, his hands clenching into fists.

Trey caught the flash of fear in his brother's eyes just before Wade moved a safe distance away from him. With an effort, Trey drew in a deep breath and released the tension that held him in its grip. He stared at his brother, prepared to beg if he had to.

"You need to go to the police, Wade. You need to do the right thing. I'll take you there. I'll sit with you when you talk to them. You need to tell them it was you. There's nothing else you can do."

Wade shook his head quickly back and forth and for just a second panic filled his eyes. "No! No way! I won't do it and you can't make me! It's not my fault. I did nothing wrong. That little bitch was all over me that night. She had her hands all over my cock. She was begging for it. She has no right to cry rape. No right at all."

Trey stared at him in disgust. "Well, she obviously changed her mind, Wade, or she wouldn't have told the police you raped her."

"Too bad for her," Wade sneered. "She shouldn't have gotten me so worked up, led me on... For fuck's sake, what was she? A prick teaser! Is that what this was all about? Well, I showed her."

A frisson of concern flashed through Trey. He stared at his brother, almost too scared to voice the question. "What do you mean by that?"

Wade's grin widened. Satisfaction flooded his smug expression. "No one cock teases Wade Walker like that and gets away with it," he said.

Trey's gut filled with dread. "What the hell are you saying, Wade?"

"Nothing! Just that she wanted it and she got it. End of story."

Nausea swirled in Trey's stomach. He thought he might be sick. His hand tightened around the back of the couch as he stared his brother. "Oh, Wade. What the fuck have you done?"

Wade's expression turned sulky. "Nothing! I did nothing! Dad told me to keep my mouth shut. I suggest you keep yours shut, too. This will all blow over, just like Dad says it will."

Trey exploded. "For fuck's sake, Wade! Wake up, would you? This is my *life* you're screwing with! You need to go down to the police station right now and tell them the fucking truth."

Wade regarded him solemnly and at last, gave an offhanded shrug. "You're not listening to me, bro. It's not my fault. Go and ask Dad. He'll tell you."

Trey had never felt fury like he did right then. He fought against the urge to grab his brother and pummel him into pulp. The arrogance, the disrespect, the total lack of remorse... It was beyond him how he could be related to such a man. He stared at Wade and shook his head in disgust.

"This is it, Wade. We're done. You might have saved my life, but I've more than repaid you for that good deed. If I take the rap for this, we're even. And I don't ever want to see you again."

———————

Wade reached up to the top shelf that hung above the kitchen counter and brought down the old flour tin he used to store his stash of marijuana. He was still pissed at the audacity of his brother coming there and demanding he turn himself in. As if he would ever do that. Not now, not ever. *What did Trey think he was? Stupid?* Yeah, probably.

Trey was just trying to protect his own sorry ass and get the cops off his back. Wade hadn't meant for the detectives to think it was Trey in the alley that night, but he couldn't say he was disappointed they'd jumped to that conclusion. It sure helped take the heat off him.

He opened the cupboard under the sink and took out his bong. Heading back to the couch, he fixed the weed the way he liked it and leaned over and took a deep drag. The pungent smoke filled his mouth and made its way to his lungs. Almost immediately, he felt better.

His brother's unexpected visit had left him feeling out of sorts. It wasn't his fault the stupid bitch had complained about the way he'd treated her. He'd fucked her. So what? She'd been begging for it only moments earlier. At least, that's the way he remembered it.

He should have called his father instead of Trey. Archibald Frederick John Walker IV would have known what to do. He wouldn't have fucked things up like his brother had. It was too late now to waste time contemplating what he should have done.

Now he had to look to the future and work out a plan for dealing with the mess as it was. But not right now. Right now he was going to kick back and relax for a while. His brother could go to hell.

Trey's blood boiled as he maneuvered the Mustang through the late afternoon traffic. He couldn't believe the gall of his brother. The man was seriously deranged! How could his brother stand by while his twin went to jail for a crime he was innocent of, a crime his brother committed? It was beyond him. And the knowledge Wade could hang him out to dry like that damaged something in him way down deep inside.

Apart from Wade's single act of bravery a decade ago, he'd always been shallow and selfish, but Trey had never dreamed his twin cared so little for him. The knowledge devastated him. He would have done anything for Wade. Over the years, Trey had proved that more than once. This was a prime example and yet, did Wade appreciate the sacrifice his brother had made and was making? It sure as hell didn't appear that way.

With a screech of brakes, Trey pulled into the circular driveway outside his father's ritzy penthouse. Leaving the vehicle where it was, he jumped out of the Mustang and strode toward the building. Recognizing him immediately, the doorman, signaled to a valet and Trey dropped the keys in the man's hands. The doorman acknowledged Trey with a respectful nod and upon his approach pulled open the heavy wooden doors.

"Good afternoon, Mr Walker. Is your father expecting you?"

"Hi, Jonah. It's good to see you. And to answer your question: No, he isn't," Trey replied in a harsh voice.

To the man's credit, his expression didn't change, not even by a whisker. Trey strode past him and went over to the bank of elevators. He punched in the button for the penthouse. In record time, he was whizzed to the top of the fourteen-floor building. The elevator *dinged* as the door slid open and Trey stepped out. His anger continued to simmer just below the surface.

He forced himself to slow his steps and drew in a few deep breaths. His father abhorred any sign of weakness in his oldest son, including a loss of self-control. The double standard wasn't lost on Trey. Wade could get away with anything. Bad behavior barely rated a mention. Trey had learned a long time ago not to let it bother him. Most of the time, it didn't.

Feeling considerably calmer, he rapped on the carved wooden panel outside his father's condominium. A Filipino housekeeper answered the door. She peered at Trey in surprise.

"Mr Trey! It's so nice to see you! Are you here to see your father?"

"Hi, Mary." He bent down and pecked her cheek. "It's good to see you, too. Is he in?"

The housekeeper, who'd known Trey since he was a baby, nodded. "Yes. But he's busy."

"Doing what?

"It's five o'clock. Time for his regular massage. Every second afternoon. Don't you remember?"

Trey acknowledged her comment with a nod. Now that the housekeeper had mentioned it, of course he remembered. It had been a long-standing appointment in his father's life ever since he'd retired.

"Don't worry, Mary. I won't stay long. I just want to talk to him. I'm sure he can manage that while he's getting his massage."

With that, he walked across the marble flooring in the grand foyer decorated with priceless antiques. Striding across the wide expanse of the open concept kitchen and living room, he headed down the wing that housed the media room, his father's library, and the den used mainly for facials, massages and such other personal things.

The door to that room was closed, but that didn't deter Trey. Turning the knob without knocking, he let himself into the room. His father lay naked on the table, with only his butt covered by a thick white towel. A large breasted, attractive blonde in a white uniform—so tight Trey wondered briefly how she could even breathe in it—worked over his father. Neither of them heard him come in and they both started in surprise when he spoke.

"Good afternoon, Dad. I'm glad I found you in."

Archibald Frederick John Walker IV came up on one elbow and stared at his son in surprise. "Trey! What are you doing here?"

After a momentary hesitation, the blonde continued to work over his father. Her slim hands with their blood red nails pounded, squeezed and scraped. She was bent low enough that her ample bosom brushed along his father's naked back. Trey was sure the gesture wasn't done accidentally.

Still, it was none of his business how his father spent his time and who he spent it with. It changed nothing about how angry Trey felt over the way his father seemed to want to let Wade get away with rape. Even to reward him...

"I've just been speaking to Wade," he said flatly.

"Oh?" his father replied, not even bothering to look up.

Trey's anger boiled over. "How could you do that, Dad? Reward him for that kind of behavior? A Porsche? Really, Dad? He raped a girl!"

His father slowly turned to look at him. The masseuse continued her work. "You don't know that, Trey."

Trey shook his head, incredulous. "He as much as admitted it, Dad."

"Ha! Your brother wouldn't know what he'd done. He was drunk and high on drugs. They both were. You told me that yourself." He coughed and then continued. "I understand you're worried about the whole thing, but don't be. A good lawyer will get this case thrown straight out. Who's representing you?"

Trey sucked in a breath and did his best to get his anger back under control. "Kiesha Munro," he replied in a steadier voice.

His father raised one eyebrow. "The aboriginal girl?"

Trey gritted his teeth. "She's a senior associate with many years' experience at the highest level of the law, Dad. She's about to be appointed to the District Court. She just happens to be a female aboriginal."

"Yes. I see. Well, she has a good reputation. Although she never appeared before me, I understand she's one of the best. If she's that good, she should get this tossed out before the lunch break and then we can all forget about it."

Once again, Trey struggled to contain his anger. He clenched his hands into fists and forced himself to breathe evenly. He didn't just want the case dropped, he wanted his name removed from any taint or whisper of suspicion. He wanted his brother to take responsibility.

"That's not the point, Dad. I didn't do this! Wade did! Why aren't you forcing him to take responsibility, for once in his life?"

His father sighed and turned his head away. When he spoke again, his voice was muffled by the towel.

"He's never been as strong or as smart as you, Trey. You know that. He was a weakling as a baby, so small and thin. He had to fight to survive. Even after he was born, the fight didn't end. We're lucky to have him here. You know that better than most. If he hadn't survived, you wouldn't be here today."

A wave of familiar guilt enveloped Trey and he fought hard against it. He shouldn't have to feel obligated to his brother for the rest of their lives. He wasn't responsible for Wade. Or his failings. *He wasn't!*

"You have to look out for him, Trey. You owe it to him. After all, he did save your life. Besides, you're capable of looking after yourself. He's not. Jail would kill him. You, on the other hand... You're a survivor. You worry too much. You'll do all right."

Trey stared at him, aghast. "Dad! Listen to yourself! I had nothing to do with this! I went to that nightclub because Wade called me. He sounded desperate. He said he needed help. Why should I go to jail for doing what was right? All I wanted to do was help him out, like he helped me all those years ago. Now I'm being crucified for it and my own family's hung me out to dry."

He shook his head. "It's unbelievable. You were a judge, Dad. You sat in judgment day after day and made decisions, fair decisions about right and wrong. Now you can't even see the right and wrong of it between your own sons! It's as if you don't *want* to see!"

His father sighed again and rolled his eyes. "Don't be so melodramatic, Trey. You won't go to jail. I already told you. Your lawyer should get rid of this for you without too much effort. You just have to go through the motions, play along. I made a few calls. Your so-called victim has form. She's done this at least twice before. If need be, we can have those men come forward and give evidence. I assume your lawyer won't object to that?"

Trey shook his head, taken aback. Heather Lockhart had cried rape before… Did that mean he was off the hook? Did it mean Wade was innocent, after all? He wished he knew.

His father sighed for a third time. "Listen, Trey. You need to relax. Let the police feel like they've had a win. Even for a little while. Don't worry. Things will work out." His father came up on his elbows and looked at him. "How's Anastasia, by the way? I haven't seen her for a while."

Trey blinked at the sudden change in subject. "We… We broke up over a month ago, Dad."

His father shrugged. "Oh, I didn't know."

Trey made a sound of disgust in the back of his throat. "I told you last time we had dinner together. How could you have forgotten?" He shook his head and turned away. "Anyway, it doesn't matter."

His father surveyed him quietly from his prone position on the massage table. "I take it you're not brokenhearted?"

Trey breathed a heavy sigh. "No. We were only casual. Things just didn't work out. That's the way it goes."

His father eyed him slyly. "Kiesha Munro's an attractive woman."

Trey started in surprise and fought against the blush that stole up his neck. He widened his eyes innocently, feigning disinterest. "Really? I hadn't noticed."

His father grinned knowingly and Trey hid a grimace. He'd never been able to get away with anything as far as his father was concerned. This time was no different.

His father chuckled. "Oh, yes you have. And the fact you're pretending you haven't, tells me everything I need to know." He followed his words with a wink. "I've seen her. She's a great looking woman, son. Beautiful, and smart to boot. As soon as this case is over, I'd say go for it, Trey."

Trey shifted uncomfortably. If he ever had a relationship with Kiesha it would be none of his father's business and he didn't appreciate him speaking about her that way. It was disrespectful. She was so much more than that. Trey glanced at the big breasted masseuse who had moved lower and now worked her strong hands over his father's ass.

With a sound of disgust, he turned and left.

CHAPTER 10

Kiesha stared out of the plate glass windows that made up two entire walls of her corner office and wished she was relaxed enough to appreciate the view. The brilliant green of Hyde Park and the bright and cheerful display of multiple garden beds normally set her at ease, but today it just wasn't happening. She'd gone over the evidence against Trey with a fine-tooth comb and despite her reputation for being the best in the business, she was at a loss about what to do.

The committal hearing was listed for next week. No matter which way she looked at it, Trey had only two choices: accept that he was the one who'd been with Heather Lockhart and argue that the sex was consensual, or put forward his brother as the suspect who'd left behind his DNA.

She'd already put her position to him and he'd refused both options. He seemed to think she could miraculously produce evidence, or stumble across a rule of law that would exculpate him without the need to involve his brother. But the truth was, there was nothing, and *he* had to know that, too. He might not have a legal background, but he wasn't stupid.

The DNA evidence was damning. There was no way to get around it without pointing the finger at Trey's twin. It frustrated her that he kept refusing to do so. Disclosing all would make this serious situation go away. And yet, he continued to resist.

With a sigh, she turned away from the window and walked back to her desk. Throwing herself down in her chair, she reached across and picked up the phone. She'd try once more to convince him to change his mind. She dialed his number from memory. He answered on the second ring.

"Trey Walker."

"Trey, it's Kiesha. We need to talk."

Something in her somber tone must have registered with him. He replied in an equally sober tone.

"Okay. When?"

"Can you meet me at Jacob's Café after four? I should be finished in court by then."

"Yeah. I'll be there."

"Good."

"Is it too much to hope you've found a loophole?"

An exasperated smile curved her lips at the hopefulness in his tone. He sounded like a needy child asking for ice cream. As much as she didn't want to dampen his spirits, he had to accept the reality of his situation.

"I'm afraid not," she replied. "I'll see you this afternoon. We'll talk about it, then."

———————

"Ms Munro, are you ready to address the court?"

Kiesha pushed her chair back from the bar table and stood. "Yes, your Honor."

"Good. What would you like to say?"

Kiesha glanced down at her notes and sent a silent prayer heavenwards that the plea she was about to put forward would be enough to keep her client from spending too much time in jail. Max Smith had pleaded guilty to a charge of sexual assault. She was there to represent him on the sentencing. Whatever she put before the court on her client's behalf by way of explanation would be taken into account by the judge on sentencing. With a prior criminal record for two similar offenses and no genuine expression of remorse, it would be no easy task.

"Your Honor, Mr Smith has an illness. He needs hospitalization, medical treatment, not prison. He freely admits he's done the wrong thing and he feels sorry for his victims." She choked the words out, even though she was far from convinced her client felt anything of the sort. She had to say something that would mitigate his sentence or he'd be facing a lengthy term in jail.

"The defendant underwent psychiatric testing, Ms Munro, and he was found to be perfectly normal. What is this illness you refer to and why don't I have any medical evidence of such before me?" Judge Campbell asked.

Kiesha blushed. It wasn't like her to speak about things she couldn't prove. It just went to show how her mind was on other things. She glanced down at her notes and regrouped.

"I'm sorry, your Honor. You're right. There is no medical evidence of such an illness, but my client feels he is unwell. He feels he loses control over his actions toward women, especially after he's been drinking. He's been regularly attending Alcoholics Anonymous and feels confident he has his urges under control. This is not his first time before the court, your Honor, but I ask for the court's leniency. I ask for a community service order."

The judge's bark of laughter sent a fresh wave of embarrassment rushing across Kiesha's face.

"A community service order, Ms Munro? You have to be kidding!"

"Yes, well, I hoped… That is, I thought that maybe—?"

"Is that all, Ms Munro?" the judge interrupted.

"Yes, thank you, your Honor." With her face burning, Kiesha regained her seat.

In short shrift, Judge Campbell summarized his findings and notwithstanding her client's guilty plea, sentenced Maxwell Richard Smith to a ten-year, non-parole period. And that was that.

By the time Kiesha hurried out of the building that housed the District Courts and made her way to Jacob's Café, storm clouds blotted out what had been an otherwise pleasant October day. As she made her way home, she couldn't help but think of Trey. He faced the exact same charge. The thought of him spending even a day in jail for a crime he didn't commit was abhorrent. Knowing he was relying on her to protect his freedom whilst tying her hands behind her back was even more alarming.

Nausea churned in her stomach. The traffic lights changed and she crossed the road shoulder to shoulder with people in a hurry to be on their way. They pushed and jostled each other, but she was oblivious to all of it. Her mind was firmly focused on her upcoming meeting. Trey's committal hearing was mere days away. She had to convince him to turn his brother in. It was the only way.

Just as he'd been the first time they arranged to meet at Jacob's Café, Trey was already seated at a table on the far side of the room when she opened the door. A scattering of people filled less than half of the tables, drinking coffee, reading newspapers, texting on phones. Trey was the only one who looked up as she entered.

His eyes flared wide with recognition and then his gaze dropped as he gave her a slow once-over. Try as she might to prevent it, heat stole across her cheeks. His gaze left fire trailing in its wake and her nipples tightened involuntarily. Her body's betrayal annoyed her, but there was no denying the way she reacted to him. She pulled her jacket closer around her and hoped it concealed all evidence of her arousal and desire. She was his lawyer. That was it. Period.

"Sorry I'm late," she murmured and pulled out a seat opposite him.

He acknowledged her apology with a casual shrug. "It's fine."

"I was in court. The judge ran overtime," she said, feeling the need to explain. "I hope you haven't been waiting long," she added.

"Only since four." He grinned. "Unlike your judge, I always run on time."

Something about his relaxed smile and the way it crinkled his eyes did funny things to her insides. As hard as she tried to steel herself against her attraction for him, he kept crashing through her barriers. At least he didn't seem to be aware of his effect on her. That was a bonus.

Drawing in a surreptitious breath, she determined to remain polite, but aloof, and ignore the flare of attraction that just wouldn't go away. It was the best for all concerned. Decision made, she cleared her throat and clasped her hands in front of her in a no-nonsense kind of way. She eyed him somberly.

"We need to talk about your case. The committal hearing is a handful of days away. I need to know what angle you're planning to take."

He frowned. "What do you mean, *what angle I'm planning to take?* You know my defense. I wasn't there. It's a case of mistaken identity."

Irritation surged through her. "You're deliberately being obtuse, Trey. We've already talked about this.

The DNA evidence places you at the scene. We have to come up with something better than 'you have the wrong man.' The jury will never buy it and I'm not staking my reputation on something so ludicrous."

He glared at her. "So this is about protecting *your* reputation, is it? What about protecting my freedom? This is my *life* we're talking about!"

"Exactly!" she shot back. "I'm glad you've finally acknowledged the seriousness of your situation! That DNA evidence is impossible to refute. We're going to look like silly jackasses claiming it wasn't you. You'll be committed for trial before you can blink; it will happen that damn quick. Now, are you willing to listen to reason, or are you going to continue to stick your head up your ass and hope this all goes away?"

Her breath came fast and her chest rose and fell in time with her breathing. She was so mad at him and his continued refusal to face reality—and to do the right thing. He was an intelligent man and though he didn't know the law like she did, he knew enough to know she spoke the truth. It was maddening how he continued to ignore what was plain to both of them.

With an effort, she got her breathing back under control and with it, her temper. When she spoke again, her tone was mollifying.

"I'm sorry. I lost my temper. It was…unprofessional. But let me say this, Trey. If our roles were reversed—if I was the one facing sexual assault charges with the same evidence against me and you were my lawyer—what would you advise me?"

His green eyes remained steady on hers. Slowly, they filled with a grudging respect.

"I'd tell you to own up to being there and then I'd fight with everything I had to convince the jury the two of you enjoyed consensual sex."

"Exactly."

Their gazes remained locked, hot and intense. She wanted to look away, but she couldn't. Time was suspended. A minute, an hour, a week... She couldn't say how much time passed, but the indefinable and invisible thing that held them enthralled was only broken by the arrival of the waitress.

It was a different girl than the one who'd ogled Trey the first time, but this female was no less immune to his charms. She smiled seductively in his direction and deliberately pressed her breast against his arm in the pretext of reaching for the menus. To Trey's credit, he barely glanced at the woman as he gave her an order for two lattés.

Hot jealousy speared through Kiesha just the same. She looked away, feeling suddenly confused and knocked off balance by her response to the man who sat across from her. She barely knew him, but that didn't seem to matter to her body. What she saw, she liked. A lot. And it didn't seem to matter that he was her client.

"You're right."

Kiesha blinked and stared down at the shredded napkin she held in her hands. She shook her head and scrambled to get a grasp on what Trey had said. "Excuse me?"

He grinned, as if totally unaware of the turmoil of her emotions. "You just want me to say it again. Admit it."

She blushed and shook her head. "No, I'm sorry. My mind wandered. I honestly didn't hear what you said."

Trey rolled his eyes and grinned again. "I said, you're right." Slowly his smile faded. "The DNA evidence could be my undoing. There's nothing I can do to refute it. Without proof of Wade's existence, I'm facing the very real possibility of being put away. If I was your lawyer, I'd give you exactly the same advice: Give up your brother, or face the consequences."

Her shoulders relaxed and she released a breath she hadn't realized she'd been holding until that moment. *Thank God! He'd seen the light. She might get him out of this mess after all...*

"The thing is though... I can't do it."

She stared at him in shock. "I... I beg your pardon?"

"I'm not going to give Wade up to the police."

Kiesha shook her head slowly back and forth in utter disbelief. "Why the hell not?"

"He's my brother. Period."

Anger and frustration once again surged through her. "This is going to go to trial, Trey. Do you understand what that means?"

"Yes."

"Then how can you sit there and tell me you're not prepared to do the one thing that could see this over for you!" she shouted, her exasperation coming to the fore.

"I don't expect you to understand," he said quietly.

"You're right! I *don't* understand! Going to trial does irreparable damage to you professionally and personally, whether we get a guilty or innocent verdict in the process."

Trey drew in a deep breath. She watched his shoulders slump as he eased it out. Once again tension gripped her insides as she waited for him to explain.

"It's my fault my brother's like he is," he began quietly. "Before we were even born, I took up all the nutrients. And the oxygen. Just ask my father. I was born nearly double Wade's weight. It was touch and go whether he'd even survive those first few months. My mother spent every night and day by his side at the hospital."

She stared at him helplessly, trying desperately to understand. *Surely he didn't blame himself for what happened in the womb?*

And yet, it seemed he did.

"I was always the stronger twin," he continued in the same quiet, faraway tone. "I could run faster, swim better and I excelled at school. I was popular in high school, captain of the football team. I always pulled the girls. Wade was always second best. Every single time. I wished like hell things were different, but they weren't. He tried so hard, but he never got there. Not once. It affected his self-esteem and he's pretty well given up trying."

He sighed. "Even now, at twenty-eight, he thinks he's never going to be good enough. It doesn't matter what I say. I can't get through to him.

"For years, I tried to tell him it didn't matter. He didn't need to try and be me. Eventually I gave up trying. He totally wore me out. Mom's death compounded matters. She was his moon and stars. He was lost without her. We both were. But Wade took it the hardest of all."

His voice had turned ragged with emotion. He looked across at Kiesha and the pain in his eyes tore at her heart. She forced herself to steel herself against it.

"It sounds like you're making excuses for him," she said softly.

He reeled back like she'd struck him. His tone turned icy. "Like I said, I don't expect you to understand."

White-hot anger poured through her. She glared at him. "Don't give me that nonsense! I have five siblings! I know all about loyalty to my family and looking out for one another. But never would I expect one of my brothers or sisters to take the blame for something I had done—and *especially* not something like *this!* It's just not right!"

Trey regarded her steadily, banked anger now visible in his eyes. "That might be true for you, but it's the right thing for me."

She held his gaze for another long moment and then finally cursed under her breath on a frustrated sigh. "Then you're going to have to accept this case will be committed for trial. There's more than enough evidence. A trial date will be set in six weeks."

His jaw thrust out at a stubborn angle. "Good. That means it will be over before Christmas."

Her anger exploded. "For God's sake, Trey! Haven't you been listening to a word I've said? If you continue to insist on this idiocy, there's a strong likelihood you'll be convicted and then you'll be in *jail* for Christmas! Don't you care about that?"

His expression remained unchanged. "Of course I care, but it's not going to happen. You'll make sure it doesn't."

She felt the weight of his gaze, saw the expectancy in his eyes, and the gravity of what she'd agreed to take on weighed heavily on her shoulders.

"You place too much confidence in me." She sighed. "I'm a lawyer. I'm not a miracle worker. And that's what you expect. A miracle. I can't just pull not-guilty verdicts out of a hat."

He shook his head. "You sell yourself too short. You might not be a miracle worker, but you're the best in this business. Everyone who is anyone knows it. Even my father, the esteemed Archibald Frederick John Walker IV, former Supreme Court judge, knows it." Trey eyed her steadily. "That's why I chose you."

"I chose *you!*" she scoffed. "Let's not forget that."

Once again, he merely shrugged. "Whatever. I'm not going to argue the semantics of it." He grinned, showing a pair of dimples. She hated that his simple action had the ability to turn her stomach upside down and inside out. Nerves fluttered low in her belly. She could see why he was a serial dater. No doubt he had his pick of women.

The thought gave her pause. *Did she want to become just another notch on his belt?* And then she remembered what Anastasia had told her. If the woman had been telling the truth, there was a different side to Trey Walker, a much needier side.

The last thing she wanted was to get involved with a man who was looking for something long term. She was about to embark on the job of a lifetime. She didn't have time for a serious relationship—with anyone.

"What happened between you and Anastasia Swift?" she asked.

The question came from nowhere. Embarrassment flooded her cheeks. She wished she could take back the words, but it was too late. Trey blinked in surprise and sat back against his chair. Her embarrassment deepened. She wished the floor would open up and swallow her completely.

"I didn't realize you were friends with Anastasia."

He spoke in a casual tone, but she sensed the heightened awareness in the sudden tensing of his body and the way his eyes didn't leave hers. She drew in a deep breath and eased it out between suddenly dry lips, wishing she'd kept her mouth shut.

Keeping her gaze fixed on the table between them, she responded in an equally casual tone.

"We're not exactly friends. She's a work colleague. Every now and then she drops into my office for a chat. We've had coffee a few times." She lifted her gaze to his. "Does it matter?"

His gaze remained hooded. "No. I just thought if she was a good friend you'd already know how dishonest she can be."

"What do you mean?"

"You were the one who raised the subject of Anastasia. You tell me."

Kiesha squirmed uncomfortably. She wished like hell she'd kept her curiosity about his former lover in check and hadn't said a word. Now she was left to explain why she'd brought the woman up in conversation. It was beyond embarrassing.

She clenched her jaw and tried to bring the discussion to an end. "Just forget about it. I shouldn't have said anything. It's none of my business. Besides, I don't want to know."

His answering smile was filled with knowing. It was like he could read her mind.

"Yes, you do."

Her heart beat madly against the wall of her chest. He'd done it again. Read her mind like he was privy to her innermost private thoughts. Heat exploded across her face. She battled through it, determined to hold on to at least a modicum of her pride. Lifting her chin, she stared him down.

"Anastasia told me you two had dated."

Trey nodded, his expression unaltered. "Yes. For a few months. It didn't work out."

"She said you fell in love with her and got too needy."

A disbelieving smile turned up the corners of his mouth. He shook his head: his gaze cool and cynical. "Like I said, if you knew her well, you'd know how good she is at lying."

Kiesha held his gaze. "Are you saying it isn't true?"

Trey's eyes burned with sudden anger. His lips curled up in disgust. "I started dating Anastasia in good faith. Neither of us were looking for anything serious, least of all me. It was one of the things that attracted me to her. We both understood from the outset that it was only casual. Then she accused me of being too needy. She felt suffocated. She needed more space. I still don't know what I did to make her to feel that way. My attitude toward her hadn't changed. We'd get together for a night or two and then go our separate ways. It suited both of us. At least, I thought it did. I can only imagine she came up with that story about me suffocating her because she didn't have the courage to tell me straight up we were done. Even still, it was weird. I still don't understand what happened."

"Were you in love with her?" Kiesha held her breath while she waited for his answer.

"Hell, no."

Her breath left her body in a rush and she hoped he hadn't noticed how relieved she was at his answer. And then she frowned. "Why would Anastasia say you were?"

Trey shrugged. "Who knows? I dated the woman for three months and I was still taken by surprise when she broke things off. I thought we had an understanding. Somewhere along the line, she changed the rules without telling me. She called me a desperado. It hurt. Especially when I didn't feel like I'd done anything to deserve the label."

Kiesha stared at him, transfixed. *Who was she to believe?* She cleared her throat. He was either clingy and far too needy, or he preferred a relationship that had no strings. It was either one or the other. There was no in-between.

So where did the truth of the matter lie? There was only one way to find out. She drew in a breath and gathered her courage to put the question to him.

"So, are you still in support of casual relationships?"

He nodded briefly. "Yes. Why?"

Her heart leaped in response to his question. *Was she brave enough to tell him how she felt?* The tingling awareness between her legs reminded her how long it had been since she'd had sex. She leaned forward and rested her chin on her hands. Locking her gaze with his, she answered him.

"I've always thought casual sex was underrated. I mean, what is there not to like? You find someone attractive; you hook up for the night and then you go your separate ways in the morning. No broken hearts, no difficult emotions. What could be simpler?"

His green eyes darkened with desire. Neither one of them looked away.

"Do you have any idea how turned on I am right now?"

His voice was low and husky with need. His pupils were dilated and his well-formed lips were parted on a soft intake of breath. Her heart hammered and her nipples tightened, intensifying to need in her core.

The waitress arrived with their coffees, but they didn't acknowledge her. Kiesha was powerless to break the indefinable something that drew them to each other and she could only guess Trey felt the same.

And then the heat in his gaze intensified and it was like she was burning from the inside out. It had been that way the first time she'd seen him. Their initial meeting had been held in the safety of her office. Now that they were on their own time, surrounded by strangers, anything was possible.

"My cock is so hard it feels like it's going to detonate," he rasped. "I want to fuck you so bad."

His coarse language should have disgusted her, but had the opposite effect. Liquid heat pooled between her thighs. Her clit vibrated with need.

Was she brave enough to issue him an invitation? Could she be that brazen? It wouldn't be the first time...

Of course, she'd never before slept with a client, but she was a woman who went after what she wanted. There was nothing wrong with that.

She was his lawyer and he was her client, but there was no dispute about an imbalance of power. He'd been calling the shots all along and both of them knew it. It wasn't exactly proper, but they were on the same side. She wasn't contemplating sleeping with the enemy. Besides, if she couldn't touch him or feel his hands on her soon, she'd just about explode.

Before she could lose her courage, she blurted out the words: "Would you like to come back to my place? We could...have a drink... Discuss the case...?" Her voice drifted off.

His eyes flared with heat and the way he stared at her left no doubt about how he felt. His gaze probed hers. It was like he was trying to make it clear to her that if he accepted her invitation, they'd be doing much more than discussing the case.

She gave an imperceptible nod and a fresh wave of desire ignited in his eyes.

"Let's go," he murmured.

With his gaze still on hers, he reached for his wallet and tossed down a handful of bills. He pushed away from the table and stood. She did the same. He reached for her hand and in silence they left the café. An instant later, he dragged her into a side alley and pressed her against a brick wall. She gasped in surprise and then gasped again at the molten heat that burned in his eyes. And then his lips descended.

They were warm and soft and pliant and moved hungrily over hers. She returned his passion, kiss for kiss, until both of them were breathless. He pushed her hard against the wall and she was left in no doubt as to the extent of his attraction. His cock was a solid hard length against her belly.

"Can you feel how much I want you?" he murmured, his voice low and husky.

She stared up at him and nodded. Her heart beat a mile a minute. "Yes. But not here. Let's go home."

With a final kiss, he dropped his hands to his sides and reluctantly stepped away. Kiesha straightened her clothes. She reached up and touched her swollen lips. The need deep inside her continued to throb and she lamented the loss of Trey's body against hers, but they were in public—albeit in a dim alleyway. Still, there was enough light from the waning day for people to see them and though she was adventurous when it came to her sex life, she preferred it to happen in the privacy of her bedroom.

In silence, Trey once again reached for her hand and together they walked out of the alley. The rush-hour traffic was heavy and the crowds had strengthened as people made their way home. But all of the hubbub surrounding them dimmed to a hum. Flooded with anticipation, she could hear nothing over the loud and erratic beating of her heart.

Chapter 11

Trey offered to drive them home in his Mustang. Kiesha was quietly impressed with his choice of car. Though shiny and red and flashy, it also had an understated classic feel about it that surprised her. If she'd been asked about the kind of car Trey Walker might have driven, she would have guessed he'd be more into the latest Audi sports car or even an Aston Martin, depending on his budget and how much his father kicked in the tin. Still, something told her he stood on his own two feet and preferred to pay his own way.

"I restored it myself," he said with quiet pride, noticing her interest.

"She's a beauty."

"Thanks. She goes like a dream. Get in. I'll show you." Trey grinned and the sheer brilliance of it had her grinning back. The dread in her stomach that had been an almost constant companion since she'd read through the brief suddenly lifted and she found herself feeling lighter and happier than she had for a long time.

With good old-fashioned manners, he opened the door for her and stood back until she was seated. He closed it behind her and then jogged around to the driver's side. Sliding behind the wheel, he turned to her.

"Where to?" She gave him her address on the lower north shore.

The engine purred beneath her feet. Trey drove with confidence as he wove in and out of the heavy rush-hour traffic. The black clouds that had threatened suddenly split open with torrential rain. It hammered onto the roof of the car and made conversation impossible. Before she knew it, they were pulling up outside her complex. As suddenly as the downpour had started, it stopped and she breathed a grateful sigh. Still, the storm had left the late afternoon darker than usual. The lights of the Mustang picked up the sleek modern lines of her building.

"Nice," he commented, taking in the dark gray, cement rendered walls and the formal manicured gardens that surrounded the building.

"Thanks. I like it," she said.

Trey climbed out of the car and went around to her side and opened the door. He stood back to allow her room to exit and then he surveyed his surroundings. Lights shimmered on the harbor, which was only a stone's throw away.

"I bet you have a great view," he murmured.

She nodded. "Yes. There are some things worth the extravagant mortgage."

He chuckled. "Tell me about it. I live at Bondi."

She smiled. "Nice," she murmured, repeating his earlier word.

Their eyes caught and held. Rekindled desire sparkled in his green eyes. Her belly did a somersault. She remembered their moment of unbridled passion in the alleyway and shivered with sudden need.

He took her hand and led her toward the gated entryway. She punched in her code on the security keypad and the door swung open on well-oiled hinges. Together they walked up the cobblestone path that led to her building.

And then she was beset by a wave of nerves. He was her client. They were still at odds about his defense. Was it wise to complicate matters by sleeping together, even if it was nothing more than casual sex?

What if things got complicated? What if he demanded more than she could give? He'd denied Anastasia's accusations of his neediness, but what if his ex-lover was telling the truth? Kiesha was determined to climb to the top of the legal ladder and was well on her way to getting there. She didn't have time to put into a serious relationship.

Then again, she wanted to be a wife and mother someday. She couldn't put that off forever. After all, she'd turned thirty the last birthday. But she also wanted to reach the pinnacle of her career. She'd worked hard to get where she was. She wasn't about to forfeit her chances of attaining it for the sake of something as elusive as love. She wished she could have it all—both love and a fulfilling relationship and a strong and satisfying career—but she wasn't foolish enough to believe it was possible. At some point, a choice needed to be made. So far, she'd chosen her career, but would that be enough in the future?

The thoughts circled round and round in her head, driving her insane. Before she knew it, they were standing outside the bank of elevators that would take them up to her apartment. With a determined effort, she shook off her despondent thoughts and snuck a glance at Trey. His face remained impassive, but heat still glimmered in his expressive eyes. She wanted him and he wanted her. They were two people who found each other attractive planning to spend the night together. Nothing more.

Quit overthinking it, Kiesha…

The thought no sooner formed in her mind when Trey turned and squeezed her hand. "You're thinking too much, Counselor."

His green eyes held hers captive. His reassurance filled her with confidence and a fresh wave of desire that left her nerve endings tingling. This was all about the here and now and doing what felt right. She winked at him.

"You're right."

His hand snaked out and drew her close against his side. She felt the hard warmth of him through her skirt, from her hip all the way past her thigh. Another shiver of desire went through her and just like that, her doubts dissolved into nothingness. She wanted him and he wanted her.

They were two consenting adults. *What more was there to it?* Like he said, she was overthinking it. Right now, all she wanted to do was feel.

After giving him a brief tour of the stylish and comfortable two-bedroom apartment, she met him out on the balcony with a bottle of Merlot and two glasses. Handing him one, she opened the bottle and poured the wine. He murmured his thanks.

"Cheers," she said and touched her glass to his.

"Cheers," he murmured.

She sipped at the wine and felt the warmth of it slide down her throat and settle in her belly. The alcohol eased her nerves although it also went straight to her head. She remembered she'd skipped lunch in order to meet with her client and now it was going on for six. Her stomach rumbled. She cringed with embarrassment.

Trey merely chuckled. "I guess it's almost dinnertime. Would you like to go somewhere and eat?"

She shook her head. "If you don't mind, I'm just as happy to whip up something here. I make a mean stir fry. Are you hungry?"

He grinned and moved closer. "Starving." He eyed her meaningfully.

The breath caught in her lungs. She stared at him as he approached her until there was barely an inch of space separating them. Evening had settled in. Though the rain had stopped, the storm clouds had swallowed up the light. The only source of illumination came from the light that spilled out from her living room behind them.

Still, it was enough for her to see the heat that sizzled in his eyes and the sensual curve of his lips. He wore a striped polo shirt and jeans. The clothing fit him every bit as well as his tailored suits. He looked like a man who was comfortable in his own skin, no matter the occasion and right now he was in her apartment and there was a burning question in his mesmerizing green eyes.

Her body leaped in response and her nerves tingled all the way down to her toes. Without hesitation, she set their wine glasses down on a nearby table and stepped right into his arms. His lips were as soft and warm and sensual as they'd been the first time he kissed her. He had kissing down to a fine art. Unlike the unrestrained passion he'd exhibited in the alleyway, this time he tasted and sipped and explored her mouth, taking his time, as if he wanted to get to know every inch.

It wasn't enough. With a groan of impatience, she took his head in her hands. Framing his face, she kissed him with all the need that had built up inside her. He growled low in response. Her tongue stole inside his mouth. She deepened the kiss and did some sensual exploration of her own.

With another husky growl, his arms came around her and pulled her close. His erection pressed hard against her belly. Tingling need surged along her nerve endings. She pressed back against him and her hands slid from his face to tighten around his neck.

With their mouths joined and their bodies pressed tightly together, the heat between them increased to an inferno until they were both breathing hard with need. Releasing her hold on him, Kiesha shucked off her jacket. He immediately reached for the buttons on her blouse and had them released in no time. She tugged at the hem of his shirt and dragged it up over his head.

A tanned washboard stomach taut with muscle met her heated gaze. She reached out and ran her fingernails across his flesh. His flat stomach clenched and his nipples pebbled at her touch. She watched in fascination. He was male perfection and she couldn't wait to taste him.

Bending her head, she touched her tongue to one of his nipples and then took it in her mouth. She heard his sharp intake of breath.

"God, that feels good." His voice was low and husky. His hand fisted in her hair.

She laved the small bud with her tongue and then turned her attention to its twin. Once again, his breath hissed through his teeth. Knowing how much he enjoyed her ministrations filled her with a sense of power and an overwhelming desire to be as close to him as two people could be.

"Let's go inside," she whispered, her own voice husky with need.

Without replying, he bent and picked her up in his arms. Striding with ease down the corridor, he turned into the room she'd shown him briefly earlier and deposited her on the bed. In short shrift, he pulled off his boots and his socks and loosened the fly on his jeans. He sat down on the edge of the bed to pull them off.

At the same time, she reached behind her and undid the button on her skirt. Sliding down the zipper, she shimmied out of it and tossed it to the carpet. Her silk blouse quickly followed. Panting slightly, she lay back down dressed only in her underwear. She was thankful she'd chosen to wear her lacy black matching bra and panties and not the sensible cotton underwear she sometimes did.

He lay down on his side next to her in his bright red Calvin Klein boxer shorts. The fabric cupped the taut cheeks of his buttocks and emphasized the strength of his erection. Unable to help herself, she reached out and dragged her fingers across the long hard length of him through the fabric.

He sucked in his breath and she smiled, filled with satisfaction. She wondered what it was about this man that made her want to linger over his reaction to every single feeling, every movement, every sensation. It had never been that way before.

In the past, sex had been a means to an end. A mutual satisfaction, a physical release. It had never left her with a yearning to know every inch of her partner's skin, to taste, to nip, to savor. Though her body burned with unfulfilled need, she wanted to take things slowly. It was like she was discovering sex for the first time and every new thing brought wonder.

She brought her face up against the warm skin of Trey's chest and breathed him in. His expensive cologne was sweet and spicy and tickled her nostrils. She kissed her way down the smooth planes of his pectorals. A scattering of dark blond hair covered his well-defined muscles. She raked her fingers through the soft strands and lower, across the tautness of his belly and lower still.

Snaking her hand under the elastic waistband of his boxers, she encircled the thick hard length of him with her fingers. Warm and smooth and silky, she felt the power he held in check. Squeezing and sliding her hand up and down his shaft, she reveled in the feelings the evidence of his desire generated inside her. He very clearly wanted her, just like she wanted him.

Without warning, he flipped her onto her back and she released her hold on his cock. With his knees on either side of her hips, he straddled her. Reaching down, he slid his hands behind her back and expertly undid the clasp of her bra. He tugged it loose and tossed it over his shoulder.

Her breasts sprang free, large and bouncy. He stared down at her with eyes that were almost black with desire. She sucked in her breath and her heart pounded. And then he touched her.

His finger traced her cleavage and then moved across to focus on one of her breasts. Tracing a path around and around her rosy nipple, he finally bent his head forward and took the aching nub in his mouth. The hot wet lushness of his mouth around the tortured flesh nearly brought her off the bed. She moaned in need and tossed her head from side to side, lost to everything but the feel of him doing exactly what she wanted.

And then he switched to the other side. Once again, she was lost. His hot mouth, moist and insistent, sucked and stroked and tasted. At the same time, his hand moved lower, slid across her belly and onto her mound. Tangling briefly in her curls, his hand moved lower still, until his finger stroked her soft folds.

And then his fingers slid inside her, stretching her. She gasped from the feel of it. His fingers matched the strokes of his tongue. In and out, round and round, the pressure built up inside her until she thought she would scream with the need for release.

"Please, Trey. You need to stop. I can't take it anymore."

He paused and looked up at her. "Do you really want me to stop?"

"No," she admitted.

He smiled and shook his head and continued his sensual onslaught. She moved restlessly beneath him, needing to feel more than his fingers inside her. As if sensing the direction of her thoughts, he released her nipple at last and sat back on his haunches. With his fingers still moving rhythmically inside her, his cock strained at his boxers. She wanted to reach out and touch him, to drive him wild the way he'd just done to her, but he shook his head as if reading her thoughts.

"Oh no, you don't. If you touch me again, I'll explode."

With that, he removed his fingers, leaving her bereft. Quickly, he discarded his underwear and after sheathing himself with a condom he pulled out of his wallet, returned to her side. She watched as he positioned himself between her legs. His cock pressed at her entrance and then withdrew. She whimpered, filled with desperate need.

"Do you want me?" His voice was low and husky. She stared at him in disbelief.

"Of course I want you. Now hurry up and fuck me, will you!"

Her coarse words both shocked and excited her, and she could tell they excited him, too. His eyes flared wide on a burst of desire and his cock quivered with need.

He pushed the engorged head in a little further and silently she urged him on. Lifting her hips, she moved restlessly beneath him.

In one savage thrust, he was inside her, stealing her breath. They gasped almost simultaneously. Her heart thumped hard against her chest. Giving her time to get used to his invasion, Trey lay still above her, panting. She savored the sensation of his cock deep inside her, stretching her as wide as she'd ever been. It was wonderful, magical, but all of a sudden, she needed more.

"Please, Trey," she begged. "Please, fuck me."

He muttered a curse and began to move in and out of her, each thrust faster and harder than the last. She clung to his shoulders and rode the waves as desire continued to build inside her. Higher and higher she climbed as the tension held her in its grip. Faster and faster Trey pounded.

Her nails dug into his shoulders. Her breath was harsh in her ears. Then she was there, at the peak of the cliff and all of a sudden, she toppled over. He went still, holding her close. She went into free fall, gasping for breath, crying out in relief. She clung to him as her body melted against his.

As the last muscle spasm around his cock ceased, Trey once again began to move inside her. With a look of fierce concentration on his face, his hips thrust forward over and over. She urged him on with murmured words of encouragement, clinging to his shoulders. Moments later, he cried out in triumph and found his release.

It was a long moment later that he rolled onto his side, bringing her with him. Slowly, their breathing returned to normal. Kiesha knew she should be flooded with regret, but she couldn't bring herself to feel it. Sex with Trey had been everything she'd imagined and more. Client or no client, she couldn't wait to do it again.

The storm from the evening before had been chased away through the night and Trey came awake slowly to the early morning sunlight filtering through the open curtains of Kiesha's bedroom. His arm had gone numb where she lay on it, but it was a feeling he welcomed. He smiled slowly, filled with the wonder of what had happened between them.

He'd known right from the start she was special and she hadn't disappointed. He'd been with countless women, some even more beautiful than she was, and yet none of them measured up to

Kiesha Munro. There was something about her, something indefinable that drew him. He was unable to explain it, but he'd sensed no matter how many times they made love, he'd never get enough.

The feelings she generated inside him were so unfamiliar they frightened him. At the same time, he wanted more. After enduring countless broken hearts and disappointments in his younger years, he'd steeled his heart against wanting anything more. But that was before Kiesha. He couldn't imagine only wanting another casual, meaningless encounter. The very thought made him want to cry out in protest. He didn't want to share her with anyone. Not now, not ever.

He turned on his side and propped himself up on one elbow. He looked down at her. His gaze drifted over her profile at the golden smoothness of her skin, the high cheekbones, broad nose, full lips. His gaze moved lower.

The sheet had fallen off her shoulders and was pooled around her waist. One perfect round breast was exposed to his gaze. Unable to help himself, he reached out and stroked her dusky pink nipple. It pebbled beneath his touch.

His cock stirred to life, hardening almost instantly. He moved until her soft ass was cradled against him. His hand moved lower, across the silky smoothness of her stomach and lower still, to tangle in her curls.

Her silky folds slid against his finger. He stroked until she was wet again. Slowly, he worked his fingers inside her. She moaned and pressed against him. Her eyelids fluttered open.

"Good morning," he whispered.

She turned on her side to face him and smiled. "Good morning."

With a gentle sigh, she lay on her back and let her legs fall open. It was the only invitation he needed. Moving over her, he kissed his way down her belly and then buried his face against her womanhood. He breathed in her musky scent and then licked her silky folds, paying special attention to her clit.

The tight little bud was swollen with need and he lavished it with loving attention. Kiesha moved restlessly beneath him, her hands fisted at her side.

"Trey, you're driving me mad," she breathed, moving her head from side to side.

Renewing his efforts, he captured her hips with his hands and held them still while he buried his tongue deep inside. He stroked and lapped at her femininity, loving the taste of her on his lips. Over and over he stroked her until she tensed beneath him and finally cried out her release.

A long moment later, she came up on one elbow and smiled down at him, her face glowing with satisfaction and wonder.

"That was amazing," she murmured. "*You* are amazing."

He shrugged, feeling inordinately happy with himself. "I aim to please."

"Oh, you did that all right," she replied, grinning.

He moved up to lie beside her. His cock stood stiff and proud. Her grin widened and a teasing looked shone in her eyes.

"Now, it's my turn."

Her hand slid across his stomach and tightened around his cock. He groaned and closed his eyes, bracing himself for what was to come. She didn't disappoint.

On her haunches, she positioned herself near his hips and took his cock into her mouth. Her tongue slid around the engorged head, licking and swiping and prodding. She dipped her tongue into the sensitive slit and his hands tightened into fists, but she was far from finished.

Her mouth opened wider and she relaxed her throat and took all of him in, as far as she could. Her lips tightened around his shaft and then slid up and down. His balls were heavy and tight with the need for release. If she kept up that rhythmic sucking, he'd come right in her mouth. He squirmed against her and groaned and tried to pull away, but she was having none of it. Instead, her grip tightened on him and she sucked all the harder.

"I'm going to come if you keep that up," he gasped, his breath coming fast.

"So, come."

Two simple words and yet they sent his nerve endings exploding with fire. With a groan of relief, he closed his eyes and concentrated on nothing but the sensations created by the magical ministrations of her lips. Desire built until it reached a fever pitch. His fists clenched. His breath came fast and then he reached the climax.

With a shout of triumph, he found his release and poured his seed down her throat. She sucked and squeezed and licked him until she'd drained every last drop. With a sigh of relief and satisfaction, he fell back against the pillows, utterly spent.

CHAPTER 12

The sun had risen higher in the sky when Kiesha woke for the second time. For a moment, she panicked, thinking she was late for work and then she remembered it was Saturday. Unlike the first time she'd woken, feeling sated and relaxed, spying Trey spread-eagled and naked beside her now filled her with doubt and self-recrimination.

What had she been thinking? Okay, she could get over the fact he was her client. Having sex with him probably wasn't the best move she'd made, but they were both above the age of consent and there was most definitely not a power imbalance.

But what if he read more into this than what she was prepared to give? They'd both agreed it was casual, but what if he'd changed his mind? She felt thoroughly loved and thoroughly satisfied. She'd never enjoyed sex quite as much. She could only suppose he felt the same way.

What if he wanted to do it again, on a regular basis? She wasn't against the idea, but where did casual stop and a relationship begin? The lines would become blurred and it would happen before she realized... Her life as she knew it would be blown off course, sabotaged and she'd have only herself to blame.

She should never have slept with him...

"You're thinking too much again, Counselor."

His quiet words were followed by a wry grin. With his dimples in evidence, the way his lips turned up was sexy enough to curl her toes and sent a hot shaft of desire tingling through her. With her silent regrets still vying for attention in her head, she fought against the feeling.

"This was such a bad idea, Trey."

Hurt flashed across his face and a sinking feeling made itself known in her stomach. *Maybe Anastasia had been right. He couldn't do casual. It was written all over his face...*

To his credit, he recovered quickly and offered a nonchalant shrug. "Why do you say that?"

She stared at him. She could hardly remind him of their agreement while they were still wrapped naked in each other's arms. It wasn't right. She latched onto the first thing that came to mind. "Because. It just was. You're my client."

"So?"

She shook her head. "It's not right."

"Who says?"

She made a sound of exasperation. "A lawyer isn't supposed to sleep with her client."

He eyed her steadily. "Why not?"

"There is an inherent power imbalance between a lawyer and client."

"I see no such imbalance here, do you?"

He opened his eyes wide, an innocent expression on his face. She offered a grudging smile. His words merely reflected what she already believed. She didn't know why she was giving him such a hard time over it. Probably because she felt guilty that he might think after the night they'd spent together that there could be something more permanent between them.

She compressed her lips against a sudden surge of panic. Trey must have seen something in her eyes, because he leaned over and tenderly cupped her cheek in his hand.

"What is it, Kiesha?"

She grimaced and wished he wasn't so observant. *Why couldn't he be the kind of man who took everything at face value, or one who accepted her words without comment? Why couldn't he be the kind of man who didn't bother probing deeper, or feel a need to discover the truth?* Most men would be relieved to get out of answering the awkward questions after a spontaneous night of sex. It seemed Trey Walker wasn't one of those.

Her shoulders slumped on a heavy sigh. As if sensing her capitulation, he drew her up close against his side and pressed a soft kiss on her forehead. Unexpected tears filled her eyes. She had no defense against his tenderness.

"What's going on, honey?" he whispered.

She buried her face against the warmth of his chest. "Last night was so great. More than great. It was amazing. But I don't do long-term relationships.

I don't do relationships, period. I don't want you to get the wrong idea about us. It was just casual sex, right?"

She threw him hopeful look from beneath her lashes and was startled to see another flash of hurt in his eyes. She bit her lip.

"What we shared between us could never be described as casual sex, Kiesha. At least, not for me. I've done casual sex. So have you. I won't believe you if you tell me what happened last night was the same as every other time. Last night was amazing. I've never felt like that with anyone. When I say that it sounds trite and silly, but it's true."

Her breath caught at the sincerity in his face. She stared at him, taken aback.

"I like you, Kiesha Munro. I *really* like you. More than I should. How does that make you feel?"

He'd opened his heart to her and she didn't know what to say. How could he fall so hard and fast and how could such hard-and-fast feelings be relied on?

They barely knew each other past the physical. Oh, he was smart and loyal and brave. He'd come to the aid of his brother and had also offered help to a woman he didn't know. Those were admirable traits, but there must be more to Trey Walker, just like there was so much more to her that he didn't know. He couldn't possibly expect her to state her feelings about the two of them so soon. In fact, she'd rather not talk about them at all.

"What about the case?" she asked, buying time.

He frowned. "What about it?"

"I'm your lawyer. It's probably not going to look good if people know we're...together."

He shrugged. "Who cares? Besides, we can be discrete. No one needs to know."

She stared at him, filled with uncertainty. It was one thing to have sex with a man when you were certain it was a one-off, spur-of-the-moment night of casual sex that both parties would walk away from the next morning. It was quite another to consider Trey might have developed serious feelings for her, or at least to consider he had. *Was this the desperation, the neediness Anastasia spoke of?*

Kiesha needed time to examine it from every angle before she'd be in a position to make a decision and he needed that time, too, whether he knew it or not. And then there was the small issue about her upcoming appointment to the bench and the fact she wouldn't have time for a relationship...

With a quiet sigh, she wrapped the sheet around her and climbed out of bed. Feeling like a coward, she murmured something about needing a shower and escaped into the bathroom, locking the door behind her.

Trey turned his head away from the barrage of cameras and journalists that followed him up the steps of the District Court building. It was too much to hope this would remain private. After all, his father was a former Supreme Court judge and the alleged victim was apparently the daughter of a prominent Sydney family. To have the former judge's son accused of sexual assault was too juicy and sensational for them to ignore. No doubt he'd make the six o'clock news. The certainty of it made him grimace.

"Mr Walker, did you rape Heather Lockhart?"

"Mr Walker, will you be pleading guilty to the charge of sexual assault?"

"Mr Walker…"

The questions came at him from all sides. Ignoring them, he continued without pause up the steps, across the wide main foyer and into the security screening area. Only then did the hubbub of the media subside. No one got through to the courtrooms without going through security— journalists and cameramen included.

Trey emptied his pockets of his keys, wallet and phone and dropped them into the basket. He put the basket onto the conveyor belt and then walked through the security screening, trying not to feel like a criminal.

No doubt Kiesha was already in the courtroom, getting ready for the upcoming hearing. He hadn't spoken to her since Saturday morning when she'd refused to talk to him about what had happened between them. It still chafed him. He'd opened his heart to her, put it all on the line, and she'd escaped into the bathroom as if the apartment were on fire.

When she'd finally emerged, she was so cool and polite it was obvious she wasn't prepared to discuss the matter any further. He didn't need to be told twice. Quickly and quietly, he'd gathered his things and left.

Now they were about to come face to face for the first time since the weekend. He planned on being just as cool and unruffled as she'd been, but the message hadn't gotten through to his heart. It pounded in anticipation and his belly filled with a rush of nerves. Despite the way they'd parted, he couldn't wait to see her again.

Locating the courtroom where his case was to be heard, he pulled open the double wooden doors.

Kiesha sat at the bar table with her back to him. He took a moment to appreciate her straight, slim shoulders and the graceful curve of her neck. Now he knew what the soft skin behind her ears tasted like, he'd never look at her the same way again. His body stirred in response and he resolutely forced the tempting thoughts away. This most definitely wasn't the place or the time.

She looked up as he approached. For a moment, an unguarded expression filled with pleasure and a hint of vulnerability crossed her face and then it was gone, replaced by the cool and professional demeanor he'd expect when she was in work mode.

She nodded in greeting. "Mr Walker, it's good to see you."

He returned her greeting with the same formality. "You, too, Ms Munro."

"I'm afraid you need to sit in the dock," she murmured and indicated an area behind her.

Turning away, he made his way to the space set aside for the defendant. It was a solitary seat surrounded by wood paneling that separated him from the rest of the people gathered in the courtroom. The moment he sat down, he felt like a criminal.

Kiesha pushed back her chair and moved toward him. She came to a stop in front of him. Her perfume, sweet and exotic, filled his nostrils, reminding him of the intimacies they'd shared. Once again, he forced his mind away from that direction.

"Is something the matter, Counselor?" he asked, deliberately maintaining his tone of casual disinterest.

"I appreciate this must be difficult for you and completely unfamiliar. Do you have any questions?"

"Will I get to give evidence today?"

She shook her head. "No. This is all about testing the prosecution's case. The Crown Prosecutor will call his witnesses and do his utmost to convince the judge he has enough evidence to take this to a jury. I'll cross examine those witnesses to the best of my ability."

"And then you'll make a very eloquent appeal to the judge to have this case dismissed," he quipped. He widened his gaze deliberately and threw her a look of innocence. "Right?"

Irritation flashed in her eyes. He could almost hear the sound of her teeth grinding together.

"Don't be obtuse, Trey. We both know that's not going to happen. Now, I need to confirm your instructions. Given the DNA evidence placing you squarely with the alleged victim—inside the victim, no less—I assume you're prepared to concede you were there, but that the sex was consensual?"

Though it went against everything inside him, he nodded. "I think that's the only way."

He watched her open her mouth in protest and then close it. Of course it wasn't the only way. Revealing the existence of Wade was the other option and one much more preferable to his lawyer. Too bad he wouldn't allow himself to feel the same way.

He could almost feel her anger and frustration, but he wasn't willing to give her what she needed. Misguided or not, his loyalty had to be to his brother and that was all there was to it. And then he remembered what his father had said about Heather Lockhart's history.

"Kiesha, there's something you should know. Heather Lockhart has done this kind of thing before. Cried rape, I mean."

Kiesha's eyes widened in shock. "How do you know that?" she whispered.

Trey shrugged. "My father did a little digging."

"I'm not sure I want to know how he came by his information, but we can't afford to ignore it. We'll have to have proof at trial, of course, but for now, I might be able to use this to shake her up a little bit."

A sharp rap on the wood paneling that lined the wall behind the bench indicated the arrival of the judge. Kiesha returned to her seat. With a sigh, Trey did the same. One way or the other, this nightmare was about to be determined. He only hoped he could live with the outcome.

The prosecution started with the two detectives who'd attended the scene. Both Craigdon and Boule reported the circumstances surrounding their callout and what they'd found. Both officers confirmed they'd spoken to the alleged victim, Heather Lockhart. Both confirmed she'd told them she'd been raped by the defendant, who was also questioned at the scene.

"Detective Craigdon, how did the defendant respond to the allegation of rape?" the Crown Prosecutor asked.

Craigdon looked briefly at Trey and then his gaze returned to the prosecutor. "He denied it. In fact, he denied even knowing Ms Lockhart."

"Was any DNA evidence recovered from the scene?"

"Yes. A rape kit found the presence of semen inside Ms Lockhart's vagina."

"And whose DNA was it?"

The detective paused and looked straight at Trey. "The report came back with a 99.9% finding that the DNA belonged to the defendant, Trey Walker."

The judge looked up and frowned at Trey, a disapproving look in his eyes. Trey flushed with embarrassment. He hadn't thought about how hard it would be to sit there and to have everyone look at him like he was a criminal. Silently he cursed Wade.

Three more witnesses followed. All of them said much the same thing. Sam Frost, the barman,

Naomi Marchant and Heather Lockhart all gave evidence placing him in The Chill Factory on the night in question. Once again, Heather accused him of being the man who'd raped her.

Kiesha tried her hardest to discredit each witness, but it was an uphill battle. Once or twice she managed to score a direct hit. Through skillful cross examination, she succeeded in getting both women to agree they'd been drinking heavily that night and were also under the influence of illicit drugs. They couldn't be sure who they'd spoken to that night or who had accompanied Heather outside.

Heather flat out denied she'd cried rape in the past. Without direct evidence to refute the denial, Kiesha was forced to back down. Trey was left wondering how good his father's information was.

Regardless of these concessions and despite Kiesha throwing every trick in the book at them, both women maintained they were certain the man they'd been with that night was Trey Walker.

At the conclusion of her cross examination of the final prosecution witness, Kiesha returned to her seat with her head bowed. Looking neither left nor right, she appeared focused on the files in front of her. Trey watched her, his heart beating fast and his gut heavy with dread. If he were a betting man, he'd place money on the prosecution winning this one. And that meant he was on the losing end.

This is bad...

The somber thought came from nowhere, but he wasn't surprised. Kiesha had told him so all along. He'd stupidly refused to listen. When the judge cleared his throat and declared there was sufficient evidence to commit the case for trial, Trey bowed his head and cursed.

Fuck.

CHAPTER 13

Kiesha busied herself packing away her files, her notepad and other items of stationery into her leather briefcase. She was acutely aware of Trey seated in the dock not far away. His bail had been continued, but he had yet to move. It was almost like he was in shock.

The hearing hadn't gone well for him. No surprises there. At least, not for her. And there shouldn't have been any surprises for him, either. They'd been over the evidence time and time again. He was well aware of the strength of the prosecution's case against him. Committing the matter for trial seemed almost like a no brainer. It was obvious to all concerned there was enough evidence to suggest Trey Walker had committed the crime. Now the judge had made that formal and there was no getting away from it.

From the corner of her eye, she spied Jett Craigdon approach the bar table. Given that the

Crown Prosecutor had already departed, she could only imagine he was there to see her. She acknowledged him with the briefest of polite smiles.

"Detective Craigdon, what can I do for you?"

"I came to congratulate you on a job well done."

She grimaced. "Apparently it wasn't good enough."

He shrugged. "You couldn't honestly have expected a different outcome?" His gaze slid to include Trey who had sat forward and appeared to be listening intently.

Kiesha threw the detective a surly look. "I believe the defendant did not rape Ms Lockhart. I also believe in innocence until proven guilty. Are you finished gloating?"

He held her gaze. "Not quite." From the inside pocket of his jacket, he pulled out a thumb drive and handed it to her.

"What's this?" she asked, staring down at it.

"CCTV footage from The Chill Factory taken on the night in question. We only received it yesterday. It provides for interesting viewing."

He smirked and dread settled heavily in her stomach. The confidence in the detective's manner told her all she needed to know. Whatever had shown up in the footage sure as hell wasn't going to further Trey's case. She'd bet on it.

Without another word, she took the thumb drive from him and tossed it into her briefcase.

"I'll see you around, Counselor," Craigdon murmured and with a jaunty wave in Trey's direction, casually strode away.

"Bastard," Trey muttered.

Kiesha sighed. "He's only doing his job. He has no reason to believe you didn't do it. All the evidence points to you, and only you."

"Yeah, well he doesn't have to take so much pleasure from someone else's misfortune," Trey replied sourly.

Kiesha spun on her heel and glared at him. *"Misfortune?* Is that what you call this? You're going to trial on sexual assault charges and from what happened in this courtroom, every person present thinks you did it! No wonder the officer in charge of the case is acting like he's just won the lottery. He thinks he has this one in the bag and quite frankly, so do I."

A flash of panic flooded his face. She was filled with a short burst of satisfaction. *Good. Let him wonder about what life might be like if he's tried and convicted. It might be the wakeup call he needed...*

"If you don't mind, I'd like to watch the footage."

He was more subdued than she'd ever seen him. Something must have finally gotten through to him. Still, they were making progress. For once he hadn't expressed utmost confidence in her ability to get him out of this. *Perhaps he finally believed she wasn't a miracle worker, after all?* The thought left her feeling a little disheartened.

Don't be stupid, Kiesha. It's best he approach this realistically. You can't perform miracles, pure and simple, and that's what he's going to need to get out of this one. Period.

The late afternoon sunlight cast long shadows across the pavement as Trey and Kiesha made their way back to Sydney Legal where Kiesha had agreed they'd watch the footage together. He walked beside her. She matched him stride for stride. She was tall for a woman, almost as tall as he was. She had no trouble keeping up.

They entered the marble foyer of Sydney Legal and made their way over to the bank of elevators. A few people stood there waiting. They threw sideways looks at him. Two of them even frowned. Trey wasn't sure if they recognized him or if it was his imagination that they appeared to condemn him with their eyes.

Thankfully, the elevator arrived a short time later and he hurriedly followed Kiesha inside. She took him straight up to her floor and hustled him into her office, as if she also couldn't bear the scrutiny.

This time, he barely noticed the spectacular view. Instead, with a heavy sigh, he strode across the room and threw himself down on the couch on the far side of the room. A flat screen TV he hadn't noticed the first time was mounted on the wall opposite.

"Would you like a drink?"

He looked at her. She'd barely spoken on their way over. He could tell she was also upset about the outcome of the hearing, but she hadn't shown any surprise. Though he had hoped for a dismissal of his case, he wasn't really surprised by the outcome either. Still, it didn't make things any easier to bear.

He nodded in response to her question. "Thanks, a drink would be great. I'll have a scotch, if you have it."

"Ice?"

"No, I'll take it straight."

A short time later, she approached him with two drinks in her hand and offered one to him. He reached for the glass and their fingers brushed. He was sure he heard her sharp intake of breath. It matched the sudden uptake of his heart and the blood that rushed through his veins. She might pretend they were nothing to each other in the cold harsh light of day, but neither of them could deny there was something between them, something electrifying. He only hoped she'd see it that way someday.

But now wasn't the time or place to dwell on their relationship. The judge had just committed him to stand trial on sexual assault charges. And now the officer in charge of the investigation had produced CCTV footage of the night. He could only imagine that whatever was on the thumb drive backed up the prosecution's claim.

He took a sip from his drink and savored the warm burn of the whisky as it slid down his throat. Setting the glass down on the small table that stood beside the couch, he leaned back and drew in a fortifying breath. Best get this over with.

"Okay. I'm ready. Bring it on."

Kiesha threw him a glance that was mostly unreadable. He thought he saw a flash of admiration, but she quickly averted her gaze and he was left to wonder. She leaned over and inserted the thumb drive into the USB port on the TV. Using the remote control, she opened the file and pressed play.

Trey sat forward, suddenly tense. The grainy, black-and-white footage showed what he guessed was the inside of The Chill Factory nightclub. There were obviously several cameras installed in various positions around the room. Footage switched from one camera to another, until they covered most of the room.

Wade was seated in at the bar. There were two girls by his side: Naomi Marchant and Heather Lockhart.

"He looks so much like you," Kiesha murmured, her gaze fixed on the screen.

Trey remained silent, feeling grim. She didn't have to tell him how much he and his twin looked alike. Looking at Wade was like looking into a mirror. It had been that way all his life. He stared at the threesome.

They were throwing back drinks in rapid succession. At one stage, Wade pulled something out of his jacket. He waved it in front of the girls. The grainy footage didn't show clearly what it was, but each girl held out her hand.

"The ecstasy tablets," Trey muttered.

Kiesha nodded. "It looks like it."

A little while later, Wade stood. The girls did the same and followed him to a booth in the far corner of the room. Drinks and conversation continued to flow. Then Naomi stood and a moment later, walked away. Wade and Heather continued drinking. Heather moved closer to his brother. Her hand stole into his lap, hidden beneath the table. She grinned and looked back at him. From the wide smile on his brother's face and the way he'd thrown his head back, Trey could only guess what was happening.

He threw a sideways glance at Kiesha, but her gaze was fixed firmly on the screen. The only telltale sign that she was aware of what was more than likely unfolding was the faint pink blush that covered her cheeks.

He grew hard at the thought of Kiesha giving him a hand job like Heather was giving his twin. They were in public, albeit a dim dark booth in the back of a crowded nightclub. Still, the thought of doing such a thing was exciting.

"No one can deny they were on friendly terms at that point," Kiesha murmured.

With an effort, Trey forced his thoughts away from his fantasies and concentrated on what she was saying. "You're right. She's all over him." He paused and then added, "Just like he said."

At some point, Naomi returned, although she didn't regain her seat. She stood beside them for a few moments of conversation and then turned with a brief wave and left. The couple seated in the booth became much more amorous. They embraced and began to kiss. Hands and tongues were everywhere. It was indecent.

Then Wade waggled the same small plastic bag in front of Heather's face. Trey watched as both of them swallowed more pills before Wade grabbed Heather's hand and tugged her to her feet. She scrambled out of the booth. Her black leather miniskirt had ridden high and she flashed a firm butt cheek to the cameras as she passed. If she wore underwear at all, it must have been a G-string.

"Charming," Kiesha muttered.

And then the screen turned black.

Trey tried to stem his disappointment. He was hoping for more, something that might support Wade's story that the two of them had engaged in consensual sex. "Is that it?" he asked.

To his relief, Kiesha shook her head. "No. There's another file."

She leaned forward and, using the remote, found and opened the second file. She pressed play and a few moments later, more grainy images filled the screen. These were much darker and less clear than the other ones and it was obvious the footage had been taken outside the building. The golden glow from a nearby streetlight and the dim lights on either side of the back door of the nightclub were the only sources of illumination.

And then Trey noticed the outline of two people standing against the brick wall of the nightclub. Most people wouldn't have been able to identify them, but Trey knew instantly it was

Wade. The girl wore a dark miniskirt and there were flashes of long blond hair. It wouldn't take much to persuade a jury to accept that the couple making out was Trey Walker and Heather Lockhart.

A fresh wave of nerves flooded Trey's body and settled like concrete in his gut. His fists clenched as he sat on edge, waiting for what might unfold. It was like watching a scary movie when you've pretty much guessed the ending, but you don't know for sure. Kiesha appeared equally tense beside him. Neither of them spoke.

The security footage showed Wade kissing Heather on her lips and then he moved to her neck. With her head flung backwards, it appeared she was enjoying it, however, the next moment, she wrenched away and vomited at his feet.

"Shit," Trey muttered. Kiesha remained silent.

Wade handed over his handkerchief and Heather wiped the vomit from her face. Trey expected his brother to help the girl out of the alley. After all, it was obvious she was in no condition to continue what they'd started. Instead, Trey watched in shock as his brother pushed the woman up against the wall. She twisted her head from side to side, trying to avoid his kisses, but it seemed he was having none of that.

In horror, Trey watched his brother tug savagely at the girl's skirt until it was up around her hips. He fumbled with the front of his jeans and a moment later, his hips thrust forward. It was clear they were having sex.

It lasted less than a minute, but it was the most harrowing thing Trey had ever seen. *This was his brother!* The man he loved with everything he had. His stomach churned with nausea and he thought he might be sick. With a gargantuan effort, he held the nausea down and forced himself to watch to the end.

When the act was over, Wade stepped away and Heather dropped to the ground. Trey watched while Wade pulled out his phone.

"That's when he called me," he said quietly, filled with loathing.

"There goes our defense," Kiesha murmured.

Once again, the screen went black.

Trey frowned and turned to Kiesha. She looked as sick and pale as he felt. "What happened after that? The cameras should have still been recording. They would've showed me arriving. The police, the ambulance. It should've all been there."

Kiesha's expression grew thoughtful. "You're right," she murmured. "Why did the footage stop there? Were the police that confident with what they'd seen, they didn't bother looking past it?"

"You must be right," Trey said, "otherwise they'd know about me. They'd know someone else attended that scene. Okay, I could have run off again before they arrived, but it should've at least thrown up some questions. They mustn't have watched the footage through to the end. It's the only explanation."

Kiesha nodded. "You're right. But where does that leave us? If you're still unwilling to put your brother forward, it doesn't matter whether they saw that footage or not."

Trey was already shaking his head before she'd even finished. "We've been over this before, Kiesha. I'm not going to turn my brother in."

"Oh, for God's sake, Trey! Grow up! Did you just see what he did? He *raped* that girl! We both know it and so do the police. The jury will take one look at that footage and they'll convict you on the spot. Not only will they accept you were there, they'll also accept there was no consent. You're dead in the water! I don't know what you expect me to do!"

She pushed away from the couch, wringing her hands in agitation. Trey understood exactly how she felt. If their positions were reversed, he'd feel the same way. In fact, he'd already told her as much.

But nothing about the footage, as disgusting and horrifying as it was, changed his mind. He was sickened by what Wade had done, but he wasn't going to be the one to turn in his twin. The best he could hope for was that Wade would come to his senses and turn himself in of his own accord, or someone else would view the video further.

"I'm sorry, Kiesha. Yes, he did an awful thing and the very thought of it sickens me. He deserves to be punished, there's no doubt about it, but I can't be the one to do it. He's my brother. He saved my life. This changes nothing," he said quietly.

She turned on him, her eyes blazing with anger. "Then you're a fool, Trey Walker! And you'd better get used to only three squares a day and one hour in the sunshine because that's going to be your life for the next five to seven years—and you know it."

Her breath came fast. Twin spots of fury colored her cheeks. She spun on her heel away from him, as if she couldn't stand to look at him a second longer. She took two steps, three, away from him and then spun back around. If he hoped her anger had abated in that time, he was sorely disappointed. Instead, the fury in her eyes blazed stronger than ever.

"And in case you didn't hear, the trial's been set six weeks from today. You'd better start saying goodbye to everything you cherish because it's going to be a hell of a long time before you see them again."

The night had settled around him when Trey pulled up outside his brother's apartment building. The darkness hid a myriad of sins in the front yard, but Trey was sure the overgrown grass, cracked pavement and discarded trash he'd seen on his last visit were still there. The air was still cool and fresh, even though summer was just around the corner. Still, it did nothing to ease the hot anger that burned with a vengeance in Trey's gut.

Every time he thought of what Wade had done he got furious all over again. If he hadn't seen it with his own eyes, he'd never have believed it.

Wade had sworn to him he hadn't touched the girl and then when the DNA evidence proved that to be a lie, he swore the sex had been consensual. Now that had also been proven a lie.

Trey was shattered. He wanted to howl with the pain from his brother's betrayal. They were not only brothers, they were identical twins! They'd shared the same placenta! Had been as close as two people could get! How could Wade have risked his life to save Trey from a burning car only to betray him with lies? Wade knew what was at stake and it was as if he didn't care...

The only sensible thing to do was to turn him in to the police, but somehow he just couldn't do it. Surely his brother would see sense and do the right thing, the *only* thing. Surely once he became aware Trey knew the truth of what had happened, he'd realize he had no other choice. That was Trey's only hope.

Feeling grim, he climbed out of the Mustang and locked it. He glanced around, but in the dark, he couldn't spy his brother's new sports car. He'd have to take his chances and hope Wade was in. If he weren't, Trey was going to spend the rest of the night driving from one known haunt to the other until he found him and forced him to explain.

To Trey's relief, Wade buzzed him inside and answered his door on the third knock. For once, his brother's eyes looked clear and the clothes he wore, though wrinkled, were clean. It was the last thing Trey noticed before he stepped forward and shoved his twin hard against the wall.

"Trey! What the fuck...? What the hell are you doing?"

Trey glared at him, his breath coming fast. "You little shit! You told me you didn't touch that woman! Instead, I find out you raped her! You disgust me!"

Panic flashed in Wade's eyes. He shook his head back and forth in vehement denial.

"No, Trey! You've got it wrong! I swear!"

If Trey hadn't seen the security footage for himself, he would have likely fallen for the sincerity in his brother's eyes. Instead, Wade's continued insistence he was innocent only fired Trey up more.

"Quit lying to me, Wade!" he shouted. "I saw you rape her! It was all caught on camera, you stupid fuck!"

As Trey's words sank in, Wade's eyes opened wide in shock. He went limp against the wall and probably would have fallen if Trey hadn't been holding him up. Trey stared at him with a savage satisfaction.

"Yes," he snarled. "I see you get what I mean. The police have the tape. They gave it to my lawyer. There's no doubt it's you and Heather Lockhart and she sure as hell doesn't look like she's enjoying your attentions. Coupled with the DNA evidence, the jury is going to take one look at it and will bring back a verdict of guilty. There's nothing surer."

Wade began to snivel. Trey shook his head in disgust. His brother had always been weak, but this was taking things too far. It was time for Wade to grow up and take responsibility for his actions.

"You need to go to the police and tell them everything, Wade. An early guilty plea will reduce your sentence by as much as a third and you'll be doing the right thing, the *only* thing acceptable."

Wade's eyes flared with sudden anger. "Acceptable to who? You? Dad? Your lawyer? What about *me*? I'm the one going to be spending the next few years in jail. Have you given any thought to that?"

Trey clenched his jaw in frustration and glared at his brother in disbelief. "You're the one who raped that poor girl, Wade. You committed a heinous crime and you deserve to be punished. Stop acting like a spoiled child crying over a broken toy. This is serious! This woman's life will be changed forever and not in a good way. You and you alone are responsible for that!"

Wade's expression grew sulky. "It wasn't my fault. She was all over me in the club. How was I to know she'd changed her mind?"

Once again, Trey stared at his twin in disbelief. "You're kidding me, right? Anyone watching that security footage can see she resisted your advances. She threw up right in front of you... What was she supposed to do, pull out a gun?"

"Fuck, Trey, you make this sound like I'm a monster! I was wasted! So was she! I didn't know what the fuck I was doing."

"Well you should have thought about that before you got yourself to the point where you could no longer make rational judgments. You forced yourself on this woman and everyone who watches that tape will know it. You were thinking clearly enough to call me and right now, *I'm* the one in the firing line. The police don't even know you exist. But that's about to change. You're going to march on down there this minute and tell them everything."

Wade's jaw jutted out at a stubborn angle Trey was all too familiar with. "And what if I refuse?" he said petulantly.

Trey saw red. Tightening his grip on his brother's shirtfront, he once again shoved Wade hard against the wall. "You're going to go to the police station and you're going to hand yourself in. No ifs, buts, or maybes. *You* did this, Wade, and you need to man up and take responsibility."

Tears filled Wade's eyes. He shot Trey a pleading look. "I'm sorry, Trey, I really am, but I can't go to the police. There are certain things I'm just not capable of doing—like going to the hospital. I've never even been able to drive past the emergency room without thinking of Mom. I get shaky and lightheaded and I feel like I'm going to be sick. Even the smell of the place brings it all back. It's the same now. I can't go to the police. I can't turn myself in. Jail would kill me. You know that as well as I do!"

Trey stared at him in disgust. "And yet you're more than willing for me to face that possibility. You'd be delighted if I stepped up and took the rap for you over this. It's happened so many times in the past—I've come to your rescue and cleaned up your mess—you've come to expect it as your right! I should never have started doing it in the first place. That was my bad. And Dad's.

You've lived your whole life expecting other people to take responsibility for your screw-ups and we've done it, time and time again. Well, not this time. I've drawn the line. This time, you're on your own. Either you get yourself down to the station and tell them the truth, or I will. This is where it ends, Wade. Period."

Wade glared at him. "And to think I saved your sorry ass. This is how you repay me." His lip curled up in disgust.

Trey stared at him, aghast. "You think I should cop every piece of shit you throw my way from here to eternity because of a single act of bravery?"

Wade smirked. "Bravery! Ha! If you only knew the truth."

Trey's eyes narrowed on his brother. "What the hell is that supposed to mean?"

"Trey. Trey. Trey," Wade crooned. "The smartest kid in college and yet not smart enough to work out what happened the night he and his girlfriend nearly died."

A cold feeling of foreboding shivered along Trey's spine. His gaze remained locked on Wade. He didn't want to know what his brother referred to, but as if standing outside his body looking on, he heard himself reply.

"You're talking shit, Wade. We both know what happened. I blacked out and swerved over the middle line. I collided with an oncoming car. Thank God the other driver wasn't hurt. The doctors couldn't explain what caused my temporary loss of consciousness. My blood alcohol level was zero.

Same for drugs. No one knows what happened that night."

Wade's grin widened. "That's where you're wrong, bro."

Ice froze in Trey's blood. The feeling of dread increased. "W-what are you talking about?"

"I spiked your drink that night. I laced it with Rohypnol. It's fast acting, in and out of your system in a flash. That's why it didn't show up on any toxicology results."

Trey stared at him in shock. "What the hell...? You *drugged* me?"

Wade smirked. "Yep."

Trey shook his head, shocked and bewildered. "*Why?*"

"You've always been the perfect son, the perfect brother, the perfect friend. Nothing you ever did turned to shit. And you didn't even want me around the two of you that night. It was obvious. I had to do something to mess up your perfect life."

He stared at Wade incredulously. "So you drugged me and then let me drive home? Angie and I could have been killed!"

"That was the plan."

Once again, Trey reeled back in shock. His eyes were so wide they hurt. He blinked and shook his head in an effort to clear it. *Surely he hadn't heard right?*

"W-what did you say?" he stammered.

Wade's expression turned petulant. "You heard me. I'd had enough of my perfect brother. I wanted you out of my life. Once and for all."

Trey felt like he'd been slammed over the head with a steel pylon. He couldn't have been more taken aback. His brother had just admitted to trying to murder him and make it look like an accident. He'd almost pulled it off.

But why had he bothered coming to Trey's rescue? He could have left him in that car to die. Moments after Wade pulled them both out of the vehicle, it had exploded into flames. Confused and reeling, Trey put the question to him.

"I was traveling right behind you," Wade explained. "I was the first one on the scene. I could hardly drive on by without offering assistance. It would have been a dead giveaway. But don't you worry, I was cursing you out the whole time. You were meant to die in that crash and that would have been the end of it." He paused. His lip curled up in disgust. "I couldn't even get that right."

Trey shook his head, completely at a loss. "B-but you even donated blood. Without it, I would have died. I'm AB negative, like you. The hospital didn't have enough. You dragged me from the burning vehicle and then gave me your blood. For someone who wanted me dead, you did all you could to save me."

Wade's lip curled up in disgust. "Don't you get it? How could I refuse? Dad knew we shared the same blood type and so did the doctors. We're identical twins. Anyone who knows anything about identical twins knows they have identical blood types. I had no choice. You were bleeding out and desperately needed a transfusion. Dad had me prepped even before the doctors came and made the request."

Shock beyond what Trey could handle suddenly brought him to his knees. A cry of pain and disbelief tore from his mouth as he slid down the wall and collapsed in a heap on the floor. He hugged his knees close and tried to come to terms with all that he'd just learned.

"Why, Wade?" he cried, his voice hoarse. "Why did you hate me so much? We're brothers! I loved you with everything that I had! All my life I've stood up for you, defended you, even when you didn't deserve it—and now I find out that during all the time you resented me so much you actually set out to *kill* me." He shook his head, the enormity of it breaking something deep inside him.

Wade's expression turned sullen. "What do you expect? You were the golden child. Not in Dad's eyes, but certainly to everyone else. I couldn't have been more different. No one liked me. Not in school, not in college. I had no friends. I couldn't do anything right."

Trey stared at his brother, still reeling.

Wade's lower lip trembled with emotion, but Trey refused to feel sorry for him.

"You went out of your way to make people dislike you, Wade. You brought it on yourself. What about the time in the third grade when you stuck spaghetti up your nose and then inhaled. You had sauce all over your face. You were a mess. No wonder all the kids thought you were weird. You *were* weird. You did weird stuff. And you did it deliberately.

"Time after time I'd defend you. I lost count of the number of fights I got into because of you. There were many times when I even took the blame for you. Especially when it involved a casual teacher who couldn't tell us apart. I did all I could to look out for you, protect you, stand by you, love you, but you didn't make it easy. You've never made it easy. And then you saved my life—at least, I thought you did—and I felt even more obligated to stand by you, to help you out."

Wade sneered. "Yes, there was never a day that went by that you weren't wearing your red satin cape."

Trey stared at him in disbelief, unable to fathom the depth of his brother's jealousy.

"Oh, Wade." It was all he could manage.

Anger flashed in his brother's eyes. "Don't 'Oh, Wade' me! You should have known what it was like for me, always being compared by others to my perfect twin. Never quite measuring up. Dad did his best to compensate, but he's my father. It's his job to smooth over the rough patches. I wanted to be liked and respected by my peers! And it never happened. It ate me up inside. Made me do things I'm not proud of."

"You mean like spiking my drink?"

"Yeah. That...and a few other things."

Trey came alert. "What other things?"

Wade shrugged and stared at the floor. Trey came slowly to his feet. His gaze narrowed on his brother.

"What other things, Wade?" he repeated grimly.

"You always got any girl you wanted. None of them would give me the time of day. It was as if I was invisible and yet, we're identical! How could they like you and not me? It never made sense to me and used to get me so mad! It still does."

A fresh wave of foreboding slid through Trey's veins. "What did you do, Wade?"

His voice was low and brooked no resistance.

Wade sighed. "While I'm in the mood for exchanging confidences, I might as well reveal all my secrets."

The dread in Trey's gut increased tenfold. He could barely bring himself to stand there and wait for Wade to speak. His fists clenched at his sides.

"It started back in high school. I'd get hold of your phone and send texts to your girlfriends. I'd pretend they were coming from you. I'd wait until you'd been dating for a few weeks and then I'd start suggesting they might like to make some improvements—you know, with their appearance and such. I told Lucy Jones she should lose a few pounds. I suggested to Josie Warren she might like to think about getting a boob job. Shit like that."

He shrugged as if what he'd just admitted was of no consequence. Trey was incensed.

"You have to be fucking kidding me! I thought it was *me* they were turned off by; something I'd done that made them suddenly go cold. And all this time it was *you!* Who else did you play games with?"

Wade looked completely unperturbed by Trey's anger. "All of them. I texted Angie after the accident to apologize and to admit I'd been drinking that night. She replied by telling me—you she never wanted to see you again. Then there were all those college girls." He chuckled. "Didn't I have fun with them? You made it so easy. You always left your phone on the charger at some point during the day or night. Sharing a room with you made it so simple. I sent messages and then deleted them from your phone. It was so much fun watching the fallout."

Wade's grin widened. He slowly shook his head. "And then there was Anastasia. She was a really nice piece of ass. I fucked her one night. Of course, she thought it was you. But it was my downfall. I fell for her and I fell hard. I wanted her to love me. *Me*, not you. I hacked into your phone and sent her message after message, telling her how I felt. I bared my soul to her. It was a mistake.

"She turned nasty. She refused to see me. I went on a bender for a week after she told me in no uncertain terms to get lost. She broke my heart. The only thing that consoled me was that her anger was directed at *you*." He smirked.

Trey saw red. He jumped up and ran at his brother and shoulder-charged him straight into the nearest wall.

"*Oomph!*" Wade grunted as the wind was knocked out of him.

Without pause, Trey raised his clenched fist and swung it. Inches from his brother's face, he halted the action. With his breath coming hard, he blinked back tears of hurt and disappointment.

"How *could* you?" he cried, his voice hoarse with pain. "How could you *do* such a thing?

You're my brother! I thought you loved me! At the very least, I thought you had my back! All these years I've felt obligated to you for saving me and for just as long you've been doing your best to sabotage my life!" He dragged in a ragged breath. "Words can't describe what you've done to me, Wade. You've ripped my soul apart. I can't imagine a time when I'll ever want to share the same air with you again. Now, you're going to take your sorry ass down to the police station and you're going to tell them exactly what you did to Heather Lockhart. After all the wrongs you've done to me, it's the least you can do. Understand?"

Trey glared at his brother. His breath came fast. His chest heaved with emotion—anger, hurt and bitter disappointment. He held onto a sliver of hope that Wade would redeem himself and do the right thing. He didn't know what he'd do if his brother let him down again.

The seconds dragged into a minute. Two. Finally, Wade's shoulders slumped on a heavy sigh.

"Okay. I'll do it."

Trey almost collapsed in relief. His head sunk forward and landed on his brother's shoulder. He fought back sobs of relief.

"Thank you, Wade," he gasped between harsh breaths. "Thank you. You don't know what this means to me."

Wade patted him awkwardly on the back. "It's all right, Trey. I'm sorry. For everything. And you're wrong. I know exactly what it means to you."

Chapter 14

Trey left his brother's apartment with mixed emotions. He was beyond devastated by the revelations his brother had shared about the cruel interference Wade had made in Trey's love life, but he was also quietly hopeful that his troubles of the past couple of months would soon be over. Wade would do the right thing. He had to. Surely after all he'd done, he'd come good in the end. Anything else was inconceivable.

He tugged out his phone to call Kiesha and then paused. Despite the fact they'd spent the night together, she'd made it clear she wanted to keep their relationship on a professional level. They hadn't shared anything personal since the morning he'd woken in her bed. The entire day spent together in the courtroom during the committal hearing had been no different. No one present that day would have had a clue she was anything more to him than his lawyer and it was obvious that's the way she wanted to keep it.

With a sigh, he dropped the phone back in his pocket and climbed into the Mustang. He wanted desperately to talk to her, to tell her about what Wade had said, but he wasn't sure he had the right to and he sure as hell couldn't take a rebuff.

No, he'd call her in the morning, during office hours. He'd let her know about the most recent developments and nothing else. After all, she was the one who insisted on keeping their relationship professional. Telling her now wasn't going to change anything. Besides, it was probably best to wait until Wade had actually attended upon the detectives. It had taken some doing to get Wade to come forward. Trey didn't want to jinx things by calling ahead of time. He'd call Kiesha when he had something definite to share. He only hoped, for once in his life, Wade wouldn't let him down.

Wade checked his reflection in the mirror of his brand new Porsche and was pleased with what he saw. He'd taken care to shower and shampoo his hair and had left it to dry naturally in a riot of curls. He was dressed in Levis and a Ralph Lauren polo shirt. He slipped on his Maui Jims and smiled at himself. It was a smile of confidence, charm and authority. He looked nothing like the kind of man who might rape a woman in a dark alley in the middle of the night.

With a final check in the mirror, he climbed out of the Porsche and locked it with the remote.

Strolling down the street, he arrived at the City of Sydney Police Station and took the stairs two at a time. With his shoulders back and head held high, he walked through the double automatic doors and strode up to the counter.

"Can I help you?"

He eyed the fresh-faced constable who stood behind the counter. "I'd like to see Detective Craigdon."

"Do you have an appointment?"

"No."

"May I have your name?"

"Wade Walker. Tell him I want to talk to him about my brother, Trey."

The constable nodded and picked up a phone. He spoke quietly into the receiver. A moment later, he ended the call and looked back at Wade.

"Detective Craigdon will be out in a minute. Please, take a seat."

Wade wandered over to the row of hard plastic chairs that lined one wall. He perched on the edge of one of them and looked around the room. It was a reasonably modest space. The walls were stark white, but were mostly covered with posters depicting the dangers of drinking and driving, domestic violence and how to use a helpline for alcoholics anonymous. There was also a stand holding several brochures on similar subjects. A potted plant stood in the corner closest to the counter. From the drooping of its leaves, it was in desperate need of water.

A few more minutes went by. A surge of irritation went through him and he jumped to his feet and began to pace.

Where the hell was Craigdon? Before Trey had left his apartment, he'd given him the detective's name as one of the head investigators. He'd also told him where he could find him. Only it seemed like the man was taking his sweet time to come and see him. It had been at least ten minutes since the constable had phoned him. Every second he delayed only served to piss Wade off more.

He was almost at the point of leaving when a door he hadn't yet noticed, opened into the waiting room and a tall, dark-haired man about Wade's age walked out. His gaze landed on Wade. He did a double take.

It was laughable. In fact, Wade couldn't help it. A chuckle escaped. He could almost hear the detective's brain processing the scene before him. The dumb fuck had no idea Trey had an identical twin. What a joke.

Enjoying the moment way more than he should, Wade strode toward the man and held out his hand. "Wade Walker. You must be Detective Craigdon."

"Mr Walker," Craigdon replied, shaking his hand, still looking dazed.

"Please, call me Wade."

The detective nodded and then, as if gathering himself, invited Wade to follow him. Turning on his heel, Craigdon headed back through the door where he'd appeared. Wade followed the detective down a long corridor from which several interview rooms branched off. About half of the doors were closed. Finally, Craigdon ushered him inside one of the small rooms.

Immediately Wade felt like the walls were closing in. There was something about the tight confines of a starkly furnished interview room inside the bowels of the police station that set him on edge. It wasn't the first time he'd been interrogated by the police. The last time had only been a year earlier. A different police station and a different detective, but the interview room was the same.

The walls of the small room were painted a dark gray and matched the scarred gray table and four gray plastic chairs that filled the room. Sophisticated camera and audio equipment was mounted high on the wall in one corner. The air-conditioning had been turned lower than necessary and Wade shivered involuntarily.

"Take a seat," Craigdon offered.

Swallowing a sudden rush of nerves, Wade sat and did his best to maintain his relaxed air.

"Do you mind if I bring in one of my colleagues? Detective Boule has been working with me on your brother's investigation."

Wade offered a casual shrug. "No, not at all."

Craigdon left the room and returned a short time later with a much older, heavyset detective who introduced himself as Harry Boule. Wade surreptitiously wiped his hand on his jeans before shaking the man's hand. Once all three of them were seated and Craigdon obtained Wade's permission to start recording, the interview began.

"Mr Walker, for the purpose of the audio, could you please state your name, address and date of birth."

Wade did as he was requested. The detectives also took turns in identifying themselves. Craigdon then took charge of the interview.

"Mr Walker, do you know a man by the name of Trey Walker?"

"Yes. He's my brother."

"In fact, you're identical twins, aren't you?"

"Yes."

Craigdon must have already worded up Boule because the older detective's expression didn't change. Not even an eyelash flickered.

"You're aware your brother has been charged with sexual assault and has now been committed to stand trial?" Craigdon asked.

Wade's gaze remained steady on the detective. "Yes."

"Has your brother talked to you about what happened that night?" Again, the question came from Craigdon.

"Yes."

Both detectives sat forward. Wade swallowed a smile.

"What has he told you?" Craigdon asked.

Wade saw the tension around the detective's mouth. The man was on edge wondering what the hell Wade was going to say. They weren't stupid. They had to know identical twins carried identical DNA. They could see their case disintegrating before their eyes. He almost laughed aloud.

"He called me the night it happened. I arrived at The Chill Factory about twenty minutes afterwards."

For all their years of experience hiding their emotions, both detectives stared at him in shock. Boule's mouth had fallen open. Wade understood how he felt. His announcement was totally unexpected and had taken them completely unawares. They were the detectives who'd conducted the investigation and yet they didn't know Trey Walker's brother had attended the scene. It was an embarrassing blunder, to say the least.

Craigdon was the first to recover. "So, let's get this straight. Your brother called you outside the nightclub, before the police or the ambulance arrived?"

"Yes. I was on my way home. He called and told me he was in trouble. It was after one in the morning, but what was I to do? He's my brother. Of course I went to him."

"How did you get there?" Craigdon asked. "The only car I recall seeing in the vicinity that night was a Mustang that was registered to Trey."

"My car was in the garage for a service. I caught a bus to the top of the hill and walked the rest of the way."

"So Trey told you he was outside The Chill Factory in Darlinghurst?" Boule asked.

"Yes."

"And that's where you found him?"

"Yes. In the alleyway. He was with a woman."

"Did you know her?" Craigdon asked.

He looked straight at the detective. "No. I'd never seen her before."

"What happened next?" Craigdon asked.

"Trey was in a panic. The girl was lying on the ground. He said something about her falling over. I went to her and checked her out. She was still breathing, but appeared semi-conscious. Trey told me she'd been drinking."

"Then what happened?" Boule asked.

Wade sighed, keeping up the pretense of concern. "I thought the girl might need medical attention. I called the ambulance."

Craigdon narrowed his eyes and looked thoughtfully at Wade. "We arrived within minutes of the ambulance. Only your brother and the woman were there. What happened to you?"

Wade sat on his hands so he wouldn't be tempted to squirm. Once again, he kept his gaze steady. "I left before you got there. I heard the sirens and knew the ambulance wasn't far away. I managed to snap my brother out of his daze and he assured me he could handle the situation on his own. It was late. I was tired. There was nothing more I could do. So I left."

Craigdon and Boule shared a long look. Wade could almost hear their thoughts. They were trying to work out how the hell they'd missed knowing their man's brother had been on the scene. Trey had told him about the security footage, but the cops must not have watched it all the way through. If they had, they'd have seen Trey arrive and would also have seen Wade leave.

After Trey left him the evening before, Wade had spent some time formulating a plan. He'd assured his brother he'd attend the police station and turn himself in.

Of course he had no intention of doing such a thing. He wasn't that stupid. A confession that it was him in the alleyway that night would see him sent straight to jail. Brother or no, he couldn't bring himself to do it. Not even for Trey. *Especially* not for Trey.

Thinking about what Trey had told him about the CCTV footage, Wade had eventually come up with a plan that covered that eventuality too. He took a punt that the footage outside the nightclub would be too grainy and dark for the detectives to identify which one of the twins had left. It was only his word against his brother's that things hadn't happened the way he'd relayed. So far, it looked as though both detectives believed him. A little of the tension that had been coiled inside him ever since he'd come up with his plan began to ease.

Until Craigdon frowned and once again narrowed his eyes at him.

"Your brother was charged more than a month ago. Why are you only now coming forward?"

Wade managed a nonchalant shrug. "I didn't think I had anything vital to add. I still don't."

"Then why come forward at all?" Boule asked.

"I'm a good and decent citizen. I pay my taxes on time. I just thought you should know I was there."

Craigdon continued to eye him balefully, as if trying to get to the bottom of who Wade Walker was and why he was there. Wade held his nerve and carefully kept his expression neutral. When Craigdon finally relaxed back into his chair, Wade breathed a surreptitious sigh of relief.

"Thanks for coming in, Mr Walker," Craigdon said. "We really appreciate it. If you remember anything else from that night, or if your brother shares any further insights, please don't hesitate to contact us."

He pulled a business card from the inside pocket of his suit jacket and handed it to Wade. With a murmur of thanks, Wade took the card and held it a moment between his fingers before slipping it into the pocket of his jeans. The detectives pushed away from the table and stood. Wade followed suit.

Craigdon held out his hand and Wade shook it. "Thanks again for your time, Mr Walker."

Wade acknowledged the comment with a nod. Boule showed him out. Wade left the building with a bounce in his step and a grin that stretched his lips wide.

———————

Jett Craigdon tapped the end of his pen on the gray Formica table in the interview room that had recently been vacated by Wade Walker. Harry Boule had returned and now sat across from him. Both men were still recovering from the shock of discovering Trey Walker had an identical twin brother.

Jett shook his head in disbelief, trying to make sense of it.

"I don't understand why the hell Trey Walker wouldn't tell us about his brother the first night he was arrested. Not only was his brother on the scene, but it's his identical twin! He must know they carry identical DNA. He could have offered that information right at the outset and our jobs would have been so much more difficult. We might not have even had enough on him to lay charges! Coupled with the fact he had a witness who verified he was with her in the hours before this happened, it just doesn't make sense that he'd keep silent about this." He looked at his partner. "What's your take on this?"

Harry looked thoughtful. "I'm not sure. This has caught me as much by surprise as it has you. It's true that the existence of an identical twin is going to muddy the waters. Our eyewitnesses might not be able to tell them apart and we sure as hell can't rely on the DNA any longer."

Jett compressed his lips, feeling grim. "There's something about Wade's explanation for coming forward that doesn't ring true, but I can't think for the life of me what he has to gain by meeting with us. It's odd, to say the least. The truth is, it could have been either one of them. Even though Trey had that other woman who claimed he was with her earlier in the night, it's still possible he left her earlier than either of them said and then went to the nightclub." Jett sighed. "We need to know for sure which one of them was involved. It's the only way we can proceed."

"How are we going to do that?"

"We can start with the phone records. Wade Walker said he received a call from his twin about twenty minutes before he arrived on the scene. He also says he called the ambulance. Those calls should show up on his phone records. If they check out, that's a tick in favor of Wade's story. Then there's the security footage." Jett grimaced. "We made a mistake not watching it right to the end. We need see if he turns up like he says he did."

Boule looked at him, his expression grave. "And if he doesn't?"

Jett stared at him. "We'll deal with that if and when it happens."

Boule shook his head. "I still don't understand why the hell Trey Walker didn't tell us about his twin the night we arrested him. Or at the very least, before the case went to court. What was his lawyer thinking by withholding this from us? We'd never have gotten past first base, let alone get the judge to commit the matter to trial if Wade Walker's existence had been public knowledge. It would have gotten Trey off the hook, at least in the short term until we worked out who the hell was there when it counted that night."

Jett regarded him thoughtfully. "Yes, something's off. I can only assume Kiesha Munro was as much in the dark about the existence of her client's identical twin as we were. Nothing else makes sense."

Boule sighed and rubbed at a tight spot at the back of his neck. "What looked like a straightforward case has suddenly turned to shit. My head's still spinning from these revelations. It's too early to make sense of anything."

Jett nodded grimly. "Yeah. I guess it's back to the drawing board."

Boule shot his partner a wry smile. "I hope you weren't thinking you might get home early today."

It was Jett's turn to sigh. "You're right. I'd better break the good news to my wife. Only this morning Danielle was giving me a hard time about how I haven't been home on time all week. I guess we can add another day to that."

Boule winked. "I'm glad it's you and not me. I wouldn't want to be on the other end of Dani's tongue-lashing when she gets mad."

Jett grinned. "She's even touchier at the moment. She's a matter of weeks from giving birth to baby number two. We're all walking around on eggshells."

"Ouch!" Harry chuckled. "I guess that means you need to get off your ass and get this case solved real quick."

"Roger that."

CHAPTER 15

Kiesha finished writing the last of her notes in Stephen Painter's file and closed it with a sigh. She'd recently represented him on a number of fraud charges. The police had accused him of obtaining money under false pretenses, mainly from shopping malls and the like. According to the police facts, Painter had misrepresented himself to members of the general public as an employee of a popular charity for which he was ostensibly collecting donations. Instead, he was pocketing the cash.

From the outset, he'd sworn to her it wasn't him and she'd believed him. After all, he was her client. It was her job to believe in him and defend him to the best of her ability—and defend him she had.

Unfortunately, the weight of evidence against him had been substantial, not the least the CCTV footage from security cameras in the mall which showed him approaching unsuspecting shoppers, time and time again, asking for and receiving donations.

The police had produced a legitimate representative of the charity who denied any knowledge of Painter or his association with their organization. It took the jury less than an hour to find him guilty of twenty-seven counts of obtaining a financial advantage by deception. Though not a large amount in total, he'd stolen a total of two-hundred-and-forty-six dollars and thirty cents and had been sentenced to a month in jail. It could have been a lot worse.

Kiesha was pleased it was over. It was one less case on her plate. In a couple of months, the year would be over and with it, her time at Sydney Legal would come to an end. She felt a little sad about leaving behind the career she'd built up at the firm, but at the same time, she looked forward to starting a new chapter of her life and what better way to do it, then as a judge of the District Court.

Once again she was filled with wonder as she thought about her new appointment: the first female aboriginal District Court Judge of New South Wales, Kiesha Munro. She still found it hard to believe.

The thought of her new job filled her with an equal measure pride and nerves. She was comfortable and confident in her role as a defense attorney at Sydney Legal. It would be a whole different ball game as a member of the District Court and it would involve a steep learning curve. Knowing the law from the point of view of a defense lawyer was one thing. Looking at it through the eyes of a judge would be altogether different. Still, she hoped she'd be given a helping hand by her fellow judges and that in time she'd be as comfortable and confident in her new role on the bench as she'd been seated at the bar table.

With a quiet sigh, she dictated the final letter to Stephen Painter, thanking him for the opportunity to represent him and outlining the terms of his sentence. Finally, she dictated her bill and then set aside the file in her "finished files" basket. Blindly, she reached for the next one.

Trey Walker.

It had been nearly twenty-four hours since they'd argued and she hadn't heard from him since. Every time she thought about it, she got annoyed and frustrated at his unwillingness to tell the police about his brother. He could so easily have made all this go away and yet he refused to do so.

How long was he prepared to wait? Until the jury had handed down a guilty verdict? Until the judge had passed sentence? Until he was behind bars? Just what would it take for him to overcome his admirable but totally misguided loyalty toward his twin?

It just didn't make sense to her and she was just as certain it wouldn't make sense to most people. She'd spoken to one of her brothers, Devon, about it. Devon was also a lawyer and knew all about difficult clients and making them see sense. When Kiesha had called him the other evening and explained her current situation, he had been at a loss to explain or provide a remedy.

'What the hell's wrong with the man? Does he have rocks in his head? Who wouldn't do everything they could to help themselves? Especially if they're truly innocent of the crime. He's going to end up with his ass in jail the way he's going,' Devon had said.

Kiesha thoroughly agreed, but there was nothing she could do about it. Trey Walker was a stubborn man and he refused to budge from his position. She was at a loss as to what to do. She couldn't bear the thought of an innocent man going to jail, or a guilty one getting away scot free. It went against everything she believed in. It was even harder to accept that very thing might happen to someone she cared about and on her watch. It seemed there was nothing she could do about it.

The phone at her elbow pealed and, distracted by her thoughts, she reached over and picked up the receiver.

"Kiesha Munro."

"Kiesha, it's Detective Jett Craigdon."

"What can I do for you, Detective?" she asked.

"Listen, the reason for my call is there has been a new development in the Trey Walker case."

She tensed, and every one of her senses came on high alert. "What kind of development?"

"Detective Boule and I received a visit from a Mr Wade Walker this afternoon. It turns out he's your guy's identical twin brother."

Kiesha's breath caught in her throat and her heart began to pound. *Wade had turned himself in at last!* Trey must've finally gotten through to him and made him see sense. But why hadn't he said anything to her? Why hadn't he called her and told her Wade was going to confess?

She was filled with a fresh wave of annoyance that quickly turned to self-disgust. She'd made it clear to him the morning after they'd spent the night together that he meant nothing to her at all. What else did she expect? She was his lawyer, but of course he was keeping his distance. He'd been in the middle of baring his soul to her and she'd hightailed it to the bathroom. *What a coward.* She hadn't been able to bring herself to talk to him about it again. It wasn't fair to him and it definitely wasn't her usual behavior.

It was just that he'd caught her unawares and his revelations about how he felt about her were totally unexpected. They'd agreed it was only to be casual and somehow, as the sun rose, for Trey it had turned into so much more. She hadn't been prepared for such a sudden change in heart and she'd panicked. It wasn't her proudest moment, but what had he expected her to do?

Their night together had been amazing, magical in every way, but until the next morning when he'd confessed his feelings for her, she'd had no clue he felt the same indefinable connection she did.

They needed to talk, *really* talk about what happened between them and what it meant for them going forward. But not right now. Right now, she had to deal with the fact Wade Walker had finally come forward to the police. A wave of hope flooded through her at the thought this nightmare might soon be over.

She cleared her throat and responded to the detective's announcement. "I see," she replied calmly.

"You don't sound surprised."

"I'm not sure what you want me to say, Detective. I was aware of the existence of Trey Walker's identical twin brother. I was instructed not to say anything about him."

"I see. That explains why you failed to mention him to us, though it would have saved you and your client a lot of grief. It's been bugging me and my partner all afternoon. But enough of that. I called to tell you Wade Walker had plenty of interesting things to say, not the least that he was in the alley that night with his brother."

Kiesha gasped quietly in relief. Wade had not only come forward, he'd also told the truth! She couldn't believe it! Trey would soon be set free!

"Oh?" she replied, maintaining her casual tone.

"Yes. Apparently your guy called his brother right after the rape. He was in a state of panic, begging for help. Wade did as any good brother would and turned up to offer his assistance. He even called the ambulance. We're still waiting on his phone records to confirm this, but we checked the security footage again and it seems his story pays out. The two people in the alley are joined by a third and then one of the twins leaves the scene. Unfortunately, both twins wore similar clothing that night and the footage is too grainy to determine the exact identity of the twin who departs, but it's exactly how Wade Walker said things played out."

Kiesha's eyes were so wide with shock it was almost painful. Her heart thudded and her chest was so tight she could barely breathe.

Wade hadn't told the truth at all! In fact, he'd twisted it to his own advantage. Of course the security footage showed the other twin arriving, but it sure as hell wasn't Wade. She wanted to scream out her frustration, to tell the police exactly what had happened, but it wasn't her job to do so. Her last instructions from her client were to keep Wade the hell out of it.

But surely Trey didn't know about his brother's latest betrayal? Surely he wouldn't continue to insist on this blind loyalty when it was obvious Wade had no such compunction to protect his twin. In fact, Wade had just thrown his brother under the proverbial bus. Kiesha could only hope the phone records proved Wade's story was rubbish.

With her thoughts in turmoil, she struggled to find something to say. *Should she disregard Trey's explicit instructions and tell the police what she knew?* Breaching a client's confidence could see her disbarred and there was no guarantee Trey would thank her for it. In fact, there was the very real possibility it would make things even worse between them. She squeezed her eyes tightly shut, vacillating back and forth. The detective finally broke the silence.

"Nothing to say, Counselor? Maybe you knew this all along? It's been part of your game. Keep the police in the dark for as long as possible. You were going to produce the twin at the last minute, weren't you, right after the prosecution had presented their case? It would have been a masterstroke, a magic trick that would have left the jury and everyone else gasping. An identical twin with identical DNA. The case would have been dismissed and the police and prosecutor would have been made a laughing stock. Is that what you had planned, Counselor?"

His voice was dangerously low and quiet and Kiesha felt a shiver of apprehension run down her spine. Craigdon was an excellent investigator. Anyone or anything showing him up as less than the consummate professional wouldn't go down well.

"I made no such plans," she responded icily. "If you must know, I've worked my butt off trying to convince my client to alert you to the existence of his twin. He's refused to consider it. I was hoping you'd make the discovery on your own." She drew in a breath, her chest rising and falling with her tension. *Did she have the courage to take this a step further? To say what needed to be said? Would Trey forgive her for betraying his brother? Would she forgive herself if she didn't?*

The questions hammered inside her brain until she couldn't stand it a second longer. And then she came to a decision.

"The thing is, Detective Craigdon, Wade Walker is a liar. He's told you exactly what happened that night, only he wasn't the one who came to the rescue. That was Trey." She paused and then added. "Identical twins carry identical DNA, but do you know they have different fingerprints?"

The words hung between them. It was almost as if the detective was as stunned by her revelation as she was. And then he found his voice.

"Interesting. Very interesting. I didn't know that about identical twins."

"Yes, I took the opportunity to research the subject. It has something to do with the separate umbilical cords and the random stresses on the fetus in the womb. That's what makes everyone's fingerprints unique, even those of identical twins."

"We didn't bother checking for prints at the time," Craigdon responded thoughtfully. "We had the eyewitness accounts and the DNA. We thought that would be more than enough to put the perpetrator away... Fortunately, it's not too late. The clothing worn by the victim is still here in the evidence room. A leather skirt and a corset top, I believe. Let's hope for your guy's sake we find some usable prints."

"How long will it take?" Kiesha held her breath waiting for his response.

"A week, maybe less. It depends on how backed up they are at the lab."

She eased the air out of her lungs on a quiet sigh. *A week.* Not so long. With a bit of luck, the police would find Wade's fingerprints. Then Trey would be free of this nightmare once and for all and the right man would be punished for his crimes.

After thanking the detective for his call and receiving his assurance he'd contact her as soon as he had results on the fingerprints, she hung up the receiver and stared into space, trying to come to terms with all that had happened.

Perhaps Trey wasn't aware his brother had attended the police station? Maybe that was why he hadn't told her about it. Maybe it had nothing to do with their strained relationship at all.

Wade had met with the detective earlier that afternoon. *Maybe Trey wasn't the one who'd managed to convince his brother to turn himself in? Who else had Wade been talking to, or had he come to the despicable decision all on his own?* She wished she knew. Either way, she needed to check in with her client.

Unable to put it off any longer, she picked up her cell phone and found Trey's number. He answered the call after the second ring.

"Ms Munro, what can I do for you?"

His voice was clipped and polite. His lack of warmth filled her with sadness and disappointment. An image of the two of them loving each other, full of passion and need, flashed through her mind. That felt like a lifetime ago. It was her own fault he was now emotionally distant. She was the one who'd thrust him unceremoniously aside. She grimaced and forced the memories from her mind.

"When was the last time you spoke to your brother?"

"Last night. Why?"

"What did you talk about?"

"Does it matter?"

His dry reply had her clenching her jaw in annoyance. *Surely they'd moved past this polite kind of back and forth?*

"It matters," she replied through gritted teeth.

There was a beat of silence on the other end of the phone and then she heard Trey sigh.

"I guess I should have called you already. I went over to his place yesterday, after I left you. We talked about the case. I'd already told him about the DNA they'd found. I also told him about the CCTV footage. He realized the game was up."

She tensed and held her breath. "What did he say?"

"He told me he was going to turn himself in to the police; tell them the truth about what happened that night. I assume he's done that."

Kiesha's heart stuttered and her belly filled with dread. She couldn't imagine the pain her next words would inflict. But there was no getting around them. They had to be said.

"I'm sorry, Trey. Wade attended the detectives this afternoon, but he didn't confess to the rape. Quite the contrary. He pointed the finger squarely at you. And they believe him."

———————

Trey stared across the wide expanse of ocean visible from his balcony window and saw nothing but the face of his Judas brother. It had been tough enough coming home last night and replaying every second of their conversation. It was now crystal clear why he'd never been able to hold onto a girlfriend. Wade had sabotaged his relationship with each and every one. Even Anastasia. Trey was utterly relieved he hadn't yet made a mention of Kiesha to his brother. She was the only woman who truly mattered. He couldn't bear the thought of Wade using deceit to turn her against him.

And then he'd discovered that just when he thought his brother couldn't get any lower, he betrayed Trey yet again. He was almost beyond being able to comprehend that Wade, his own flesh and blood, had gone to the police and lied about what had happened that night in the alley. And not only lied to save his own skin, but had deliberately placed Trey in front of the firing squad. The traitor had all but pulled the trigger. If he didn't already know the lengths his brother went to in order to assuage his jealousy, he wouldn't have believed it.

"Fuck! Fuck! Fuck!" he cursed savagely.

His fists tightened around the steel railing until pain radiated up his forearms. *What the hell had Wade been thinking?* How had he come to the point where he thought it acceptable to betray his brother this way? All Trey had done was come to his brother's aid, just like he thought Wade had done a decade earlier, and this was how that brother repaid him. It filled him with so much pain and sadness it was almost more than he could take.

The sound of his phone interrupted his dark thoughts. Frowning, he tugged it out of his pocket and checked the screen. It was his father. He answered the call.

"Dad."

"Trey, how are you doing? Listen," his father continued without pause, "you haven't heard from Wade lately, have you? I've been trying to get hold of him all day. I've left a ton of messages, but he hasn't replied. I—"

"No, Dad, I haven't, but I need to find him ASAP and when I do, I'm going to kill him."

His father laughed a little uncertainly at the vehemence in Trey's tone. "What's the matter, son? Had a tough day?"

"No, Dad, but I tell you what, when I get hold of my brother, he's going to know all about what it means to have a tough day." The iciness in his tone registered with his father. He stuttered and stammered and finally found his voice.

"What the hell are you talking about, Trey? What's Wade gone and done now?"

Trey's dry laugh was humorless. "I don't know where to start."

"You're talking in riddles, Trey. Have you been drinking?"

Trey made a sound of disgust. "Not enough." And then he sighed and took pity on his father. "I don't feel like going into the details now, Dad, but one thing you should know is that I have irrefutable proof my brother, your much-loved son who can do no wrong, is a rapist."

"H-how do you know that?"

"The whole thing was caught on CCTV cameras. It's plain for everyone to see."

"Oh, hell." The abject disappointment and sadness in his father's voice almost gave Trey pause. His father wasn't exactly in his prime. *Was his heart going to hold up to further bad news?* Trey would just have to take the risk. He couldn't keep this agony inside him a second longer. His father had to know.

In succinct sentences, he laid it out for Archibald Frederick John Walker IV just what his golden child had done, all the way back to the beginning. When he was finished, he was met with silence. Long tense moments passed before his father spoke again.

"How sure are you of your source of information?"

"Dead sure. I got it straight from my lawyer," Trey replied grimly. "She took the call from the lead detective who spoke to Wade. It doesn't get any closer to the source than that."

"Fuck, Trey. I can't believe it! That lying, sniveling son of a bitch! To think I defended him! How the fuck could he do something like that?"

All of a sudden, the fight went out of Trey. He was emotionally stretched to the limit and beyond exhausted. It was only early evening, but it felt so much later. His head pounded and his gut ached with a sadness so deep he couldn't ever imagine getting over it. Betrayed by his own flesh and blood. *How could things get worse?*

His father continued to rant. "Where the fuck is he? Wait until I get my hands on him! The little fuck! Fancy turning on your family like that, your own flesh and blood! It's reprehensible! Unforgivable! He's crossed the line so many times and I didn't know."

"Yeah, well good luck finding him. I haven't been around to his place. Last night he told me he'd turn himself in. Instead he implicated me completely for a rape I didn't commit. Until a short time ago, I was oblivious to all he's done. Right now, I'm beyond having the energy to go out and find him, but you're welcome to go in my stead. Let me know when you locate him."

Trey ended the call and dragged himself inside. With a heavy heart, he made his way across the living room and threw himself down on his couch. With his arm flung over his eyes, he let the anguish he'd held back ever since he'd taken Kiesha's call slide slowly from beneath his eyelids.

Pain and devastation trickled down his cheeks and dripped onto his shirt. His heart had been ripped out by his very own brother, his much loved, much adored twin. Trey's life would never be the same again.

Chapter 16

Archibald Frederick John Walker IV, or "Archie" to his friends couldn't remember the last time he'd felt so angry. He was combusting from the inside out.

After all he'd done for his youngest son and this is how he repaid him...

It was beyond infuriating. Wade had been given every opportunity, every favor, every hand-up Archie had at his considerable disposal and still Wade had thumbed his nose at all of it. And now Archie discovered Wade had been sabotaging Trey's life all along, at every opportunity he could get. They were twins, for Christ's sake! It was unforgivable.

Archie hadn't wanted to believe his youngest son, or any child of his, could be capable of rape. When Trey had first come to him with the accusation, he'd brushed it off. He was sure there was another explanation. Perhaps the woman's boyfriend had discovered her little dalliance with Wade and she'd felt the need to accuse him of taking her by force in order to save face. It wouldn't be the first time a woman had cried rape to save her hide.

But then Trey had told him about the security footage. Having the whole sordid episode caught on tape was something else. According to Trey, anyone watching the footage would be left in no doubt the woman hadn't given her consent. It was deeply disappointing. He'd raised his sons better than that. At least, he thought he had. He'd paid for the best nannies money could buy to see to his young sons' education and social grooming. It seemed that wasn't enough. Now he had to face the reality that his youngest son was also capable of planning a murder.

It hadn't always been easy, being a single, older first time father, especially one who spent more time at work than at home. But, he'd done his best for his sons; he really had. In addition to the highly qualified nannies, he'd paid for the finest private school education at his disposal. He'd showered them with gifts. He'd introduced them to important people and had gotten them entry into the best university in town. And where had it gotten him?

His elder son, Trey, had taken everything on board and had taken it to the next level. He'd excelled in school and had graduated top of his class. He could have had his pick of jobs at illustrious advertising agencies and in the end, chose Baker & Saddler, a firm well established in Sydney with a more than respectable reputation. Though Archie had been disappointed his oldest son hadn't followed him into law, he was proud of Trey's achievements nonetheless.

But with Wade, things had always been different. He'd been given the same opportunities, the exact same advantages and invitations, but he wasn't interested in achieving or in making a name for himself, other than for all the wrong reasons. He'd been in and out of trouble for a fair portion of his life.

Thanks to Archie's esteemed judicial position and a few well-placed bundles of cash, all but a few minor traffic incidents and a single drunk driving charge had evaporated like magic.

Of course, it hadn't been quite that easy and Archie knew that one day the favors he asked for from his friends in law enforcement would be called in, but it had been worth it to help smooth his youngest son's way.

It was true that Archie had never been able to force Wade to take responsibility for his actions. It seemed every time Wade did something untoward, he always had an excuse that seemed legitimate enough that Archie ended up letting things slide. It had given Wade a sense of expectation that no matter what he did, his father would make it go away.

It was his fault that Wade felt that way and now he wished he'd handled things differently. Trey had pleaded with him on more than one occasion for him to do just that. But Wade had been such a weakling. For months after his birth, no one even knew if he'd live.

His mother was almost beside herself with happiness at that news. Eileen had spent every waking hour seated beside Wade's incubator, holding his tiny hand, praying, singing and praying some more for her son's recovery. The prayers had paid off. Eventually they were allowed to bring Wade home and he'd only continued to improve.

Though never the same size and capability as his older brother, he did well enough. No one really connected Wade's acting out and his sometimes socially unacceptable behavior with the fact the boy felt inferior to his twin. Trey certainly didn't treat him any differently and Archie liked to think he and Eileen hadn't, either. If anything, they probably overcompensated by showering him with love.

And where had it gotten them? Wade had grown into a spoiled and petulant child who became a spoiled and petulant adult—and it was all Archie's fault. If he'd spent more time with his son... If he'd resisted the boy's constant demands for things... If he'd forced Wade to take responsibility for doing the wrong thing—even once.

Of course, Eileen's untimely death hadn't helped matters. She'd died from meningococcal— was gone before anyone had a chance to catch their breath. He'd been spending a pleasant few hours with his current mistress when he took the call. He could still remember the shock of it.

Wade had been unreasonably attached to his mother and had taken her death hard. For months afterwards, he'd acted out worse than ever. But Archie had made excuses for the boy, blaming the escalation of his bad behavior on his mother's death. And perhaps there was some truth to that, but his mother had been dead more than twenty years and Wade was still acting out. Now he'd not only admitted to setting Trey up for a car accident that could have killed him and his girlfriend, Wade had also actively encouraged the police to find Trey guilty of rape. That was simply unforgivable.

With an impatient squeal of tires, Archie turned his silver Aston Martin DB9 into Wade's street. Accelerating up the steep incline, he cursed when he couldn't find a parking space close. He eventually found one more than a block away and was forced to walk all the way. Why Wade insisted on living in such a dump was beyond him.

He'd tried hard to persuade his son to live somewhere more exclusive, but Wade dug in his heels and would have none of it. He insisted he was more comfortable among people who understood him. Each time, Archie had fought to hide his hurt.

But now, standing before Wade's front door with its cracked and peeling paint, his anger at his son returned full force. He hadn't bothered to call ahead and let his son know he was coming. Wade hadn't returned the last five calls. *Why would he answer this one?*

With a muffled curse, Archie pressed the buzzer in the foyer of Wade's building.

"Wade! Open up! I need to talk to you."

It took longer than he had patience for, but Wade eventually buzzed him in. By the time he reached Wade's floor, he was out of breath, which only made him more disgruntled. He thumped on Wade's door and waited a second or two and then thumped on the door again. He was just about to lift his fist a third time when the door opened. Wade stood there looking clean and respectable in a designer polo shirt and jeans. He looked like any other rich and successful twenty-something enjoying a relaxing night in.

And then Archie peered closer at his younger son and noticed his dilated pupils and the telltale flush on his cheeks. He snorted in disgust. Wade was both high and drunk. The knowledge only fired Archie's anger hotter. He pushed his son in the chest, forcing him backwards.

"What the fuck, Wade! You're a snake and a rapist and now you've laid the blame on Trey!"

Wade's eyes opened wide in surprise. He blinked once, twice, as if he was trying hard to process what his father had said.

"What the hell, Dad—?"

"Don't 'what the hell' me, Wade. You heard what I said. You were meant to tell the police the truth about what happened that night, not do your utmost to get them to convict your brother! It's fucking piss weak!"

"I... I didn't. You've got it wrong. I—"

Archie's temper snapped. He pushed his face into Wade's. "Don't lie to me!" he snarled. "Trey's lawyer had a call from one of the detectives you met with this afternoon. She told Trey all about how you went to the police and pretended you were Trey in the alley that night! You told the detectives it was *you* on your way home and Trey who called, desperate for help." Archie shook his head in disgust. "And that's not all you've done. Trey told me everything. I can't believe you did it! Betrayed your own flesh and blood! What kind of a man are you?"

Before his eyes, Wade collapsed into a sniveling mess. He stumbled down the hallway and fell upon the couch.

"I'm sorry, Dad! I didn't mean it! I didn't mean any of it! I just wanted to put a dent in Trey's oh-so-perfect life, that's all. I didn't mean for him to die in the accident! Why do you think I gave my own blood? As for the rape, it was never meant to get this far, but Trey wouldn't leave me alone. He kept on me and on me to go to the police. So I did."

"He meant for you to go and confess and man-up to your responsibilities!" Archie shouted. "Not for you to turn traitor! You spoiled little shit!"

Wade's wails of devastation grew louder. He hugged a cushion to his chest and sobbed. "Please, Dad! You have to believe me! I... I didn't know what I was saying. I was high. I can't even remember what I said..."

Archie shook his head, filled with loathing. "You disgust me! You lily-livered son of a bitch! You're always making excuses! Well, I've had enough! Get off the drugs and get clean or stay out of my life for good! I don't need a son like you!"

A look of shock and horror flooded Wade's face. His eyes opened wide and tears poured down his cheeks.

"No, Dad! No! You don't mean that! Please, say you don't mean that!"

Archie looked at him, his heart breaking, but he strengthened his resolve. This time, he wouldn't weaken. Wade needed to be taught a lesson. Some things had to be learned the hard way.

"You told me you didn't rape that girl, Wade," he said quietly. "And yet the security tapes tell a different story. Just another one of your stunts. I can't believe a son of mine could do such a thing."

"I didn't—"

Archie held up his hand. "Save it. All I want to know is why. Why did you do it? Why did you force yourself on that poor girl? There are plenty of women looking for cock. You don't have to force yourself on a reluctant one."

"She wasn't reluctant, Dad! I swear! She was all over me!"

Archie shook his head, so tired he could barely stand. His son's lies and continual refusal to face the truth had wearied him beyond measure. The worst of it was knowing he was largely responsible for creating the whining, petulant, spoiled brat of a man who stood before him. There was nothing more he could do. With feet that felt weighted down by lead, he turned and left.

A soft knock on Trey's door snagged his attention. Sometime during the evening, he'd fallen asleep on the couch. The knock came again a little louder and he blinked and sat up. The night had fully descended. The sky was as black as tar. It wasn't broken by the twinkle of a single star. He could barely distinguish the ocean from the horizon. Lights from passing freighters stood out like beacons.

He glanced at his watch. It was a little past nine. Not late, but not early, either, especially for a caller. Hoisting himself off the couch, he padded barefoot to the front door. He peeked through the security hole and was surprised to see Kiesha standing on the other side. It had been hours since her phone call and more than a day since they'd seen each other. He was unsure how he felt about seeing her outside his apartment.

What had brought her there? Was it curiosity, or pity? Or was she there because she cared? And if so, did she care as a friend, or something more?

He hated that he didn't know the answers and hated even more that how she felt about him mattered so much. He was usually the one in charge, the one calling the shots in his relationships. This thing with Kiesha was so different from the way things normally were: it had him all off keel. Throw in the issue with his brother and it was no wonder his head was in a spin.

Swallowing a sigh, he undid the deadlock and opened the door.

"H-hi," she said uncertainly.

"Hi."

His tone was carefully neutral, neither welcoming nor uninviting. She was the one who'd turned up on his doorstep. Let her be the one to make the first move.

"Can I come in?" Once again, hesitance dogged her voice. It just went to show he wasn't the only one feeling off-balance. The knowledge cheered him up. He nodded briefly and stood back to allow her to enter.

She moved into the foyer and then stepped to one side to let him pass. Padding along the cool tiles, he turned and led her into the open concept kitchen and living room. He heard her quiet gasp and acknowledged it with a silent flash of pride.

The entire wall of his living room was floor to ceiling glass and showcased the magnificent view of the Pacific Ocean. Though the black night concealed most if its magnificence, he was sure she could imagine what it would look like with the morning sun shining in.

"You have a nice place," she commented, looking around her.

"Thanks. It's comfortable."

She gave a slight grin. "I'd say. It's definitely comfortable."

He moved toward the well-stocked bar he kept in the corner of the living room.

"Would you like a drink?"

She nodded. "Thanks that would be nice. A gin and tonic would be lovely."

He walked behind the bar and fixed them both a drink then handed one to her. Their fingers brushed. He heard her quick intake of breath...

For endless moments, their gazes meshed and a world of unspoken questions and answers passed between them. He saw both longing and uncertainty in her blue eyes. He could only guess she saw much the same thing in his. And then she looked away and sipped from her drink and the spell between them was broken.

"I'm really sorry about your brother, Trey," she murmured.

He shrugged and forced back a wave of pain. "He made his own choices. It's too bad we all have to live with them."

"What he did to you is unforgivable. I had to come over and reassure myself you were okay. If one of my brothers betrayed me like that, I'd be a mess."

Trey compressed his lips so tightly against a fresh surge of anger he tasted blood. Kiesha didn't know the half of it. Just the thought of what Wade had done sent his emotions spiraling out of control. He still couldn't believe his brother, his *twin*, had done such things.

"What did you tell the police?" he asked.

"I told them Wade was lying; that it was you who was the last to arrive on the scene."

Trey grimaced. "We're identical twins. From memory, both of us were dressed in jeans and light-colored T-shirts. They're not going to be able to tell us apart."

Kiesha nodded. "Yes. The detective said as much. Right now, it's only your word against your brother's. They're curious about why you didn't tell them about Wade in the first place. It seems awfully convenient to the detectives for you to suddenly produce an identical twin brother on the eve of the trial."

Trey shrugged, but looked away. Guilt surged through him. Right from the outset, Kiesha had urged him to tell them about Wade and he'd refused to do so out of loyalty and obligation to his brother.

Loyalty, huh! What a joke! It seemed Wade felt no such noble emotion toward him. Trey should have told the police the truth right from the outset and forced Wade to accept responsibility for what he'd done. Now, who knew what was going to happen…?

"I'm sorry," he whispered, his voice hoarse with emotion. "I should have listened to you. I should have told them about Wade. I should have—"

"Hey, don't beat yourself up about it. You did what you thought was right and…I admired you for it. You have many admirable qualities, Trey Walker."

She'd walked slowly toward him as she spoke, closing the distance between them until they stood less than a foot apart. The heat from her body mingled with his and filled him with a deep yearning. The blue of her eyes had deepened to cobalt and the need in them seemed to reflect what he felt deep inside.

He'd never felt so emotionally connected to a woman. After the callous way he'd been treated by women in the past, he'd vowed never to let himself feel that way again. Now he knew the truth about those relationships, but he couldn't rewrite the past. All he could do was look to the future, a future he wanted to include Kiesha.

Somehow, what he felt for her transcended the merely physical and went to what really mattered.

He wanted to claim every inch of her—her body, her mind, her heart. *If he spoke the words aloud, would he send her running for the hills, like the last time?*

There was only one way to find out.

CHAPTER 17

Trey stared at her with eyes that burned bright with hunger. "I'm glad you came over," he murmured.

Kiesha stared back at him. Her heart pounded. Her mouth went dry. Her palms were clammy with nerves. She couldn't work out why she was nervous. It wasn't as if the two of them hadn't already gotten naked. Okay, so it had happened at a time when they were both seeking a physical release and an emotional attachment hadn't been a consideration. At least, that's how it had been for her.

But now, things were different. She knew him so much better, knew the person he really was. The depth of his love and loyalty to his brother blew her mind. Even now, he wasn't ranting and raving about the betrayal, but seemed more resigned and deeply weary. Oh, she'd caught the flash of anger in his eyes, but those emerald orbs had also been filled with pain. The worst of it was, there was nothing she could do to alleviate it.

Or was there?

The thought popped into her mind and took root. Coming to a sudden decision, she closed the scant distance between them and planted her mouth squarely on his. She felt his momentary start of surprise and then a second later, he gathered her in his arms. Groaning against her lips, he tightened his hold on her and kissed her like he was a man starved for contact.

With her breasts crushed against his chest, she kissed him back with all the passion she felt inside her. Warm and pliant, his lips moved over hers and when his tongue pressed against her mouth seeking entrance, she willingly opened it and welcomed him inside. He thrust in his tongue and swept it back and forth, tasting, seeking, loving. It was heaven. It was hell. It was the most exquisite torture.

His erection pressed against the juncture of her thighs, flaming the fires that ignited in her core. She tightened her arms around his neck and pressed against him, earning herself another of his hoarse moans.

"Oh, hell, Kiesha. I'm so turned on I'm about to explode."

His husky words, muttered against her ear, filled her with excitement. She kissed him hard again and then pulled slightly back and framed his face in her hands. She hadn't planned to fall in love with him and she didn't even know if that was what she felt, but she wanted him, yearned for him like she'd wanted no other and she sure as hell didn't want him to stop.

"I don't want you to stop, Trey," she breathed and watched his eyes darken with desire.

Without another word, he bent and scooped her up in his arms and padded down the hall. Past one room and then the other, until they came to a door that stood open at the end of the hall. He strode in and deposited her on the biggest bed she'd ever seen.

The faint yellow glow from a lamp that stood on the nightstand cast intimate illumination around the room. The pale blue-and-white bedspread beneath her felt as soft as silk. A floor-to-ceiling sliding glass door opened up to another balcony. She spied two white wicker chairs before Trey came down beside her and all of her attention shifted to him.

He kissed her softly, tenderly on the forehead, her nose, her cheeks before once again finding her lips. Their first few frantic moments of togetherness had passed and it seemed like they'd wordlessly given themselves permission to touch and feel and breathe.

His hands skimmed over her ribcage and then circled her waist. With an impatient noise in the back of his throat, he tugged at her blouse until it came loose from her skirt. Then he started on the buttons and it wasn't long before he spread the fabric wide, exposing her lacy white bra to his gaze.

"You're so beautiful," he whispered.

His voice held awe and wonder and she believed him. He followed through with the most tender of touches, running his fingers lightly up and down the shadow of her breasts, tracing the lacy mounds and then back again. He reached around and undid the clasp of her bra. He tossed aside the lacy fabric and watched as her breasts sprang free.

Once again, he traced the soft mounds, only this time he paused to stroke her nipples. Heat surged through her and centered in her core. Still he stroked and the little nubs pebbled beneath his touch. The ache between her legs intensified.

She moved restlessly against him. "Trey, please. You're driving me insane."

"That's the idea," he murmured. "Relax and enjoy it."

Closing her eyes, she blew out her breath and did as he suggested. He shifted his head, his mouth tracing a path over her skin. From one nipple to the other and then lower, across her ribcage, over her flat stomach and lower still.

His fingers reached behind her and undid the button and zipper of her skirt. She lifted her hips and assisted him to slide the clothing off her hips. Her white lacy panties quickly followed and finally she was naked.

Desire glowed in the depths of his eyes, sparking an answering need deep inside her. His head bent low and the next instant his tongue touched the most intimate part of her and slowly began to stroke. She clenched her hands into fists against the indescribable pleasure of it.

"Trey!" She gasped.

His answering smile was slow and oh so sexy. "Do you like that?"

She grinned back. "You know I do."

"Then what are you complaining about?"

She opened her eyes innocently. "Who said I was complaining?"

"Minx," he muttered and returned his attention to her clit.

Long unhurried lashings with his tongue were followed by shorter, sharper pokes. All the time, his hand massaged her mound. The pressure built inside her until she felt like she was going to explode. Trey glanced up at her and as if sensing how close she was to the edge, slowly, reluctantly moved away. At once, she felt disappointed.

"Trey! Please, don't stop!"

"I want to feel you come on my cock," he stated.

In short order, he disposed of his clothes and sheathed himself. His cock jutted hard and impressive from his groin. He moved and positioned himself between her thighs, spreading them even wider. She eagerly encouraged him and braced herself against his invasion.

Instead of thrusting into her, he ran the tip of his cock up and down her wet slit. Over and over, until the head of his engorged erection glistened with evidence of her need. The sight of it sent her desire skyrocketing and her core filled with liquid heat. She moved restlessly against him, urging him to take her.

"Please, Trey. Fuck me. I need to feel you inside me."

His lips quirked upwards in a grin. "This isn't all about you, sweetheart."

She groaned in frustration and reached for him, urging him down on top of her, but still he resisted. Once again, he swiped his cock up and down her slit. Lifting her hips, she tried to encourage him to enter her, but he only slid his cock in the tiniest bit. Hotter and hotter, her desire flared and greater and greater was her need. When she was at the point where she didn't think she could stand it another minute, he bent forward and with a harsh groan of triumph, surged forward and filled her to the hilt.

Both of them gasped from the exquisite feel of it. They stared at each other, eyes wide with wonder, unable to look away. It wasn't the first time they'd been together, but it was the first time Kiesha felt loved.

Slowly, Trey began to move and she felt each thrust deep inside her. The tenderness in his eyes, the passion, the need, all of it, triggered something inside her, something new and unfamiliar. She wanted to pause and reflect on the feeling, but right now there was no time.

Faster and faster, deeper and stronger, each thrust was harder than the last and then there was nothing or no one but Trey. The strain on his face was telling. She felt the tension inside her, too. Her fingernails dug into his back. A cry of relief skated on her lips.

And then she was there at the pinnacle and she cried out with all the wonder she felt inside. Stars burst behind her eyes. Her muscles clenched around his cock, milking him for all he was worth. At the same time, he found his release and with a groan he collapsed on top of her. She relished the feel of him, the warm weight of his body, the spicy scent of his cologne.

Slowly, they returned to earth.

Trey turned to look at her. "That was..."

"Amazing," she finished.

"Absolutely."

He grinned softly and pulled her close against his side. She snuggled into his warmth. They were silent for a long time before Trey finally spoke again.

"I really appreciate all you've done for me, Kiesha."

His murmured words, muffled against her hair, filled her with emotion. She came up on one elbow and kissed him softly on the mouth.

"I wish I could have done more."

He grimaced. "You did everything you could. I'm the one who refused to listen. If it wasn't for my faith in my brother and my willingness to protect him and help him at all costs, I would never have found myself in this mess."

"You weren't to know he'd turn on you like that. You expected him to be as good and honorable as you are. If your circumstances were reversed, you would have come forward right away and owned up to your actions."

Trey grimaced. "I would never have gotten myself in such a predicament in the first place." He shook his head. "I still can't believe he raped that girl. If I hadn't seen the proof with my own eyes no one would have convinced me he was capable of it."

"None of us know what we're capable of until we do it, or what anyone else is capable of either," she said quietly. He opened his mouth as if to argue and she pressed a finger against his lips.

"*Shh*. I understand. You're everything a man should be with too many good qualities to count. You could never force a woman. Of that I have no doubt."

Trey sighed heavily. "You're right on the last count at least, and it saddens me and shocks me every time I think about what my brother did. That he was capable of such a terrible thing… And that he'd try to lay blame on me. And you don't know the half of it. Wait until I tell you what else he's done. You won't believe it… It's shaken my faith in him. I doubt it will ever be restored."

A surge of sadness went through her. She could only imagine what it felt like to be faced with the awful and indisputable reality that your brother was such a monster. And though she was curious about what else he had yet to reveal, she didn't push. She trusted that Trey would tell her when he was ready. She pulled him close.

He pressed a kiss against her hair. "Thank you for coming over. It's nice to know you care."

She stared at him. "You're right. I do care. I care a lot."

She smiled softly as the realization set in and saw the sudden light that shone in his eyes. For the first time since she'd arrived, he looked at peace. He half-sat up and his hand traced along her naked shoulder and slid down along her arm. His fingers brushed the side of her breast. She shivered with need.

His hand moved lower, across her belly and lower still. His fingers tangled in her damp curls and her legs fell open of their own accord. A moment later, he stroked his way down and inside her silky folds. His fingers found her clit, already swollen with need. He circled the little nub and she groaned.

"Trey, it's late and I have to be at work early in the morning."

"But you care about me. You care a lot. Are you sure you're ready for sleep?" he murmured and leaned forward and kissed her on the mouth.

She murmured against his lips and then gasped as his fingers plunged into her warmth.

"You're so wet, babe. It doesn't feel like you're ready for sleep. It feels like you want more of my cock."

His erotic words, coupled with the rhythmic stroking of his fingers filled her with heat. She melted against him, powerless to resist his wordless call. Silently, he sheathed himself. Then he moved and positioned himself between her legs and without hesitation, plunged inside her once again.

She stretched around him, warm and fluid, and clung to his muscular shoulders. He moved slowly, in no hurry this time. In and out, his hips moved back and forth, filling and withdrawing. She met his thrusts head on, eager for more. They'd climaxed only moments earlier and yet she felt a fresh wave of hot and urgent need build inside her once more.

"Look at me," he commanded softly.

She reluctantly opened her eyes. He stared down at her, his gaze filled with tenderness. In fact, his expression almost looked like one of love...

No, he couldn't love her. It was too soon. They barely knew each other. And yet, she felt something for him she'd never felt before... *Was it possible he felt the same way?*

He'd told her the first time he liked her way more than he should. *Had he fallen in love with her? And had she fallen in love with him?* If this was what love felt like, she wanted more, more, more!

She smiled at him, filled with the wonder of it and he slowly, tenderly smiled back. Staring into each other's eyes, he continued to move inside her. The fire between them continued to burn until at last they reached the peak. They orgasmed together showering themselves in tongues of fire as they cried out and collapsed on the other side.

"I love you, Kiesha Munro," he mumbled, sounding half-asleep.

She tensed and a wave of panic engulfed her.

Trey Walker loved her. A relationship was the last thing she needed. The timing was all wrong. What the hell was she going to do?

And then she forced herself to relax. A gentle smile filled with wonder tugged at her lips. *He loved her.* Trey Walker *loved* her. Somehow, they'd make it work.

Detective Jett Craigdon poured himself a cup of strong black coffee from the machine in the staff tearoom and headed back to his desk. It was his fourth cup of coffee since he'd arrived at work at six that morning. It was now a little past nine.

He'd had a rough night. His two-year-old was teething and spent most of the time either crying or tossing restlessly in bed between him and his wife. To make matters worse, Dani was up and down to the bathroom. Their unborn baby was making its presence known. He was bleary eyed and weary beyond measure and now needed all the help he could get to make it through the day.

Nodding greetings to a couple of other officers, he rubbed a hand across his face and paused to chat with Harry Boule.

"Big night, Craigdon?" Harry ribbed with a knowing wink.

Jett grimaced. "I wish. My kid's teething."

Harry chuckled. "That's your story, anyway."

Jett gave him the finger and turned toward his desk.

"By the way, that fingerprint report in the Walker case came back from the lab."

Harry's casual comment was enough to stop Jett in his tracks. He spun on his heel and then winced at the pain that arced through his head. He strode back to Harry's desk.

"That was quick. I only sent off the request yesterday. Why didn't you tell me earlier?"

Harry shrugged. "It only just hit my desk. You were in the tearoom so Zoe handed it to me."

Harry offered him a single piece of paper. Jett snatched it out of his hand and scanned the contents.

"Two partial prints were retrieved from the black leather miniskirt. Both good quality prints. Both were matched to..." He looked up at Harry.

"Wade Walker," Harry finished.

"Shit." Jett shook his head. "I ran a check on him. He's in the system for other minor violations. We should have looked at him harder. I can't believe it was that prick all the time. He came in here and gave us the sad story of how he'd come to his brother's aid, helped the poor guy out in his time of need. And all the time, it was him who'd raped that woman, him who'd made the SOS call to his brother." He looked across at Harry. "It's unbelievable."

Harry grimaced. "Yeah, who needs friends when you have a relative like Wade Walker?"

"How did we do with the phone records? Did they come in, yet?"

"No, but Telstra promised we'd have them today. I'd bet my pension the first call for help came from Wade Walker's phone."

"And no doubt the call to emergency services came from Trey's number." Jett cursed again.

"We have enough for an arrest warrant without the phone records," Harry said.

"Yeah, but we might as well wait until we have everything. I doubt Wade Walker's going anywhere anytime soon. He did a great job deflecting blame to his brother. He must have been supremely confident he'd get away with this. He must have known we wouldn't be able to tell him and his twin apart in the CCTV footage.

"Too bad for him he didn't know about the fingerprints on the skirt. No doubt he probably didn't think about us being able to prove the origin of the phone calls, either. He doesn't come across as the brightest match in the box."

"You're right. I think he's almost certain his brother's going down for this. He came in and shared tidbits of information with us to make sure of it. What a germ."

Jett compressed his lips into a grim line. "You have that right." He sighed. "At least Kiesha Munro will be happy. Her high-profile client is in the clear. It's a nice way to bring her career as a lawyer to an end."

Harry nodded. "Yeah. It sure provides a nice sound bite for the six o'clock news. If she wasn't headed for the District Court she could just about name her price."

"She'll likely be sorely missed at Sydney Legal," Jett commented. "But I wish her all the best. She's a good lawyer and she's worked hard to get where she's going. To have an aboriginal woman finally on the District Court bench is a step in the right direction."

"Yeah. I agree. Hopefully this is the start of many similar appointments."

"Let me know when those phone records come in," Jett said. Once we're sure, I'll make the call to the esteemed Ms Munro and give her the good news."

Harry waved in acknowledgement. Jett sipped from his coffee and wandered off in the direction of his desk. Pulling out his chair, he stretched out and stacked his hands behind his head. With his feet on his desk, he sighed and closed his eyes. Oh, for a few minutes peace and quiet so that he could catch up on some much needed rest.

He spared a thought for Dani who was still at home with their son. She'd had as much sleep as he had and she now had to deal with the toddler and her advanced pregnancy all day on her own. He thought he had it tough…

It was nothing compared to what his wife dealt with all day. He made a mental note to stop off at the florist on his way home and bring her some fresh flowers. It wouldn't make up for her tough day with their son, but it would bring a smile to her face and that was almost as good.

Chapter 18

Kiesha rubbed the knot that had formed in the back of her neck and leaned back in her chair and sighed. The kink had developed from working on the pile of files on her desk for far too long without a break. It was barely eleven in the morning and she was already well and truly over the day.

She'd spent long hours throughout the night making love with Trey every which way there was and though she wasn't complaining, when the alarm on her phone went off at six, she'd groaned in disbelief. Even now, despite the more-than-pleasant way she'd whiled away the hours, she was still silently bemoaning her lack of sleep.

The last time she'd pulled an all-nighter had been as far back as her college days when she'd stumbled into bed with a fellow law student. Her distant memories of those times couldn't compare to what she'd shared with Trey.

He was such a considerate and expert lover. Each and every time they'd reached for each other during the long, sweet hours of the night, he'd seen to her pleasure first and foremost and his consideration had greatly pleased her. She didn't think any of her past lovers had such good old-fashioned bedroom manners.

Coupled with that, he was everything she wanted in a man: He was kind, compassionate, intelligent, sexy and oh-so-physically attractive. He was the whole package and though she was still coming to terms with the idea of having a relationship with him, she couldn't believe he was hers.

His murmured words of love hadn't been repeated and she hadn't found the courage to raise the subject before she'd hastily dressed and headed out the door. They'd promised to catch up later and she looked forward to exploring the matter some more.

If anyone had asked her a couple months earlier if she was interested in a steady relationship, she would have laughed and told them no. She was headed for the bench. A whole new chapter in her life was about to open up. Working as a District Court judge would be exciting and definitely challenging. Once in the position, she wouldn't have time to put into a new relationship, no matter how much she wanted a husband and family one day. It was as simple as that.

But Trey had landed in her life when she was least expecting it and he couldn't have come at a more inconvenient time. She'd thought she'd represent him, clear his name and then they'd go their separate ways. She never dreamed he'd fall in love with her or that she'd fall in love with him. It was damned inconvenient, but she wouldn't have it any other way.

She was in love with him... There, she'd admitted it. Despite everything, she'd given her heart to Trey Walker and she couldn't be happier. Her lips tugged upwards in a wide smile and she even giggled at the thought. *She was in love with Trey Walker.* She couldn't wait to tell him.

Digging in her handbag for her cell phone, her search came to a halt when the phone on her desk began to ring. With a quiet sigh, she reached over and answered it.

"Kiesha Munro."

"Ms Munro, it's Detective Jett Craigdon."

Kiesha's heart skipped a beat at the sound of the detective's voice. The last time the man had called, he'd been the bearer of bad news. She couldn't help but wonder what it would be this time. "What can I do for you, Detective?"

"I just thought you might like to know, we managed to obtain some fingerprints off the clothing worn by Heather Lockhart."

Kiesha's hand tightened around the phone. Her heart pounded so loudly, she almost missed the detective's next words.

"The prints matched some in our database. They belong to Wade Walker."

Her breath escaped in a rush. She was filled with a surge of relief so overwhelming, she was left feeling dizzy. The detective continued, unaware.

"We also checked the phone records. It's obvious Wade Walker lied to us when he told us he was the one on his way home the night his brother called. The call originated from Trey Walker's phone. What's more, it was Trey Walker who made the call to emergency services."

"Just like he said," she replied coolly, finding her voice at last.

"Yes, well, you could have saved us a lot of time and trouble if your client had only told us about the existence of his brother right from the start."

She frowned in indignation. "He—"

"Save it, Counselor. I don't need the lecture."

She reluctantly closed her mouth. After all, what good would it do? The good news was Trey would be released from all charges and the case against him would be dismissed. It would be over once and for all, and that was a good thing.

"I'll draft the motion to dismiss right away," she said. "Have you notified the Crown Prosecutor?"

"Not yet, but I will."

"Thank you. What about Wade Walker? Has he been arrested yet?"

"No. We're putting together an arrest team now. We aim to pick him up later this afternoon. Until we do, I'd appreciate it if you could keep this to yourself. We don't want him to get wind of our interest too soon."

"Of course," she agreed, "but I'll need to inform my client of the latest developments. It's not fair to keep him in the dark."

"That's your call, Counselor. I won't stand between you and your client and I understand you'll want to give him the good news as soon as possible. Let's just hope he keeps his mouth shut."

"I'll speak to him about it. I'm sure he'll understand the need to keep things quiet, at least until after his brother's been arrested."

"Thank you, Counselor. I appreciate your support."

After a few more moments of general conversation, Kiesha ended the call. She hung up the receiver and could barely contain her excitement when she once again dug in her handbag for her phone. She couldn't wait to tell Trey about the fingerprints. He was a free man at last. Well, almost. Save for the formal paperwork being filed and a final court appearance.

Her hand closed around the device and she brandished it in the air triumphantly. A moment later and with a smile on her face, she found and dialed Trey's number.

Trey collected his takeout coffee cup and murmured his thanks to the waitress who'd served him. Heading out of Jacob's Café into the bright sunshine, he immediately reached for is Maui Jims. Summer was fast approaching and with it the warmer weather. Soon it would be pleasant enough to hit the beach.

The thought of Kiesha in a skimpy black bikini made his mouth water and his body tightened instinctively. Their second night together had been as magnificent as the first. She was a passionate and sensual lover who was just as adventurous in bed as he was.

Kiesha.

He still couldn't believe he'd told her he loved her. It was true, of course, though he still marveled that it had happened so quickly and completely. But he hadn't meant to frighten her off by revealing the depth of his feelings so soon. She'd made it clear the last time they were together that she wasn't in this for the long haul, nor was she looking for a relationship. She'd just been given a huge break in her career. She didn't have time for distractions. But last night, she'd told him she cared. A lot.

Were they just words, or did she actually mean them?

He understood where she was coming from. A judgeship in the District Court, no less. Even if she wasn't the first female aboriginal District Court judge, it would still be a big deal.

Still, he hadn't planned on falling in love with her. He hadn't planned on their paths crossing at all. But they *had* and *he* had and now he didn't know what she was going to do about it.

She'd dressed and left his condo in such a rush that morning, he didn't have a chance to raise the subject—or to tell her the whole sordid story about Wade. She'd muttered something about being late for work as she'd pecked him on the cheek and hurried out the door. It was a less than satisfactory end to their amazing night of love and lust, but that's what happened. He'd come into the city with the hope of meeting her for lunch. *Surely she couldn't be so busy she wouldn't take a lunch break?*

The phone in his pocket buzzed against his breast. He reached in and pulled it out. He checked the screen and his heart skipped a beat.

Kiesha.

Mindful of his hot coffee, he quickly answered the call. "Hi, how are you doing?"

He grimaced at the inane question, but there was nothing he could do to take it back. Thankfully, she seemed not to notice. He'd barely finished speaking before she responded.

"Oh, Trey! Thank goodness you answered! I have the most amazing news! You won't believe what's happened!"

His heart stuttered on another beat and nervousness rushed through his veins. She sounded happy, so he guessed the news wasn't bad. But still...

"What is it?" he managed.

"I just had a call from Detective Craigdon. He's agreed to dismiss the charges against you. I'm drafting the paperwork right now. Isn't that the best news you've heard for like...forever?"

He smiled at the childish enthusiasm in her voice, but something held him back from celebrating. He needed more information. *What had happened for the detectives to suddenly change their mind? Had Wade come to his senses and finally told the truth?* He voiced that very question.

"No. They found Wade's fingerprints on Heather Lockhart's miniskirt," Kiesha explained.

"Wow. You mean they hadn't tested the clothing before now?"

"No, apparently not. Listen, where are you?"

"I'm in the city."

"Great. It's nearly lunchtime. Maybe we could grab a bite to eat? I can tell you the rest face to face."

"Yeah, I'm only a couple blocks away. Give me ten minutes."

"Great. I'll come downstairs and meet you out front."

"Sounds good."

Trey ended the call. Although he still had questions swirling around in his head, he was glad the nightmare was nearly over...and with it, he realized, went his reason for spending time with Kiesha. He only hoped she cared enough for him to want to give whatever was between them a chance—judgeship or no judgeship.

The impressive glass skyscraper that housed the offices of Sydney Legal loomed up ahead. He was right outside the glass sliding doors that formed the entryway when he spied someone familiar.

Anastasia.

He stopped cold and turned away, hoping she hadn't spotted him. Despite Wade's recent revelations, he didn't feel up to explaining and going over old ground. Besides, his heart lay elsewhere now. His hopes of avoiding her were dashed when she spoke.

"Trey Walker! Fancy seeing you here! It's been ages!"

Her smile was warm and friendly. He tensed, confused. The last time they'd spoken she told him to stay the hell away from her. Of course, she was as oblivious to Wade's deceit as he was. *Still, he had no interest in rehashing the past. He'd remain polite and get the hell away from her.* He turned and offered her a tentative smile. She immediately stepped closer and enveloped him in an exuberant hug.

"I've missed you, Trey," she confided. She released her hold on him, but remained standing close.

He shrugged, uncomfortable, unsure what she expected him to say. Her big blue eyes filled with sympathy.

"I heard you've been charged with sexual assault! To say I was shocked is an understatement. You might have been a little needier than I was prepared for, but I won't believe you raped anyone. If you need a character witness, you can call me. Anytime."

He smiled at her gratefully, a little surprised. She'd never been one for magnanimous gestures and her last few texts all those months earlier were far from flattering.

"Thanks, Ana. I appreciate the offer and the thought behind it. I won't need to take you up on it, though. As of a short time ago, the police have agreed to dismiss all charges."

Her face broke into a wide smile and once again she threw herself into his arms.

"How wonderful, Trey! Fantastic news! You must be over the moon."

"Yes. In fact, that's why I'm here. I'm taking Kiesha Munro out to lunch to celebrate."

With one hand still on his arm in a possessive manner, she eyed him slyly. "Kiesha has been representing you, hasn't she?"

"Yes."

"She and I are friends. She told me a couple weeks ago about your case. She also seemed rather taken with you. I tried to persuade her to withdraw from your case. I could tell her feelings for you would screw with her ability to represent you. Are you sure your relationship didn't spill over into something far more than professional?"

Trey frowned. He took offense at her insinuating tone. "I'm quite sure whatever there might or might not be between Kiesha and I is none of your business, Ana. You and I were over a long time ago."

A look of hurt and surprise tinged with anger flooded Anastasia's features.

"Trey! Don't be like that. Besides, I might have acted a little too hastily in that regard. You and I were so good together. Especially in the early days. I miss you so much!"

Without warning, she propelled herself toward him and pressed herself against his chest. With her hands framing his face, her lips found his and she kissed him like she couldn't get enough.

He gasped in surprise and was momentarily startled into doing nothing. At last, he reached up and extricated her hands and firmly set her away from him. Flushed and panting, she kept her gaze averted.

"Anastasia, what the hell are you thinking! Whether I'm involved with Kiesha or not, you and I are over. We were over months ago and nothing has changed that. Now, I suggest you go back inside and we'll both try and forget this happened."

With that, he turned her to face her building and swatted her on the ass, like a recalcitrant child. Instead of the embarrassment he was hoping for, she turned and shot him a mischievous grin.

"When you get over this little dalliance with your lawyer, give me a call. You know where to find me." She followed through with a wink and the promise in her eyes would have had him hurrying after her if he was the least bit interested.

Which he wasn't.

So, he merely lifted his hand in a casual wave of farewell and then spied Kiesha on the other side of the door. She stared at him, her eyes wide with surprise and hurt.

Shit.

He wondered how long she'd been there and how much of his time with Ana she'd witnessed. Enough, by the dark expression on her face.

"Shit," he murmured aloud and strode toward the entryway, eager to explain.

"Kiesha," he started.

She glared at him and shook her head. "Don't even think about it, Trey Walker! Nothing you can say will change anything. I saw the two of you together, looking very cozy. And you had the hide to tell me you two were over. It didn't look that way to me."

Panic gripped his insides. "Please, Kiesha. Let me explain. It isn't what you think."

"And what is it that I think?" she sneered. "Oh, I know we didn't talk about our relationship or seeing other people, but I didn't expect you to be back in the arms of your former lover before we'd even had the chance to sound things out."

Trey tried harder to convince her. "You don't understand. What you saw back there was nothing. It was Anastasia trying to wheedle her way back into my good graces. She told me how much she missed me and then she just kind of launched herself at me. I didn't kiss her back, I swear! I was as taken by surprise as you were! There's nothing between us. I love you! Not her!"

His breath came fast and his heart pounded with the effort to explain. The thin line of her lips had softened and she at least appeared to be listening. He tried again.

"Anastasia and I have been over for months. I don't know why she suddenly wanted to get back with me. I certainly didn't give her any encouragement in that regard. In fact, she asked me about you. She wanted to know if there was anything going on between us."

Some of the anger eased from Kiesha's face. "What did you say?" she asked quietly.

Trey blew out his breath on a sigh. "I told her it was none of her business, but I think she knows I've fallen for you." He paused and then added softly. "She's right."

He stepped forward and reached for Kiesha's hands. He pulled her so close their clothing touched. He heard her little intake of breath and saw the widening of her eyes. Though she regarded him steadily, a pulse beat madly in the side of her neck.

"I didn't plan for this to happen," he continued softly. "I didn't plan to fall in love. When I sought you out to be my lawyer it was because you were the best damned attorney there was. But the first time I walked into your office, I knew I was in trouble. You were gorgeous and smart and sassy. You stood me on my toes and turned me on my head. I didn't know if I was coming or going, but one thing I know for sure. I've never felt like this about anyone and I'll never feel like this again."

She stared at him with eyes that sparkled with emotion. A shaky smile curved up her lips. "Do you mean it?" she whispered. "Do you really love me?"

He nodded and laughed and squeezed her hands all at the same time. "Yes, I mean it. I really, *really* love you."

"Oh, Trey!"

And then it was her turn to throw herself in his arms and cover his face with kisses. This time, he embraced them, loving the feel of her pressed against him. She hadn't said any words of love in return, but right now that didn't matter. It was enough that she was here with him, in his arms, giving him all that she could. The rest could wait.

CHAPTER 19

Wade Walker was a loser. He'd been one all his life. Oh, his family had gone to great pains to hide it—bending over backwards to praise him for every single undeserving thing he did—but it didn't change anything. He was still a loser. The only time he'd been a winner was when he'd pulled Trey and his girlfriend out of a burning car. The feeling of pride his actions should have instilled in him had been suffocated by the knowledge he hadn't acted out of bravery or a love for his brother, but merely because he had no choice.

He wished he could be more like his brother. Trey was perfect in every way. He always had been. He was a winner. Everyone knew it. Wade knew it most of all. He could never live up to the kind of wonderful guy Trey was and so he didn't even try. In fact, he went out of his way to be the opposite. It wasn't any coincidence that he'd acted out at school or deliberately broke the rules. He could never hope to compete with the perfect Trey, so he became the recalcitrant Wade.

He didn't mind. In fact, it was fun not to concern himself with rules and regulations, or caring what other people thought. His father and brother forgave him no matter what scrapes he got into and they were the only people who mattered.

It had been tough losing his mom. She'd always been on his side. When he was with her, he didn't feel like a loser. Well, not as much of a loser as he usually did. She understood him like no one else did and often saw through his need to act out. He was almost himself when he was with her. After all, he had nothing to prove to someone who knew him like she did.

Trey understood the real Wade and his need to go against the system, but Trey was busy making a life of his own and lost interest in what Wade was doing. While Trey was leader of the track team and the captain of the football team, Wade was smoking pot behind the sports sheds, cutting class and snatching kisses from the seniors.

School days were long over, but Wade hadn't changed his ways. He still tried hard to buck the system, to break rules, to laugh at someone's pain. He didn't go out of his way to hurt people, but if that was a consequence of his actions, then it was merely collateral damage.

Take the incident with Heather Lockhart. He hadn't set out to rape her, but she'd pushed him to the point of no return. She'd had her hands all over him. He was drunk and high and "all sorts" of confused. It wasn't fair for her to change her mind. Anyone could see that. Anyone but Trey.

That was the problem with his perfect brother. He didn't see things the same way Wade did. Things Wade found perfectly acceptable, Trey completely disapproved of. It was annoying, but Wade had learned to live with it.

Until now.

The opportunity to make Trey feel how it was to be a loser, just once, was impossible to resist. When Wade realized Trey hadn't told the police about him, he'd been beyond relieved. He hadn't questioned his brother's loyalty. Trey's loyalty to his family had always been beyond reproach. But he'd been grateful for his brother's protection and thoughtfulness just the same. Keeping his existence from the police had been a generous thing to do, especially when it meant the spotlight became firmly fixed on Trey.

Of course, Trey had been born with a silver tongue and always knew what to say. Wade had no doubt his brother would talk his way out of any charges. He'd been as surprised as anyone when the case was committed for trial. He'd even felt a little guilty when he saw his brother's face splashed across the front page of the newspapers and saw the media hounding him on his way out of the court. But feeling all that wasn't enough for Wade to turn himself in. To the contrary.

He saw an opportunity to ensure suspicion never fell on him. He listened to Trey's anguished plea for him to attend the police station and do the right thing and he'd nodded and said all the right things and then had gone to the detectives and made sure they kept their eyes firmly on his brother. It was mean and spiteful, but what did Trey expect?

The CCTV footage was damning. There was no way Wade would escape incarceration if it was shown to a jury, and there was one thing he was sure of, and that was that he'd never survive in jail. Really, he had no choice but to turn against his brother.

Trey should never have told him about the security footage. Until then, Wade was confident the whole sordid mess would be worked out. Once he became aware of the evidence that could turn against him, there was no way he could do the honorable thing.

So he did the only thing he could do—and now his father was pissed. Angrier than he'd ever seen him and desperately disappointed. It was the disappointment that hurt the most. Of all the questionable things Wade had done in his life, his father had always stood by him. Even during the couple of times when the police were called, Archibald Frederick John Walker IV had remained staunchly loving and supportive. To see the disgust, to hear the fury, to realize the love had dried up... It was more than Wade could bear.

He'd let down his brother and his father in the most awful way and there was nothing he could do to change that. It wasn't like he could go back to the detectives and tell them he'd gotten it all wrong, that he'd lied when he told them it was

Trey who'd been with the girl that night. No, he couldn't do that.

Could he?

The very idea froze him to the spot with fear. Dread churned in his gut. His belly clenched and he rushed to the bathroom. Hot vomit spewed from his mouth and spattered all over the porcelain. With his head still hanging over the toilet bowl, he slid to the floor. The tiles were cold beneath his bare feet. He was bereft of everything other than the certainty he couldn't go to jail.

But that meant standing by and watching Trey become the patsy. *At what point would his brother's love and loyalty waver?* Surely if he reached the point where he faced a lengthy period of incarceration it would be enough for Trey to do everything he could to save himself and to hell with his stupid brother.

That's exactly what Wade would do. The truth was, if their positions were reversed, Wade would have pointed the finger at his twin at the earliest possible moment. In fact, that's exactly what he'd done. The thought shamed him, but it wasn't enough for him to man up and do the right thing.

But what if Trey did decide to spill everything to the detectives? Their suspicions would immediately turn on Wade. *Then what would he do?* He howled in an agony of indecision.

How the hell had he gotten himself into such a mess?

All he'd wanted was to have a good time on a Saturday night with a girl who was every bit as eager as he was. She should have known better than to lead him on and then simply change her mind. That wasn't fair and she got whatever she deserved.

But the law didn't see it that way and that was his major concern. Hell, the police might even be able to get copies of his phone records and prove which one of them had been telling the truth. He hadn't thought about that before he'd spoken to the detectives. Now he wondered if they were already scanning the numbers and coming to a different conclusion about exactly who was involved...

He had to get away from there. He had to go on the run. The thought came from nowhere, but it slowly crystallized into action. He scrambled off the bathroom floor and washed his face and mouth at the sink. Staring at his reflection in the mirror, he was shocked at the man who stared back at him. Red rimmed eyes and bedraggled hair. It hadn't been brushed since he'd attended the police station. He was a mess.

Still, there was nothing he could do about it now. Any minute, the cops could put the pieces together and land outside his door. He couldn't take the chance Trey might tell them the truth about what happened that night, or that they'd work it all out for themselves. He had to disappear, and quickly.

Running down the hall, he grabbed a duffel bag out of the closet and stuffed it with clothes. Tossing in some toiletries and a spare pair of shoes, he zipped it up and hoisted it onto his shoulder. The keys to the Porsche were on the kitchen counter where he'd left them. Grabbing his wallet and phone, he left without a backward glance.

Trey fitted his body closer against Kiesha's side and pulled her back against him. Though the leather couch in his living room was comfortable, it wasn't all that wide. They'd made slow and gentle love in his bedroom and now had made it as far out as the couch.

After meeting in the city, Kiesha had taken the rest of the afternoon off. She'd called her bemused secretary and requested the woman reschedule the rest of her appointments. Trey had been a more than willing accomplice to the deception and had dragged her off to his room the moment they arrived at his condo.

Idly tracing a finger up and down the soft skin of her bare arm, he sighed in contentment.

"That tickles," she murmured. He could hear the smile in her voice.

He replaced his finger with his lips and kissed his way up and down instead. "What about that?"

"That feels amazing."

It was his turn to smile. He couldn't believe how far they'd come in such a short period of time and while she hadn't said the words he longed to hear, he could tell by the way she kissed him, the way she looked at him that she felt deeply for him and it was only a matter of time. For some reason, she felt the need to hold back that last tiny part before she plunged in, and he accepted that. He was confident she loved him, even if she couldn't bring herself to say the words.

His thoughts drifted to his brother and he wished Wade had found someone special in his life. Perhaps he wouldn't feel the need to keep searching for something elusive if he was in a happy and committed relationship. Who knows, the right girl might be able to get him to turn his life around, to do good instead of harm. It was possible.

Despite the awful things Wade had confessed to, Trey refused to believe his brother was rotten all the way to the core. He was just misguided and had been let get away with far too much for far too long. That wasn't Wade's fault. Trey and his father had to take some of the responsibility for that one. After all, they were the ones who'd let him get away with it.

He thought about how the detectives had finally discovered Wade's fingerprints on clothing worn by Heather Lockhart. They'd agreed to drop the charges against Trey. The nightmare was nearly over. At least, for him. It would only be a matter of time before the police arrested Wade. The thought depressed him no end.

And then he remembered the question that had been bugging him from the moment Kiesha had called him with the news.

"What made the police decide to look for fingerprints on Heather Lockhart's clothing?" he asked quietly.

Kiesha momentarily tensed beside him. He felt her take a breath and ease it out. Finally she responded.

"I told them to check for them but they had the security tapes and would have come to that soon enough on their own."

Shock ricocheted through him. Pushing her away, he sat up and stared at her in disbelief.

"*You* told them? It was *your* idea?"

She stared at him steadily. "Yes."

He shook his head. "Why?"

She flinched at his angry tone, but continued to hold his gaze.

"The statements the police supplied me with in the brief referred to DNA testing, but there was nothing about fingerprints. I already knew that identical twins have identical DNA, but I only recently discovered their fingerprints are different. I thought it might be a way to prove you weren't the perpetrator of the crime."

He stared at her and slowly his anger subsided. After all they'd been through, all the trouble he'd gone to in order to keep his brother out of this and now the truth had come out. He was filled with an overwhelming feeling of sadness and resignation.

"I tried so hard to protect him and in the end, the evidence spoke for itself. His deeds were all caught by the cameras. They were his downfall. I wish you hadn't pointed the police in his direction, but I understand why you did."

She reached for his hand and pressed a soft kiss against his palm. "I'm sorry, Trey, I only did it because I love you. I couldn't bear the thought of you going to jail for a crime you didn't commit. I had to do everything I could to make sure that didn't happen."

He stared at her. *Had she just said she loved him?* He had to make sure.

"So, you love me, do you?" he murmured.

Reluctantly, the corners of her mouth tilted upwards. "Yes, I do. I'm not sure how it happened and it couldn't have come at a worse time, but there you have it. I've fallen in love with you, Trey Walker, and there's nothing I can do about it."

He reached for her. They both leaned forward and when their lips met, the sweetness of their kiss brought tears to his eyes.

"I'm so glad I found you," he whispered. "Neither of us planned it, but I wouldn't change things for the world."

"My career is about to take off. I—"

Trey placed a finger against her lips, silencing the rest of her words. "Yes, and you're going to be an amazing judge. And I'm going to be there for you, cheering you on, encouraging you every step of the way. I'll stay home and be the house husband, the house daddy, the...whatever... You've worked so hard to get where you are. I'll support you in whatever way you need. I'm not going to let anything stand in the way of your dreams. Not me, not our children...no one."

She quirked an eyebrow upward. "Children?"

A rush of panic surged through him. "You don't want kids?"

She laughed. "Of course I want kids! It's just... We haven't talked about any of this. It's all happened so suddenly. I just need some time to get my head around it."

The tension inside him eased and he grinned at her. "Take all the time you need. I'm a patient man."

"Good. Maybe we can talk about it in another five years."

He growled a protest and then caught the sparkle of mischief in her eyes. "You little minx," he chuckled.

With happiness shining brightly in her blue eyes, she leaned in close for another kiss. He was more than happy to oblige. From the corner of his eye, something on the TV screen caught his attention. A familiar face flashed past. He tensed, frozen to the spot.

Wade.

Kiesha pulled away from him, a frown on her face.

"What's the matter?" she asked.

Silently, he pointed to the screen. Police swarmed outside Wade's apartment block. The street was full of squad cars. Curious bystanders gawked at the unfolding scene. Handcuffed, Wade was marched down the cracked concrete path and pushed unceremoniously into the back of a police van.

Trey let out the breath he'd been holding and slowly turned to Kiesha. She looked just as shocked as he felt. In silence, they reached for each other and held each other tight.

Blinking back tears, Trey sighed. For better or worse, it was over. From now on, Wade was on his own. It would take a long time—maybe never—for Trey to come to terms with all that had happened. He was just glad he had Kiesha by his side, supporting him, loving him, making everything all right. Despite everything that had happened, he was the luckiest guy alive.

NOTE TO READERS

I do hope you have enjoyed reading Trey and Kiesha's story. If you've enjoyed this book, please feel free to leave a review for The Ties That Bind at Goodreads and your favorite digital retailer. Every review is very much appreciated.

Receive a free book when you sign up for my newsletter if you would like to receive news on upcoming stories, release dates, book launches and other snippets. I love to receive feedback from my readers. Please feel free to contact me at chris@christaylorauthor.com.au

The Perfect Crime is the next book in The Sydney Legal Series.

Here's a sneak peek:

Jessica Wolfe's career as a lawyer at the prestigious Sydney Legal was going from strength to strength until her brother, Alistair Wolfe, decided to get involved in human tissue trafficking. Alistair's subsequent arrest and conviction brought with it a mountain of negative publicity and has damaged Jessica's prospects of a partnership at the law firm. Jessica is determined to prove her worth despite her brother's criminality.

Then she receives a phone call from an old high school flame that will change her life forever...

Mackenzie Calloway is a successful property developer. A former high school football jock, he's defied everyone's expectations by scraping his way through college and graduating with a business degree. Sheer hard work, a whole lot of charm and a fair amount of luck has enabled him to accumulate wealth like he'd never dreamed possible. Then his ex-girlfriend's body is found washed up along the shores of Sydney Harbour and all hell break's loose.

Mackenzie is charged with her murder and his perfect life begins to spiral out of control. His only hope is the girl he's known since high school who just happens to be a damned fine criminal defense lawyer.

Can Jessica and Mackenzie ignore the spark of attraction between them in order to save Mackenzie from being convicted for a crime he didn't commit...?

PROLOGUE

The meaty fist came from nowhere. Taken by surprise, Mackenzie Calloway ducked, but he wasn't quick enough. The smack of flesh-on-flesh was sickening. The thin skin covering his bottom lip split under the impact. Pain shot through his mouth.

"What the hell—?" he gasped. Reaching up, he gingerly touched the wound. His fingers came away wet with blood. Before he had time to contemplate what had happened, his attacker came at him again. This time, Mack was ready.

A flurry of punches from the short and stocky man who'd appeared from nowhere outside the bar where Mack had been drowning his sorrows were met with solid deflections as Mack squared off against his attacker. The man's fists were fast, but Mack was quicker. In short order, he managed to rain a series of blows against the man's head and shoulders, until the thug cried out in pain. An instant later, the man turned tail and disappeared into the darkness.

Mack stumbled back and leaned against the red brick wall that ran alongside the building that housed the bar. It was late. Way past three the last time he'd checked. The streets of Sydney were quiet. Everyone with any sense was in bed asleep, like he should have been on a Tuesday night. If it wasn't for Pamela and her cheating heart, that's exactly where he would have been, still oblivious to the double life she'd led for as long as she'd known him.

Thirteen months and he hadn't had a clue. What kind of idiot did that make him? He thought they had something together. Hell, he'd even thought about their future. Though she wasn't exactly the marrying type, he hadn't given up hope of trying to convince her... After all, he was thirty-six and more than ready to settle down. It was almost laughable the way she'd played him. Talk about gullible.

In an effort to block the memories of their less-than amicable parting, he'd found himself in a downtown bar, drinking to forget. *What a joke.* All he'd gotten was a splitting headache from too much whisky and a sore and bloody lip. He'd be lucky if the thug hadn't chipped one of his teeth.

Gingerly, he moved his tongue around his mouth and was relieved when it appeared all of his teeth were intact. He couldn't say the same for his bottom lip. Blood continued to drip in a steady stream down his chin and onto his T-shirt. He looked down at the mess and shook his head in disbelief.

Who the hell attacks a stranger like that?

It was downright weird. He wasn't in a rough part of the city and the man hadn't even asked for his wallet or phone. Mack had merely been standing outside the bar, waiting for a cab; minding his own business, trying not to think of the harsh words that had been spoken between him and Pamela. He hadn't even noticed the man until it was too late. As if the bullet Pamela had put through his finger at the pinnacle of their argument the night before hadn't been enough.

He sighed. The week had been way past difficult and it had barely begun. As if on cue, his injured finger throbbed beneath the bandage the nurse in the emergency room had applied less than twenty-four hours earlier. He was lucky Pam wasn't a better shot. He could have lost the digit altogether. And to think he thought she loved him as much as he loved her. Ha! Now *that* was a joke!

The flash of lights from an approaching car snagged his attention. More cautious than he would have been before the attack, he pressed himself against the brick wall until he recognized the outline of a cab. Closing his eyes briefly in relief, he stepped out of the shadows and flagged the driver down. All he wanted to do was go home, take a shower and climb between the cool cotton sheets. He'd nurse his sore fists and cut lip and do his best to forget that he ever knew a woman called Pamela.

CHAPTER 1

Jessica Wolfe frowned at her computer screen with fierce concentration. Night had descended hours earlier. The office had fallen silent. One by one, her work colleagues had left to go home to their families, friends or empty apartments. But not Jessica.

With a surge of irritation, she pushed away from her desk and strode over to the window. The night sky was as black as tar, visible in small patches between the tall buildings in downtown Sydney. The road far below was illuminated by the orange glow of street lights and the silence was only disturbed by the occasional siren or passing car.

She was alone in the office. At least, alone on her floor. There might be the odd lawyer working back late in some other part of the building—some other poor sucker who didn't have a life... But she couldn't tell who else was still there from her lowly position on the fourth floor.

One of the senior partners had asked her to research a point of law and she was determined to find a loophole he could use which would allow his client to go free. She'd been at Sydney Legal for more than five years, but ever since her brother, Alistair's arrest and subsequent conviction for illegal trafficking in human organs, she'd been well and truly on the outer and her chances of one day being offered a partnership had been dealt a severe blow.

Though no one at the firm would come out openly and say it, she wasn't stupid. The firm had recently been forced to overcome negative publicity when one of the senior partners had been shot by his wife. The scandal had hit all the major media outlets and had gone viral on social media. It had been a major embarrassment.

Suffice it so say, Alexei Gianopoulos' wife was now cooling her heels in jail, just like Jessie's brother. The firm wasn't about to promote someone like her, no matter that she wasn't responsible for her brother's actions. Now it felt like she had to work three times as hard as anyone else there to prove her worth and remove the stigma her brother had left behind.

Alistair Wolfe had done his best to convince his family his actions had been done for the greater good, but no one could dispute the fact he'd made millions off the illegal deal and Jessie's chance at a partnership at Sydney Legal had been all but shot to smithereens. In the months that followed his conviction, she'd barely been able to hold her head up in the corridors of the esteemed law firm, let alone put her name forward for a partnership. Two years down the track and she was forced to concede it might not ever happen.

Though she tried her hardest to ignore the whispers and sideways glances, as far as most of her colleagues at Sydney Legal were concerned, she was just as guilty as her brother. It made things difficult for her, but she was determined to weather the storm and eventually, when the time was right, demand the secure future and the pay packet she deserved.

So here she was, still at her desk, even though it was going on for eleven on a Friday night. She was a thirty-something single woman living in Sydney. She should have been out with her friends, kicking up her heels, meeting someone special. Instead, she was burning the midnight oil in an effort to impress her bosses and claw back some of the esteem she'd previously been held in before Alistair's spectacular fall from grace.

There were only a handful of lawyers at the firm who continued to treat her as if nothing had happened. She'd counted Sally-Ann Li, Daisy Green and Abby Brown as her friends beforehand and was fortunate they'd stood by her during Alistair's trial. Even after the guilty verdict, they'd been there for her and continued to offer her their support. She was beyond grateful for their efforts but even her well-regarded lawyer friends couldn't restore the damage her brother had done to her career.

The sound of her phone startled her from her musings. Bending low, she picked up her handbag from under her feet and hunted around for her phone. Pulling it out, she glanced at the screen and frowned. It was Lachlan Coleridge.

What was her brother-in-law doing, calling her so late? All of a sudden, she was filled with dread. Had something happened to her sister, Ava, or her nieces and nephew?

"Hi, Lachlan. What is it? Is everyone all right?"

"Yes, of course. Everyone's fine," Lachlan replied.

Relief flooded through her. "I'm so glad."

"I didn't mean to worry you, calling so late," Lachlan continued.

"You're right. It is late. I should be heading home."

"I thought I might still catch you at work. That's why I called."

"What's this about?" she asked, frowning.

Lachlan sighed. "I'm at the station. Night shift. I've just arrested a man by the name of Mackenzie Calloway. He's requested a lawyer. He's asking for you."

At the mere mention of Mack's name, Jessie's heart skipped a beat. *Mackenzie Calloway.* It was a name she hadn't heard in a long, long time. Not since she was eighteen.

"Are you sure he asked for me? Mackenzie and I haven't seen each other since we left high school and even then, we didn't exactly hang out in the same circles."

"Yes, I'm sure. I asked him if he wanted to see a lawyer. He said he wanted to see you."

Jessie's eyebrows lifted involuntarily in surprise. She wasn't even aware Mack knew she was a lawyer. *Had he kept tabs on her after high school?* The thought filled her with a warmth that immediately irritated her. She and Mackenzie Calloway had been nothing to each other. She might have carried a secret flame for him, but he hadn't even known she existed. She was a nerd, a geek who always had her nose in a book. He was the captain of the football team. They'd had nothing in common.

"Has he been arrested?" she asked, curious.

"Yes. We brought him in a few hours ago. He agreed to participate in a record of interview. He initially declined the services of a lawyer, but we've since charged him with murder. Suddenly, he's interested in talking to you."

Jessie started in shock. She blinked and shook her head. She couldn't imagine the Mackenzie Calloway of her high school days being capable of murder. Still, no one knew what happened in the years after graduation. Anything was possible. Just look at Alistair. Nobody had seen that coming, least of all Jessie.

"Are you still there, Jess?"

Lachlan's voice was tinged with concern. She hurriedly responded. "Yes, I'm still here. You took me by surprise. Mackenzie Calloway's the last person I'd guess would be up on murder charges."

"Yeah, he isn't your typical criminal, that's for sure. He's a successful property developer and has substantial holdings in and around the city. He's polite and well-spoken and dresses like he's just stepped out of the pages of GQ magazine. Still, I've been in this business long enough to know that criminals come in all shapes and sizes and from all walks of life. You never can tell."

Jessie absorbed Lachlan's information, storing it away for later dissemination. Her mind snagged on the fact Mackenzie was a successful businessman, a property developer. Somehow, it jarred with her memories of the laid back, fun loving football jock who'd turned her into hopeless ball of awkwardness and embarrassment if he ever happened to glance her way.

Jessie sighed and glanced at her watch. It was already after eleven. Her eyes were sore and gritty from endless hours staring at a computer screen. Her back ached along with her neck from being bent over so long at her desk. She wanted nothing more than to switch off her computer and call an end to the night.

But now Mackenzie Calloway had once again crashed into her life. He had asked for her... *What was she going to do about it?*

"There's no need to come over now," Lachlan continued, as if reading her mind. "He'll spend the night in the cells. He's asked to see you before he's brought before the bail court in the morning."

Jessie eased her breath out on a sigh of relief and then immediately felt guilty. Mackenzie Calloway, the man she'd loved with all her heart all through her high school days, needed her and she'd blithely put him off until the morning. No, that wasn't fair. There was nothing she could do to help him at that moment. He'd just have to resign himself to an uncomfortable night in the lockup.

She wondered what he looked like. Was he still the same tall, broad-shouldered athlete, like he'd been at eighteen? Or had the years been less kind to him? Perhaps his desk job had turned the muscle into fat? Did it matter? Probably not.

All of a sudden, she was filled with a yearning to see him, but it was way past late. She was tired and far from on her game. The first time she came face to face with Mackenzie Calloway after nearly twenty years, she wanted to be firing on all cylinders. For now, he'd have to wait.

The Perfect Crime will be released on
30 October, 2018 and is available for pre-order
from your favorite digital retailer.

ABOUT THE AUTHOR

Chris Taylor grew up on a farm in north-west New South Wales, Australia. She always had a thirst for stories and recalls writing her first book at the ripe old age of eight. Always a lover of romance and happily-ever-afters, a career in criminal law sparked her interest in intrigue and suspense. For Chris to be able to combine romance with suspense in her books is a dream come true.

Chris is married to Linden and is the mother of five children. If not behind her computer, you can find her doing the school run, taxiing children to swimming lessons, football, ballet and cricket. In her spare time, Chris loves to read her favorite authors who include Richard North Patterson, Sandra Brown, Kathleen E Woodiwiss and Jude Devereaux.

You can find out more about Chris and sign up for her newsletter at her website:

http://www.christaylorauthor.com.au

9 781925 119565